JE

Jez Lowe was born in County Durham, and is a singer and writer of songs, inspired mainly by life in North East England. Much covered and much travelled, he has around twenty albums of original songs to his credit, and has been a principal writer for the award-winning BBC Radio Ballads series since 2006.

This is his first novel.

THE DILLEN DOLL

By

JEZ LOWE

Published by Badapple Books
PO Box 57,
York
YO26 8BN

www.jezlowe.com

Printed and bound in Great Britain by Clays Ltd, St Ives plc

ISBN 978-1-9998888-0-0

For Louisa Jo Killen and Johnny Handle,
who began the beginning.

DO LI A – (A traditional Tyneside song.)

Fresh I'm come fra' Sandgate Street,
Doli, Doli,
My best friends here to meet,
Do Li A,
Dolly the Dillen Dol,
Doli, Doli,
Dolly the Dillen Dol,
Do Li A

The Black Cuffs is gawn away,
Doli, Doli,
That will be a cryin' day,
Do Li A

Dolly Coxon pawned her sark,
Doli, Doli,
To ride upon the baggage cart,
Do Li A

The Green Cuffs is comin' in,
Doli, Doli,
That'll mak' the lasses grin,
Do Li A.

THE SONG.

I can't remember where or when I first heard the song. Scores of people have recorded it; hundreds have sung it in my lifetime, thousands before that. No-one knows who penned these words, nor who the woman in the song was, or what she did, to be feted in such a long-lasting, sing-able way. She has passed into history as a camp-follower, a soldier's doxy, a woman on the streets of Newcastle at the end of the 18th century, when battalions like The North York Militia ("The Black Cuffs") and The Ulster Dragoons ("The Green Cuffs") swarmed across the city on the way to European wars. Local militia groups were also springing up all over the North, established by wealthy landowners with an eye on tax-dodging and playing at soldiers. Not much has changed on that score since then, sadly. The streets and alleys that she knew haven't changed much either, despite the recklessness of short-sighted town-planners and crooked council officials, who have sliced their way through Newcastle in homage to the petrol engine and the shopping precinct. The River Tyne flows quietly past all this, doleful and serene these days, but still bears witness to the same alcohol-fuelled wildness at weekends that Dolly Coxon must have been part of, almost three hundred years ago.

The melody of the song is a curious one, and was later used to good effect on "The Liverpool Lullaby", written by a computer-science pioneer called Stan Kelly and made popular in the 1960's. A fine songwriter, he habitually used traditional melodies for his songs, and possibly heard this one from a celebrated recording by Louis Killen on a 1962 album called "Along the Coaly Tyne". The tune predates those of the music-hall ditties and parlour ballads that became a trademark of Tyneside a century later, and could likely have arrived fully-formed via the voice of a foreign sailor, echoing across the cobbles from the window of a dockside hostelry.

The coming-together of all these parts resulted in a mysterious whole, part children's rhyme, part lament, part military march. It has travelled the world over, often losing its origin on the way. Just the other day I heard it sung in a bar in Amsterdam, where it was introduced as a Dublin street song. I sang it myself once in Massachusetts, and was quizzed at length about its history afterwards by a zealous young Harvard student. Only then did I realise how little I had to tell her about it.

The story I present here could be the real one, though I have nothing to prove it. Most of the characters that inhabit this tale were indeed real people, but this could be their first meeting for all I know. Whatever Dolly Coxon's true fate, she certainly left her mark in history, and I thank her profusely for the song she left behind.

THE OTHER SONGS

Several other songs are alluded to or quoted in this story, including Here's The Tender Coming, Sair Fyeld Hinnie, Buy Broom Besoms, The Waters of Tyne, The Skipper's Wedding, The Keel Row, The Sandgate Lass's Lament, My Bonny Lad, The Collier's Rant, Byker Hill, The Skipper in the Mist and Bobby Shafto, all of which are traditional Tyneside songs.

Written sources for these and other songs include "Allan's Tyneside Songs", Frank Graham's "The Geordie Songbook" and especially "Bell's Rhymes of the Northern Bards".

The singers who led me to these songs over the years include Benny Graham, Louis Killen, Johnny Handle, Bob Davenport, Anni Fentiman, Alan Fitzsimmons, Tom Gilfellon, and so many fine local singers at clubs and sessions around Tyneside, too many to mention here, but each of them important in the journey of this story.

I've recently recorded my own interpretations and adaptations of some of these songs, and others, as a "suite" of music and words, loosely following the path of this story. It is available for reference and for your listening pleasure on a CD also entitled "The Dillen Doll", available from Tantobie Records.

ACKNOWLEDGEMENTS

Thanks to Benny Graham, Bev Sanders, Frankie Lieberman, Corrin Bramley, Steve Tilston, Pete Wood, David De La Haye, Kate Bramley and Andy May. Special thanks to Kari MacLeod for her artwork and to Lisa Kirkbride for the cover designs.

ACKNOWLEDGMENTS

THE DILLEN DOLL

This was a game for the crowded streets... Newcastle being a fine town to roam in, especially after dark... It was a working-class crowd in every street, largely cheerful because, being Saturday, they had a bob or two to chuck away; and easy with one another, because they had all got that bob or two the same hard way, or similar... none of them any better than they should be, because they all spoke the same dialect, and because this was 'canny Newcassel'."

Jack Common, "Kiddar's Luck" 1951.

CHAPTER 1

AS I CAME THROUGH SANDGATE

A thousand noises swam through the darkness. Any single one of them could have woken her. She lay still and sipped at each one, shuffling them, maybe hoping that sleep would sooth them into silence once again. A deep bell rang somewhere down by the quayside, a scuffle of something close, too near to the bed, a door closing angrily, twice, a strange scrape of iron on cobbled street, the sickening hockle and spit of a man outside the broken glass of the window, from where a high moan of a breeze now arose, followed by the flap of a ragged curtain, and another tiny rasp of movement in the corner of this room.

Then the scrape of cartwheels, for that's what it was, got nearer and louder, and a chorus of dogs barked their collective anger, like a lighting of noisy beacons up and down the street, first one, then another close by, two more, all distinctive, a gruff rasp, a yap, and now a howl cut off by a yelp, as an angry master kicked out in sleepy indignation. The yelp silenced the hollering of the other hounds into a tumble of nervous growls and grunts, and on into silence. But now the crunch and grind of cartwheels was upon her, and the eerie glow of a swinging lantern swayed across the room, stretching shadows into corners, then back and forth across the stained ceiling.

"Bastad! Ah'll skelp yer', yer shite, I'll bloody brae yer!"

That's what had woken her. Bessie Lavender welcoming in the Sabbath with her weekly scolding of her poor husband Barty, the tallest man on the quayside, but no match for the toothless, wild-eyed ire of little Bessie after a Saturday night in the Flying Horse with his fellow misfits.

"Go back to yer mother, yer little shitflea! Ye're a bloody waster!"

"Me mother's dead Bessie. Ee though, Ah loved me mother. What a canny woman. An Ah love thee an' all Bessie…"

She could picture the stooping, cowering figure of Barty in the middle of the street, tearful, from the sob in his deep gentle voice.

"Buggeroff!" snarled Bessie, and the door creaked to a slam and a rattle of a bolt.

"Orr… Bessie!" Barty moaned weakly, and she heard the scuff of his boots as he walked slowly down Pallister's Chare and off towards the river, where he'd consider drowning himself yet again before falling asleep among the discarded jute bags at the end of Broad Garth.

These were the voices of the quay, but not her voice. Her words were rounder, lighter. These had not always been her streets.

She was awake now in the pit-black room. Her long brown hair, knotted by last night's passion, lay in an uncomfortable clump between her head and the coarse pillow. Her bare legs were suddenly cold, and her feet fumbled for a corner of rough blanket, but it hardly stretched across the broad form of the man sleeping beside her. She'd rather not unsettle him by rummaging for what little warmth the threadbare covering had to spare.

The night before, she'd had fine sport with Moss. He'd come in from the Black Boy with the dregs of some brown gin in a broken bottle, and made straight for her, almost smothering her in damp gabardine and the smell of tar and tobacco. She'd feigned a coy struggle, but in truth relished his strong hands and wet mouth devouring her limp, pale skin. Her slight, skinny frame folded like a rag toy in his clutching.

"You nowt for lookin' at, Dolly," he'd said in his squinted style of speaking, "but you got ample charms and you can sing like a bird. And you please a man, you surely do."

And please him she had, lost in his long and scarred limbs and whiskered cheeks. He'd pulled off his eyepatch as they fell together on the bed, and she tried to stop herself from looking into the ragged ditch where another blue eye had once glinted in the foreign sun, but she always looked, and it always caused her to force away a shudder. Once he'd asked her why she had never enquired about the loss of the eye, but she'd answered that the remaining one was so beautiful, she never missed its marra. He'd laughed and rolled back his head, and so didn't see the flash of horror on her face, as she steeled herself against the imagined brutality that had snuffed out half of his light into darkness. Only a tiny spelk of this man's life was known to her, and exactly what had brought a brown-faced seaman from the sun-drenched colours of Genoa to the drizzle-grey banks of the Tyne, and all that had occurred before and after, remained a fearful mystery to her.

He'd first spoken to her on a Thursday night at the end of last year's summer, in the rowdy snug of The Flying Horse, where she was fitfully employed, dipping pots and trimming lamps. She'd seen him once or twice in the weeks before, usually towering over a quartet of loaders at the Sandgate side of the quay, as she'd made her way from this very room above the vinegar store, towards the Bigg Market to start her daily work. The patch of course, while not unique among the scavengers and haulers in this end of the city, had singled him out when coupled with the thick black hair and darkened features, not to mention a laugh that had shown more teeth than she'd seen on any man's mouth that she could remember. Had that attracted her, repelled or just puzzled her? She couldn't remember. Then she'd heard him talking in the snug as it emptied one night, of a dogfight he'd witnessed in Montrose. His words were long, snapped, sometimes song-like, other times sharp and broken, a raw mixture of old Tyneside, Yiddish like Ezra the Lender, and Turkish like the Shoe Market vendors in the summer. He was French, she was told by a woman at the washer; a spy from the colonies, according to the muck-picker in Pudding Chare. It had been Harrison Marley, her own employer, whom she'd heard refer to him as "Morrasso, that Roman pirate", that night as she'd stoked the fading ashes of the year's first hearth, as the motley clientele indulged in their rowdiness around her.

"Sing up Dolly!" someone had called at her from the end of the bar.

4

"Don't turn 'round, mind," Anty Proud had sneered from the corner table, "We don't want to look on yer!" There'd been a few cackles and laughs, as there had always been since that first night months before, when the bowed arch of the fireplace had first echoed with her carefree lilting, skipping barefoot around the chorus of "My Bonny Lad". It was a song she remembered from her sister Bertha, lulling her to sleep when they'd shared a cramped old cot, so many years before. That night, the gentle certainty of Dolly's singing had somehow filled that room, by way of the resonance of the stone hearth, until one by one the old keelers and layabouts and drunkards and dockers had ceased their prattle and racket, stared into their mugs and swooned off into the dreamy melancholy of the young girl's lament. As she'd suddenly sensed the massive silence behind her, Dolly had swung around, her face red, her eyes wide, fearful embarrassed.

"Don't stop now lass!" someone had hollered across the trestles, to a muttering of fond protest all round. "D'ye know "Bobby Shafto"? Or "The Skipper in the Mist"? She'd ended up singing for an hour, startling even herself as to how many songs she knew, all from listening to her sisters at night, when struggling together for warmth and sleep in their dingy attic of a long-lost childhood.

It had become a regular occurrence, not every night, but most nights, certainly at the week's end, that Dolly would be marched out from the scullery at the cundy-end of the barroom, and propped before the tall black fireplace, and encouraged to entertain these miscreants

5

with her voice like clear, clean bright tumbling water. Customers from the long bar and the block room would drift in to listen. And so it had been that night in late summer, when the tall scoundrel with the grey eyepatch and black brows had melted into the doorway, his head pulled back, tall against the brown yellowness of the barroom wall, entranced by the luring lilt of her song.

An evening or two after, she had watched him at a card table by the door, as Wool Maggie laughed too loud and too close upon his knee, forever whispering, often grasping his arm, and just as often being ignored. No wonder then, when the card game was over, and to his cost, that he'd been less than happy with Maggie's company. Dolly had passed them by, struggling with a boulder of coal for the fading grate, and Moss had risen to assist her. He'd smiled and spoken at her, words she didn't catch, but plainly coated in fondness. She thanked him, and felt him standing behind her as she'd pushed the jagged roundy into the embers and stoked them about it to encourage a new flame.

"Moss!" Wool Maggie had shouted, "Ah's goin' dry over here, mind!"

He'd ignored her. Dolly had looked across at Maggie, then up at him.

"Will you sing tonight?" he'd said, softly.

She'd felt a trembling in her body, somewhere, everywhere.

"No, not tonight. It's a bit late now. Not many in. And nobody asked me."

"If I ask you, would you gan' sing for me?" She smiled at his awkward use of words.

6

"Get away man," she laughed, "It's far ower late. They'll be lockin' up presently."

"Then somewhere else. I'd like it, to hear you sing tonight".

She stared at him. She searched blindly for an answer within herself.

"Bobby Shafto went to sea, silver buckles on his knee, Diddle diddle diddle dee, Bonny Bobby Shafto..." Barely a step or two away from them, Wool Maggie leaned on to the rough table and sang, coarsely, tunelessly, and ran out of words in an angry snarling sob of jealousy.

Anty Proud roused himself from a beer-soaked sleep by the door.

"Shut yer hole, yer sluvven," he cawed at her. "Ye sound like a dock rat gettin' pitch-forked!"

Maggie cursed at him in fine style, and leaned across to summon up a follow-up spit of contempt in his direction.

"Hew! Ye!". Marley the landlord had heard the oath and banged the base of an empty jar on the surface of the bar. "Cut the lip, or get out! Yer not in the gutter in here. Get back in the street where ye belong, if yer gonna curse like that!"

"Ah'm goin'", Maggie snarled back. She staggered to her feet and pulled her grubby shawl around her in indignation.

"Moss!" she said. "Are ye comin'? Ah'm not stayin' here to be talked at like that!"

The tall man didn't even turn to look at her.

"Oh, yes, you should go." he said. "Maybe I follow later. But you should go. Definitely." His eyes were fixed on Dolly, who turned away and stared into the dry ashes.

7

"Dolly!" the landlord called at her. "Pull that roundy off the fire and save it for the morn'. Then get away home!"

But she hadn't gone home that night. She'd woken in the dawn's drizzle, wrapped in Moss's coarse jacket and some old sail cloth, in a doorless scull-hut at the entry of a skinny alley, which, had she been able to read, Dolly would have seen to be named as "Love Lane", on the faded lettering below the upstairs window of the corner dwelling. Moss had been sitting, as she woke, lost in thought, staring with a solitary eye at the first collier brigs of the day, dancing their nimble way across each-others' wakes in the slow River Tyne. The night before, they had walked a while, they had talked a little, he had laughed at her and laughed with her, and then she had indeed sung for him, when they reached the spot where the gushing Pandon Burn joined the big river on its slow journey to the sea. They'd barely sheltered from the rain in this broken shell of wood, when she'd lain back into sleep in his arms.

And now, half a year on, she was awake again, and still she lay beside him.

A day was dawning, and with it the rattle and the ringing of the world outside this room was increasing, with real voices, working voices, mingling with the bells and cartwheels and scratched rattling of chains and shovels, the clashing of gates, the banging of doors, that all proclaimed that the city must once again stir itself.

Dolly's white flesh moved slowly in the greyness of the morning light, as she slid warily, edging her body away from his and out into the dreaded coldness of the day.

8

The hair at the base of her belly itched. Her stealth gave way to a jerk and the man snorted, spoke a word in his own tongue and breathed heavily back into slumber. Her feet found the splintered wood of the floorboards, and she was mindful of rustle of rat that she had been aware of minutes earlier. As she reached for the pale mauve shawl on the board beside the bed, his hand stretched out and gripped her bare thigh firmly.

"Where you goin' Dolly?" he rasped, his eyes still closed, his head still on the grimy pillow.

"Ah'm goin' to piss", she whispered. "Sleep on!"

He moaned and stirred his body into movement, his hairy arm rising from the tan blanket in a groaning arc.

"Sun is up,", he said in a voice still full of last night's drink, "I gotta go workin'."

"No, it's still early," she said, "Stay there. Ah'm away' to the peelin's. Ah'll wake yer when Ah'm back. Sleep on,"

"What's peelin's?" he asked.

"At the Groat Market", she replied pulling a shift, damp from the dew of the bare room over her head. "The scuff from the leeks and tatties and that, all the mildew scuffins that they cast out. There's enough to make broth from if you get there early. Ah won't be long."

She leaned back to kiss him, but he was already asleep. She dressed hurriedly to fool the coldness. One shoe was outliving the last of many repairs, and her swollen bloodied foot bore witness to the fact. Winter was almost upon them. She cast it from her mind, winced at the stab of pain in her hunched left shoulder and limped to the door. She tried vainly to lift a silent sneck, but it creaked out of its latch like it always did. She slid out of the narrow door, thumped it closed and found the stairs in the grey gloom.

CHAPTER 2

BREAD FOR ME AND MINE

King George was a dozen years into a long and eventful reign when the Coxons left a shabby hovel in Deptford on the River Wear to move the ten long miles north to the River Tyne. Wilfred Coxon had been a pee-dee lad on a Wearside keel, but was a skilled oarsman who knew the narrow river like a lover by the time he saw fit to find a wife. He took the woman known to all as Blenk, when they were both twenty-six years of age, and there were two daughters in the first two years of marriage. Wilfred was a good man, strong as an ox, and had worked hard through six winters, when Blenk showed signs of a third child, another daughter, who was born in mid-summer, at a time when work was plentiful and long in hours. When he finally returned to the family home, two days after the birth, Blenk was sitting wordlessly scraping beets by the window, and the new baby lay greeting in harsh swaddling in the opposite corner. It was small, and lay at a tilt, one arm stretched out in hunger, but the other almost still at its side. His father-in-law George Blenkinsop, a Godly man of stern disposition, had never set foot in their house before, but there he was, bowed over a crooked walking stick, similarly unspeaking and breathless from the steep climb up the gunnel to their door.

It was the old man who had given the helpless child her name.

"Ye've not long to get a baptism," he'd eventually proclaimed, looking down on the bairn from the middle of the room. "A dillen like that. It's not fit to last 'til the morn, and she's not feedin' it. Get hold of a pastor and get it christened. Ah don't want any blood of mine sufferin' in a limbo of your makin'." He moved forward, stick raised and extended towards the infant like some ghastly withered tongue. He gingerly flicked back the wrappings with a look of disgust on his crinkled face.

Wilfred despised the old man. He pushed past him and gathered the child up in his huge hands. The wailing ceased. The tiny face turned to the father's, lit by the slit of light from the open door. A tiny hand gripped the gnarled, coal-dusted finger.

"Two of them, we lost", the old man was saying, almost in triumph. "Ah know the signs. Man, a heifer would know the signs with that 'un. Get a pastor. Get it christened. Ye'll need a name. Her mother's name, Dolitha. She'll not use it long." He turned towards the door. "And keep yer hands off her!" he cackled, gesturing behind him with the handle of the stick, towards his own daughter, still wreathed in silence.

Eighteen days later, she was gone. Not the fragile child, blessed with her mother's name by holy oil and pump water. It was the mother, Blenk, the first Dolitha, who had pushed the mite into the startled arms of the middle daughter, Rose, and with a whimper of what might have been goodbye, swayed unsteadily out of the crumbling doorway, into the afternoon sunlight and away forever. Wilfred had been home by ten that night, to find Rose asleep on the floor, and Bertha the eldest clinging to the

12

baby, singing the same dandling song that he himself had sung to her when marriage had seemed a blessing, and a child a completeness.

He'd spent a day and a night searching the streets. A trader in the Blue House in Hendon had told him of a simple woman, by his account, drifting through high grass atop of the nearby cliffs, but a cautious search of the beach below had presented nothing. He'd searched again a week later when work was slack and stormy seas had prevented the colliers from coming into port, but by then his elder daughters had stopped asking questions, and the backstreet's gossips had turned their attention elsewhere.

"Little Runty", he'd called her, though fondly, as she'd persevered through an infancy and beyond, to be distinctive by the slight hunch above a weak left arm, and a slight cast in the eye on that same side, most pronounced with the tiredness of day's end. What brought more remark to her infirmity was the beauty of her elder sisters, as they approached womanhood. Rose was dark with cheeks to match her name, and Bertha was flame-haired and vivacious. Dolly relished their company, and loved her role as cupid's messenger for the local lads, all of whom treated her with bemused fondness in their clumsy attempts at wooing her elder siblings. When Rose announced her stubborn intention to accompany a Scotch tinker back across the border to set up home in Dalkeith, Wilfred feigned outrage and disdain, while in truth felt relief at being unburdened of the need to support a growing brood of unwieldy womenfolk. Dolly was distraught at Rose's departure, and drew even closer to Bertha in the weeks after.

A chance meeting with a brig rudderman in a dowdy pub called The King's Arms, situated high above the oldest Wear bridge, convinced Wilfred that more money and better conditions were to be found on the banks of the Tyne. There, the keelmen were treated like royalty, he was told, not with the customary Wearside scorn, and the hold on the coal trade by the all-powerful Newcastle Hostmen meant more security and long-lasting opportunities for men like Wilfred, skilled in the handling of the wide, shallow-draughted keelboats.

Wilfred set out for Newcastle, alone, in the early April of Dolly's eleventh year, full of certainty that a new and better life lay ahead for all of them. Dolly and Bertha waited for a week before following him, unbidden, but spurred on by worry and lack of money. It was evening when they reached the Windmill Hills of Gateshead, and looked down in wonder across the broad river to the walls, spires and twisting terraces of Newcastle, its stern grey keep watching majestically over a dockside frontage lathered with the sails and rigging of a bewildering throng of vessels of all shapes and sizes. Bertha wisely chose to shelter for the night in a tanner's hut to the west, away from the bustling north road, and the pair set off across the busy wooden bridge as the bells of St Nicholas were pealing in next day's dawn.

Visits down-river from Deptford to Sunderland had been rare and mostly unnecessary for the young girls, so to suddenly find themselves in the bustling madness of a strange city was all but overwhelming. For an hour they stood together, arms locked, against the wall of the mighty Guildhall, as a rat's nest of commotion, noise and turmoil swirled around them. Sailors, doxies, merchants of all sizes and colours, angry tradesmen, simple bewildered folk, strong women and be-wigged men, all marching with a purpose from alley ways and entries, to destinations high above the dockside, where steeples pointed heavenwards, and tall buildings leaned as if dizzy, split apart by steep stairways and gushing spigots.

A dead horse was being hauled away from the road in front of a timbered drinking house opposite them, and a large crowd had gathered to offer criticism and advice. The language was thick and fast, the accent dark and strong. It was another world.

Before long there was music, the simple strings of a box fiddle, and a short-tongued lisping voice, all seemingly coming from the middle of the broiling crowd of onlookers.

"Buy broom besoms, buy them when they're new!" it sang.

"Fine heather bred uns, better never grew!" For Dolly, it was like the summer sun coming out. She stepped forward, drawn by the melody, oblivious to what had a moment ago seemed like a cauldron of insanity. Bertha grabbed her limp arm.

"Dolly!" she hissed. "Hold on now! Where're ye off to?"

"Just to hear the man," she said. "Ah can't see where he's at."

Bertha led her across the rutted road, skirting the crammed pack of laughing, caterwauling sightseers, who

15

immediately let out a unified groan as the horse's corpse split beneath its girth as the elderly knackermen tugged too hard on the ropes wrapped around it. The crowd at the viewing side of this occurrence began to scatter in panic from the sudden stench, and cleared enough to give view to the culprit of the song. He was stood, not on the street but in the open doorway of the public house, fiddle across his arm, a wide smile on his lips, a sliver of hair left on his pate, and sightless eyes aimed high above the approaching girls.

"If Ah had a horse," he sang, "Ah'd feed it every neet, Ah'd nivor leave lyin' stone deed on the street! Buy broom besoms..."

Dolly giggled like a sprinkle at the jest, and the blind man's head swivelled sharply in her direction.

"Ha ha!" he shouted, still bowing the strings, "D'ye like that 'un? Ah'm a clever 'un, aren't Ah?"

Men perhaps five or six of them, having abandoned the entertainment of the demised animal behind them, suddenly rushed at the pub door, pushing the blind man sideways and off the tall step where he'd been standing. He fell heavily, holding his fiddle high from harm's reach and so landing his full length into a merciful clump of weeds and tar-cloth rotting away beneath the parlour's long window. He cursed in full voice. Laughs and jeers rose from the remnants of the crowd, for it was indeed a comical sight.

"Sodden again Willie!" someone jeered.

"Jangle at a blind man would ye?" he snarled. "Bastads!"

Bertha and Dolly ran to him. He pulled back, startled, but the sound of Bertha's cooing voice as she took his arm melted him and he assumed the painful look of one mistreated and misused.

"Take us up, lass," he groaned, "Ah'm certain Ah've broke summit vital! But not me fiddle Ah hope…"

"No, no," Bertha said. "The fiddle's champion, and you are too, Ah'm sure of it. Just rise yersel' up on to me arm."

He stood suddenly, wobbled a little, and turned vaguely towards Dolly.

"Here, hold me fiddle while Ah wipe mesel' down. Them bastads. Thirst! It's thirst, makes the devil out of a man!"

Dolly cautiously took the instrument into her childish hands. Before she could help herself, she twanged the gut strings stretched tight across the plain soundbox. She'd never seen, never mind held a musical instrument before, and she felt giddy at its touch.

"Hew, hew!" the blind man rasped at her. "Ah told thee to hold it, not swivel a jig out of it!"

"Sorry, sorry!" Dolly murmured, in fright.

The man melted again at the sound of a young girl's voice, a child's voice.

"Aw, go on then, play us a tune if ye have to! Ah'll have a bit dance wi' yer mother!"

Bertha tried hard to cover her laugh with false indignation.

"Ah'm not her mother, Ah'm her sister. And she cannot play for truffles! Give the man his fiddle back Dolly, now go on!"

She placed the box back into the searching, outstretched hands of the blind man, who smiled and cackled a laugh.

"Canny lass, Dolly!" he said. "Ah can teach yer, yer know! For a pot of Spanish juice and a crust, Ah can have yer scraping a French polka in no time! Now where's that door, Ah never play on the street, me. The parlour's the place for me."

They guided him the few steps to the doorway, and he went in without another word. They heard laughter from within as he pushed the high door of the barroom and edged into the gloom.

It was noon, with more bells ringing from somewhere above them where the main city stood. They were hungry. They drank from a pump across from the Guildhall steps. Local folk passing by, especially men, eyed them warily. A group dressed in blackened blue-tailed jackets and yellow waistcoats emerged from an entry a dozen yards away, and fell silent as they passed them. One made a muffled comment in their direction, and his cronies laughed like conspirators. Dolly smiled too, but Bertha knew the nature of that laugh, and perhaps had heard the comment. Her face showed sudden concern.

For an hour the two girls followed the busy riverside eastwards, past shabby barques and proud schooners, around capstans, log-piles, creels, masts stretched out in agony, rudders gathered up in pain, bewildered by the noises and smells and faces, all gathered with stern intent and purpose, while they themselves wandered without direction through the writhing mixing of commerce and

18

labour. Every time a keel floated past them on the dark water, they searched for a sight of their father, both secretly sure in the knowledge that such a sight would never come.

As the river's busy day began to thin out, they turned back whence they'd come. The shadows from the forest of sails and masts grew longer. Dolly felt tired. Bertha felt a growing anger, though with her father or with herself, she couldn't fathom. Her mind drifted. The weariness of the day was giving way to worry about the night ahead. She fretted for herself, a red-haired girl in a strange city, as much as for Dolly, a child in a cesspit of uncertainty.

Dolly! Bertha's heart leapt in horror, as she felt a sudden anguish of loss. Where was Dolly? Where had she gone? In a beat of a heart, the child had vanished. By now only a handful of people were in sight on the quay. Behind her, a few steps away, only the filthy river slid slyly by. Bertha had never felt this rushing emotion of panic before. It rendered her helpless, weak, confused. She moved slowly, her head spinning, towards the water, her eyes wide, her hands trembling.

"Bertha! Look at this!"

The child's voice was behind her, away from the water's edge, towards the stacks of bloodied fleeces that lay in waiting between a brace of upturned hulls. There was Dolly, her eye skewed to one side with fatigue, and with a hand-sized crust of bread held out in Bertha's direction. The elder girl staggered with relief.

Dolly was jabbering. "Look, it's proper bread!" she was saying. "It was a big black-heeded gull, skimmin' down that alley with it in its gob. It had rogued it from

19

somewhere up there, but it was too heavy for it. Ah was just in time mind, 'cause there was a gaggle of his marras ready to swoop down and snatch it off the cobbles if Ah hadn't got there first! It's like the manna from heaven, ye know, in the parson's story! Ah cannot credit it!"

Bertha laughed. She laughed until she sobbed, and clenched the back of her hand to her mouth. Then the pair sat on a stray fleece by the wall and tore into the crust. The quay was empty save for the odd workman and a few women struggling by with unknown burdens of heaviness and bulk. The girls felt the unwelcome whisper of cold for the first time that day.

CHAPTER 3

THE MERRY DAY HAS GETTEN PAST

As Dolly passed the spot where she and Bertha had spent their first night in the city all those years before, she didn't even give it a second glance. It had been a wool merchant then, and had been a blessing to the bewildered girls, the surrounding cobbles being strewn with the shredded cast-offs of its wares, which they were able to gather up around them and bundle into a discreet amount of warmth in the black shadow of its skewed yard-gate. It was a printer's office now, and the wares that were scattered around nowadays amounted to nothing but puddles of blue-black river water and stones stained as if bruised, at the entrance. Even at this early hour, a dim lamp glowed within, with men toiling through the night at pressing machine and paper lashing. It would be no place now for waifs seeking shelter from the harsh reality of their own innocent foolhardiness.

But there had been instances in the years in between, when Dolly had found herself taking time to give thanks for her good fortune in this bowlegged neighbourhood. There had been singular moments of realisation, mere hesitations in the clattering roll of life, when she was smitten by the fact that fate had dealt her a surviving hand, when around her so many other players in this unsteady game had fallen by the wayside. She had a paying job of sorts, a place to live, friends and acquaintances, a sprightly walk barely hampered by her physical failings, and a regular path through this beleaguered world to follow. And now also, a man to grip her tightly by the waist and hair, and match her good eye with one of his own! She'd often laugh inside herself at this thought, but not this day. The Bigg Market was already busy with women and beggars on missions like her own, to harvest the cast-off trimmings of poor quality mid-week vegetables that the stallholders scattered sparingly in their wake. Dolly's heart sank. Already a pall of disappointment draped like a salt fret over the faces of those gathered there. The stallholders frisked busily around their trestles and carts, anxious for the chance to strike out at anyone who stretched an over-zealous hungry hand in the direction of their forbidden stock. Looks of harsh resentment slapped Dolly's flushed cheeks as she joined the throng. To her right, she saw a familiar face snarling accusingly at all and sundry. It was Bella Roy, leaning brazenly against the wall of the Lamb Inn, the sharp remnants of a snapped clay pipe jabbed unfilled and unlit in her teeth.

"Ah, Dolly", she said too loudly, "Don't think ye're too late and chide yer'sel'. There was nowt for gatherin'. Them tight-arses wouldn't spare ye a gobspit if ye'd crawled from Heaton Bank, the smut wipes!"

"We owe ye nowt, ye drunken bitch!" one of the stallholders retorted from behind the safety of his handcart. Bella gutted like an alley cat and stared at him with cold eyes. He sidled a step or two further from her. She chuckled in triumph.

Bella had been the queen of the Bigg Market when Dolly had first clapped eyes on her. A striking woman with a voice like a slider's bell, she'd been amply generous to the poor and needy from behind her own stall in days gone by, and many a hungry soul, Dolly included, had been grateful for her benevolence in darker times of keelmen's strikes and weather-bound brig famines. But slowly, her fortunes had changed. Her husband Rowly had died of a dogbite while gathering produce from a keelman's allotment off Darn Crook one Christmas Eve, and though Bella gamely struggled on, bolstered by the sympathy and understanding of the entire quayside, her luck, her looks, and her devoted customers had gradually ebbed away. One by one the public houses that increasingly became her main habitats, became less tolerant of her boldness and boisterousness, until now only The Flying Horse offered her a grudging welcome, tempered by an increasingly reluctant forgiveness in the face of her more alarming outbursts, when the worse for drink.

Dolly slid proudly towards her, defiantly eyeing the scowl of the marketeers amongst the slant of tables and handcarts, and swallowing the bitter resentment she tasted at the sight of service maids and housewives emerging from Pudding Chare, purses ready, baskets poised.

"Ah should've gone earlier up to the Mill at Spittal Tongues", Dolly said. "Alice Carmichael told us she got a few fine helpings up there last Thursday. Ah was late up."

Bella looked sideways at her and smiled.

"He's a hungry man that Moss! Night and morn, Ah bet!" she said coarsely.

Dolly flushed and looked away, a certain pride stroking her embarrassment at sharing words like this with an older woman.

"Well, he'll be at work with an empty stomach the day," Dolly sighed.

"Is he still on the chutes?" asked Bella.

"No", she answered. "He's with the chaldrons, comes home stinkin' o' hossmuck every night. But it's better money for us." Dolly was relishing this homely talk between women, feeling like a true wife with a man to scold and criticise. Bella sensed the warmth between them, and the unexpected domesticity that easily oozed from the girl. Yes, she must be twenty-three or more years, but she'd always be the twisted girl with fear in her squinting, that Bella had first seen trailing behind her bold sister up the market bank a dozen years before.

That distant morning, Bertha and Dolly had awoken as one, tangled in each-others' skirts and limbs, and dry of mouth from the dust of the sheep's wool, at the clanging of a ship's bell somewhere close by. Dolly had risen and walked with curiosity towards the river, where a sizeable barque was attempting a tight turn at the very base of the bridge. A smattering of foreign-tongued shouts and clamours were echoing across the water from a handful of crew leaning over the gunwales to watch for shallow banks and smaller traffic.

Bertha had decided in the night that they must head home today to Deptford. Further searching for their errant father was pointless. If he was here, there was more likelihood of him eventually getting word to them, either by message or in person, if they were at the family house, where equally, they themselves would be in a safer and less precarious situation. They had reliable friends and relatives, Bertha reasoned, and some kind of work for herself would surely present itself before too long. She cast a wary eye towards Dolly as she straightened herself up and smacked the filthy wool strands from the folds of her skirt.

Suddenly, there was a commotion from the quay, an unnerving barrage of shouts and calls and oaths, towards which a gaggle of dockmen and passers-by were rushing. Dolly stood transfixed as Bertha approached her from behind, peering beyond her head towards the still-swaying boat in mid-stream. A heavy wooden stay had swung unexpectedly across the stern of the boat and had evidently struck a crewman on the head. He'd not gone overboard, but lay motionless on the deck, with several of his fellow crewmen surrounding him, some knelt over him, some standing helplessly to one side. The girls, along with the rest of the observers, watched in fascination as the boat edged cautiously to the mooring, and after some fuss and unfathomable discussion, the injured man was carried roughly ashore. The skipper, if so he was, babbled angrily in what could have been Dutch as the grim-faced sailors manhandled the victim. A group of local men pointed to a hut in reachable distance on The Side, where a pair of washerwomen were waving white sheets in the morning sun. The pale limp body was lifted waist high between a mixed group of locals and crewmen and transported smartly to an imposing building on the City Road end of Sandgate, adjacent to where the washerwomen had been. The whole group were

25

swallowed by its large doorway and disappeared from view.

"Is he dead Bertha?" Dolly asked in wonder.

"No, he's just poleaxed. He'll be fine." Bertha was dubious.

"Where've they took him?" said Dolly. "What's that place? It looks like a gaol or summat…"

A tiny woman in widow's black crept by them, a bottle-green rag held to her face, as if in mourning.

"That's the keelman's hospital," she said. "There's never many come out o' there. A husband and a son, I'm owed. And yon Dutchman, they only give sparse care in there to them that's not their own. He'll be washed and shrouded before noon, and in a cart for the paupers' pit soon enough!" The old woman forced a moan, a sobbing wail, and stooped even lower to pick up a rotten turnip head from the gutter by a horse trough. She wrapped it quickly in the green rag and scuttled on her way.

"Maybe that's where father is, in there," said Dolly after a moment's wise-eyed thought. "If he's fallen or been set on. He's a keelman by trade. They're sure to have taken him there! We have to go and get the missus in charge. Tell them his name and find him. That's why he hasn't got word to us. He's bad, maybe dyin'!"

Bertha sensed a rising panic in the child's voice. "All right," she soothed, her arm around her, fully expecting Dolly to bolt across the street at that instant. "Come, let's ask at the entry. They'll know if he's been there."

As they entered the white-washed hallway, no-one was in sight. Through a half-shuttered window to their left, a quadrangle of greenery peeped through, with saplings and berried bushes rustled by a confined breeze. Dolly gaped in wonder at what appeared to her to be a garden within the walls of a house. The nature of the sight before her was beyond her understanding. As she stared blankly across the plain room, a red-faced woman in grey emerged from the furthest door.

"Are ye here for the young Dutch lad?" she demanded sharply. "'Cause he's very poorly. Ye'll have to come back!"

"No, we're not," Bertha explained. "Ah'm lookin' for me father. Our father," she added, gesturing at Dolly. "He came up from Sunderland a fortnight past and we've not heard from him. We've come all the way up from the Wear to find him. He's all we have, and he's a good man."

The woman frowned. "Why, what makes ye think he's here? We only take keelmen and their bairns here, not any dock hand or tinker who bloodies his nose in a bar-scrap!"

"He is a keelman!" Bertha snapped back. "He's as good as any ye've got up here!"

"Aye, but here we look after our own!" the woman retorted.

"D'ye not have a keelman's hospital on the Wear?"

"Ah don't know," Bertha said, "Ah don't know where other to look for him. He said he was off to the Tyne, so Ah reckon he must be somewhere about. There must be reasonin' in his goin's on."

"Or he's dead and buried already!" snarled the woman in grey. The young girls stared back at her. She immediately regretted her words. "Ah'm only sayin',

27

there could be a hundred reasonin's why ye cannot lay a salt on him! He's likely back at home, wondrin' where you's have got to!" The girls said nothing. "All right, Ah'll look in the book of admissions. What's his name?"

"Coxon," said Bertha, "Wilfred Coxon. Of Deptford."

The woman fumbled with tiny spectacles that slid down her ruddy nose continually as she turned the dry pages of the largest book that Dolly had ever seen. Was this The Bible, she wondered to herself? The Bible was filled with the names of the dead, she knew that from the Sunday sermons that her mother had taken her to years before. Is this what happened to people when they were dead, that their names joined the lists of so many other strange ones in the Bible? Her heart pounded.

The woman flicked through the pages carelessly. "There was only sparse concern last week," she said. "And the week before, aside from the cull pichin' over at Shields. And that was surely before yer Father was even on Tyneside, was it not? Ye said a week past?"

"Two weeks," Dolly offered.

The grey woman studied the page with renewed interest, it seemed to Dolly. "Two weeks?" she muttered. "Two weeks, eh?" There was silence as she read. "Five men lost at Tynemouth." She paused. "Only three were brought here. And two claimed." Her redness of face looked paler, pinker now. "What name was it?"

"Wilfred Coxon", said Bertha, firmly. The woman peered closer at the page, her eyes screwed in concentration.

"Wilty, they called him," Dolly murmured.

The grey woman's eyes flickered, and raised slowly into a blank stare towards the rustling green shrubbery beyond the open window. Her spectacles slipped down, unchecked. Her hand reached slowly to her face and she lifted them carefully from her nose. She turned slowly to look at the two girls, their bleak raggedness crying out like damned souls in the white simplicity of that bleached room. Dolly would recall that look on that woman's face for many's a long year to come.

CHAPTER 4

BLIND WILLIE SHALL PLAY ON THE FIDDLE

The bed was a cold empty scene of ragged blankets and poisoned undersheets when Dolly came back to the room above the vinegar store at past ten that morning. Moss's massive boots and harsh coat were gone. The empty gin bottle lay on its side by the skirting of the room. Dolly carelessly shifted the position of the wood slats that had long failed to imitate the forgotten shreds of glass that had deserted the sole window, and soothed the meaningless stretch of threadbare calico that excused the lack of curtain at one edge. In vain she teased the tallow-tinted coverlet to reach more than two corners of the mattress, then smoothed the single bolster pillow into a central spot, though maybe more generously into the direction away from her own.

Was it some curious feminine instinct that made her behave this way? Certainly, before Moss had entered her life, she paid no more attention to the details of this room as a she-cat to the spittoon-shadowed corner of the tap-room of the Flying Horse at midnight. Now, she pined for the chance to bring order and even cleanliness to these four staid walls, even in the knowledge that they would never be more than a convenience of abject tiredness and gin-smeared lust, a seasonal escape beyond the misery of hunger and deprivation that was forever braying at its bare door.

30

The grate had not suffered a fire for nearly a week. The blackened pot was still stained within from a broth of her own making last Friday evening. The plates too bore the remnants of a forgotten meal, and she was suddenly urged to scour them dryly with a cast-off cloth, though without result. Of a sudden, she took up the cracked bucket in her strongest hand, and with a determined lope headed for the pump at mid-Side, which she straight-way saw from a distance was busy with women and high-pitched children at this mid-morning.

Dolly was a familiar face on the quayside, but the womenfolk were wary of her. They had heard their men talk of her singing voice, of her bar-room manner, and the sight of her squint and warped gait only added to her reputation. She was a curiosity and carefree spirit among a breed of women yoked by brutal men and the harsh servitude of childbirth and domesticity, in this most caustic of neighbourhoods. She found herself ignored and pariah-like as she joined the plague of maternal spite at the pump-site, a sharp retort for the sense of womanliness she had wallowed in only minutes before. She watched these females with a remoteness that comforted her. Their drooping maternalism, their slow, sagging bodies and worn out expressions, transcended her own obvious physical deficiencies to the point of reassurance. Despite everything, she could feel Moss's wide hands across her thigh, his breath in her mouth, and felt a pride that she could finally invoke such reactions in a man.

"Take a hand of a blind man!" sounded a familiar voice at her rear. Dolly's reveries melted away. Willie Purvis, the blind fiddler, was padding ignored through busy clumps of workers and gossipers at the entry to Milk Market, on his daily path from All Saints Poorhouse to the first of several quayside pubs. He was tolerated in them all except The Three Indian Kings, where songsters of a more scholarly temperament met on occasion to boast about their latest works of significance. The fever of song-making and verse-writing was at a new pitch in this town, with both poet and printer vying with each other for attention and plaudits. In the midst of all this, a ragged minstrel like Willie was an embarrassment and a nuisance in their haughty eyes, and they had objected to his constant bowing and scraping and wailing in the barroom, while they spoke of grander things in the tap-room next door.

Since their first meeting years before, Dolly was well-known to Willie, at least by voice. She called to him across the street.

"Go canny off the step there Willie, and mind the ruts in the road!"

Willie's head spun around to her direction.

"Dolly, me flower!" he cackled. "Did you say ruts or rats? Ah'm wary o' the first and bolden o' the latter. Which is it to be?"

"Ha'ad yer horses!" Dolly replied with mock scorn in her voice. "Ah'm comin' to get yer!" The women at the water watched her go, their heads slanted towards each other in whispered contempt.

As Dolly reached him, Willie held out his arm. She took it with her own weaker one, and Willie sang at the sky.

"Dolly, Dolly, Dolly the dillen doll! Dolly, Dolly…!" over and over as they walked. Dolly smiled to herself. He had first put a tune to her name years before, when she would meet him daily as she waited for the coming of the organ grinder at Wraugham's Entry. It was almost the tune that the dark-skinned organ grinder played all day long, a strange foreign melody, neither sad nor happy, but bold and strong and too queer to warrant much in the way of farthings or popular appeal. Dolly had been taken with it though, and it held her spell-bound for hours as she huddled in the doorway of Larner's glass workshop, day after solitary day.

Those had been bleak times. Orphans now, she and Bertha had been living in a garret high above Lemington Gut, near the old theatre. Bertha had found work as a quayside shaver alongside a group of older women whose costs were as keen as their razors, but who needed a pretty lass to attract more custom. One of those that had found Bertha too hard to resist was a balloted Militiaman called Hepple, who now had an afternoon grip on the girl's time when her morning's bristle-work was done. He had hours to kill also, between pre-noon muster and evening patrol, so an understanding soon developed. In time, he would coax Bertha westwards, when he eventually secured an overseer's job in the old Roman quarries at Acomb. Their courtship in the meantime was long and heartfelt, snatched at odd hours dictated by duty, and by clandestine opportunity.

This had often left Dolly at a loss for company and occupation. She wandered the chares and entries around the Wheat Market and St Nicholas Square, peering into grimy windows, marvelling at women of fashion and men of long gait, pining over bakers' benches and sweetmeat stalls, and meeting the bold, bad, and beautiful characters who haunted the same cobbles as her. Blind Willie had emerged one cold morning from Clapham and Gilpins apothecary in Silver Street as Dolly stared through the yellow glass of the frontage too near to the door. Willie had walked into her with a smack and an oath, and had recognised her voice when she offered an apology.

"Dolly is that?" he said. "Little Dolly, Bertha's dillin sister?"

"Aye, it is. Ye surprised me, stridin' out like that into the public street!"

Willie chuckled. "Ah'm long since past surprises of that nature," he said. "But if it's a busy public Ah'm facin', after a bumpin' like that, the least ye can do is to walk me to the quay."

And so the pair of them had set off through the alleys, avoiding the hurrying crush of the morning activities, Willie's ever-present fiddle in a leather bag over his shoulder. The organ-grinder's tune rang through the passages and lanes in eerie echoes and swirls as they got closer.

"Dolly, Dolly, Dolly-oh!" Willie trilled with it, mockingly, merrily. "Dolly, dillen Dolly oh!" he went. The girl was flattered by the rhyme, despite the stain of dillen – runt – that it contained.

She slowed down to listen as they approached the corner where the man churned out the tune, but Willie pulled at her harshly.

"No, no, Ah'm not givin' him ear!" he moaned irritably. "That's not respectable music. There's no skill in that. The carter's bitch could give as good as that. If ye need music to listen to, Ah'm the only man for the task."

"But Ah can't go in to pub rooms and saloons to listen to ye!" Dolly retorted. "If yer think yersel' too good for the street, then yer too good for the likes o' me!"

Willie was amused. "Why, Ah'm singin' to ye now lass! Doesn't that tell ye how good ye are in my blind old eyes? Ye have yer very own song! There's not many that can say that now, is there?" And off he went again as they turned into the Pandon Gate. "Dolly! Dolly! Dillen Dolly!" he sang, clutching her limp arm ever more tightly.

Time had been fair to them. Dolly was a woman now, but the years had made little impression on Willie's squat body and wide, lined face, and only a whitening of what was left of his hair betrayed the passing of them. He had first heard her sing in the Bunch of Grapes on Side, one mid-week evening, several winters ago, but had passed no comment as to her worth. She sensed a wariness about him when he was in earshot of a compliment handed to her by some boozy admirer, and a whiff of jealous competitiveness sometimes soured the air between them. She understood this intuitively. Poor Willie had been blind probably from birth, people said, and had struggled to an age when his talent with word and melody was his sole saviour, his meal ticket, and the foundation of his position in this soiled society. His lack of a sense so essential and taken for granted by all others, drove him to talk louder, more often, more outrageously than needs be, and any perceived threat to his place as songster-in-chief

35

pricked more than his pride; it wounded his sense of survival. Dolly respected this, and indeed respected the man himself. She had been touched, only a few weeks earlier, when he had unexpectedly laid his hand on her wrist at a beer-soaked table and offered her a song.

"D'ye know "Sair Fail'd, Hinney"?" he'd said softly. "Ye'll never have heard me sing it for public! It's a beauty of a song to listen at, but a devil of a tune to hold on to! But Ah reckon it's fit for ye. Listen up now..."

He'd leant over to her ear and crooned softly at her, in a voice that she and no-one else had ever heard him use, a tender keening, smooth around the verse, and then leaping at the top of the tune when it eventually came. Over and over he sang it, mesmerising the girl and eventually exhausting himself.

"Sair fail'd hinney", he sang, "Sair fail'd noo, Sair fail'd hinny, Sin Ah kenned thou." The words sounded more than ancient, the melody from another world. The words were a man's, but the tune was a woman's. Willie's rendition filled Dolly's head and heart. She sang it later that night, alone at the banks of the Tyne, but had yet to give it a public platform.

The water bucket still empty in her hand, Dolly left Willie at the door of The Flying Horse, and wandered back to her room. The thirst for cleaning and homemaking had abated in her, and the burden of hunger and a need to feed her man had replaced it with a vengeance. As she'd turned into the entry, a blustery rain began suddenly, and a grimy-looking stallholder was struggling with a canvas sheet to cover his meagre wares from the downpour. Dolly loped towards the scene and

36

with keenness and dexterity, grabbed the loose end of the cover and succeeded in stretching it over the contents of the cart. The man tucked it in, as a smiling Dolly stood expectantly by.

"They'll be champion now," she said. "Good job Ah was passin'."

He scowled at her and reluctantly picked up a leek, examined it, changed it for a smaller one, and threw it towards her.

"Thank you", she said, feigning gratitude. "That's no good to ye now is it?" she added, pointing to an onion that she'd managed to nudge off the edge of the cart in the excitement. "It's got hoss-shite on it, ye can't sell that." She pushed it towards a patch of manure with her foot before he had the chance to lower himself below the shaft of the cart to see it. "Ah'll try rinsin' it but Ah doubt that'll fettle it. Anyhow, the rain's stopped!"

The leek and the onion were in the bucket and she was away, and the vegetables were soon joined by a gutted fish that she spotted, out of gull's view, beneath a bonded keel oar on the nearby wagon way. It was past noon. She would get water, set a fire in the grate for boiling a stew, and eat with Moss in the hour between his return from the ballasts and her leaving for work at dusk.

Moss was working in the Byker cut, where the colliers dropped spill to suit the tidal river. Three chaldron carts were allocated twice a year to skim the thick off the riverside spoil to ward against the build-up of silt and sand, and clear a good draught for the ever-wary collier brigs in their journey to meet the keels. Moss had been with a three-man team, enjoying a leisurely pace for the last three weeks. It also brought him home early each day.

Dolly had washed her face in the last of the water, pulled a weaver's rake through her hair and pinned it, and was wearing her shawl at an angle to fool the crook in her weak shoulder when she heard a wholesome cough and spit at the foot of the stairs. Moss stooped in through the doorway. He noticed her efforts to sooth his one tired eye towards a beauty that she feared she would never possess, but that he saw plainly. He smiled and uttered something she couldn't understand, but sensed it was fondly meant. Without taking off his jacket he fell on the bed with a long groan of exhaustion. She moved towards him and sat almost primly at his side. Head back, he laid his heavy fingers instinctively on her knee.

"Is there food?" he asked.

"Some fish in a broth," she said apologetically. "Ah've wages to get tonight, so there'll be more tomorrow. And drink if you want it."

"No, you keep your money for yourself now," he said fighting off weariness. "I'll have money. I will buy you things. Food, we can always find food. Special things, that is more important."

"Food is important," she laughed. "For strength. For those workin' hands and for the insides. For…"

He placed his hand over her lips.

"I have to go tonight to talk about a job, a special job, to guide a sculler down to the north bay. On Sunday, early. I have done this before, so I think I will do it once more. For three shillings, I think."

Dolly pulled back slightly. "Are you stealin' it? Is that why they pay ye so much?" she asked warily.

"No, no, not that," he said. "It is the business of Turnbull, but not the Hostmen, so there is no "tasse", what you say for that? No money extra…"

"Tax?" Dolly asked.

"Si, si, tax, the same thing. That is why."

"But there's always tax," Dolly said. "That's what keeps the Hostmen and the clerks warm and fed, while we worry and drink our food in stews not chew it in meat. And ye could lose yer job if you're found to be goin' against the Hostmen. Or worse…"

"No, not all that, not a worry for you," Moss groaned. "It is nothing, only a "favore", You know that. And yes! Yes!" He sat up and faced her. "You can sail with me, that will be possible, and from the river, you will see all the towns and churches and all the splendid things that only the "marinaio" and stink of keelmen see. You too will see it!"

"No, a woman can't set foot on a boat, you know that!" she hissed, taken aback by the suggestion. "That could never be!"

"Yes, yes, in Genoa, the wives, the daughters, they live together on the long barges and "barcone", even the schooners, yes! It will be adventure!"

"No!" she almost shouted

"Come, it will be a magical adventure. You will wear my jacket. You will be a man for a day! No woman before will have such an adventure. You will be a hero for a whole day!"

39

Dolly stopped herself. This man could be child-like and wild at times. She let the conversation crumble into tiredness and walked to the window. She stared out, through the gloom of crooked roofs and twisted alleys, to where a bare mast or two reached up from where she knew the river lay.

"Such a thing could never be," she said to herself.

CHAPTER 5

O BRING ME THE BOATMAN

The vast waters, brown and powerful, mocked her, surrounding her with their coldness and unrelenting lapping, like the evil chattering of unseen devils and sprites. The flimsy wood and the misplaced confidence of the mere mortals around her gave her no comfort. These were the greedy waters that had claimed her father, had enslaved him in life, and then had choked him in death. They had broken her heart, and now perhaps were bent on stilling it forever. And yet that very heart was now locked in a tormenting conflict of fear and thrill, of lust for life and terror of death, at battle at once within her. The sky beyond drew her towards the pale promise of hope and freshness of a new day. Dolly suddenly felt her fingers and wrist ache from the grip in which they were locked, and in her weaker limb, she tasted a strength that had hitherto been unknown to her. She turned her head cautiously to look at Moss, just behind her left shoulder, and he caught her eye. He grinned. He seemed to know.

Saturday night had been a squall of noise and anger, bolstered by the drunkenness of new ale. Dolly gladly avoided her gaffer, Harrison Marley, all night, after she had heard him barking spluttered obscenities at his wife Jessie early in the evening from halfway up the mildewed staircase that led to their lodging. The entire pub had heard raised voices coming from the scullery at around eight o'clock, but all the later row and ruction amid that beer-swilling mob had absorbed whatever followed behind the skewed inner door. Needless to say, when Harrison did emerge to face the public, his demeanour was foul and menacing, and he'd spent the whole night at the parlour end of the bar, scowling into a mug of beer, and scheming drowsily with Anty Proud, himself more than happy to lean a conspiratorial ear, if it meant a share of spite's wayward access to the barrel.

Jessie Marley never emerged at all that night, so Dolly, along with May the long-suffering barmaid, were left to dodge between the two barrooms, slopping and pouring, splashing and foaming, penny raking and soaking, and all the while taunted by the angry thirst of a roaring room-full of uneasy end-of-the-week revellers with no homes to go to.

There was no singing to be done that night. The caustic atmosphere brought on by the landlord's smouldering fury had stained the evening with a bubbling unease that flicked across every face and tarnished every conversation. But at one point, during an unexpected lull across the bar, Dolly felt herself wondering if the entire agitation was *her* doing, anxious as she was about Moss's plans for them both in a dawn that lurked a mere few hours away.

The dark room and rough bed were both empty when, hours later, she wearily pushed open the familiar door, and she stared at their stillness for a moment, her mind weaving its way through possibilities and excuses, until finally she lay down alone, her shawl still wrapped around her, and slid off into sleep. Moss was in the room when she woke, and darkness still in charge, causing him to bump noisily into the bed-leg, and hiss some homespun curse into the black dampness.

"Are ye hurt?" she whispered, "What are ye doin'? There's a candle…"

"No, no, we have to be leavin'", he said. "It's so early, sorry, but we must leave. A long day for us." She saw his mouth shape a smile as her better eye mellowed to the gloom. She forced herself to rise, her mind slowly focusing, her body slowly coming to life.

The empty garths and cobbled entries echoed to the clump of Moss's boots, but Dolly's light feet and worn shoes made hardly a sound, and frankly would have fooled no-one, despite the massive reefer jacket she was wearing, and the bottle-blue wool cap that was pulled down across her brows. They passed not a soul as they made their way to the river. Again, it was only a spice-box of noise that peppered the moonless night. A baby's cry from a dimly lit upper room, a retching cough behind a privy door, the dull chime of a hearth-clock down an alleyway to a hovel beyond, and the lone bark of a dog, all bouncing through the warren of streets, from somewhere far or near. Moss strode with resolve, and Dolly limped after him like a shadow, her mind a mixture of bewilderment and dread. She tried not to fear what lay ahead of her, and tried equally not to wonder why this man had so insisted on her presence. Had he insisted? Had he explained? Was that true desire that sparked in his eye, or a twisted plait of schemes and secrets that fired his enthusiasm? On they tramped, the one-eyed man and the lame scarecrow. Another clock, with much more authority, chimed a count of four somewhere in the city above them. Yet another, or perhaps the echo of the first, sounded somewhere far off to where the wind now blew, and then they were at the river's edge, and further downstream than Dolly had ever ventured before, away to where the slope of houses falling from Byker lay sleeping and still.

Dolly became aware of a solitary figure standing hunched against the chill by the water's edge. A large row-boat rocked and bobbed a yard or so into the water. There were no other crafts moored within earshot, though Dolly knew that the smooth river was said to cheat noise and stretch the senses. She was peering nervously about her, when Moss's voice broke the silence, close to her suddenly, near enough to her face that she smelt the dark stain of tobacco on his breath.

"Say nowt," he panted. "No voice. And wait."

She stood fixed, as Moss wordlessly approached the other man, and the two of them busied themselves at the mooring. Dolly stared at the river, as the fear inside her absorbed the greater width, the new closeness, the overwhelming expanse of its presence at this point of its existence. Ship-less, bridgeless, free of quay and jetty, the mighty Tyne had come here to stretch a strength that was usually stifled by the constraints of its familiar role, as servant to commercial endeavour, a mere quarter mile upstream.

Suddenly, Moss was motioning to her with an agitated gesture to join him. With a walloping heart, she hobbled over to where the other man was already stepping from the water's edge into the boat. Moss motioned for her to do likewise. She felt the grasp of the icy water around her feet. She lifted her better leg over the wooden rim and all at once she was afloat, uncertain, unbalanced, cowering halfway between standing and sitting, and finally finding the smooth flatness of the rower's board, which she gripped with sweating hands and tightened legs. She heard water playing among the wood beneath her feet, and then the boat lurched as Moss stepped in and they skimmed slowly into the midstream. The air grew suddenly colder. Dolly gasped for breath. It came, and she sank to accept that she was gliding to an inevitable life's end. There was nothing she could do now. The river would claim her, like it had claimed her father and likely her mother, and a hundred more. And a hundred of hundreds more before them. There was some comfort in that company, at least.

She felt the nudge of Moss's clenched fist against her shoulder. He was manoeuvring the long oars behind her, while the other man handled those in front. The huge sculler seemed empty apart from this trio of silent humanity. She gingerly turned to look at Moss. He was working hard at the task. He threw his head in the direction of the shore they had just left. She gazed away in that direction. The grey glow of a new dawn was just beginning to cast it in a silhouette of floated buildings, stocky cottages and rows of block-built warehouses, a holy place topped by a castle's roof, a spike of a spire, a square-rigged vessel tilted at a tumbling angle, dragged by madmen on to dry land, terraced smacks lined up with their hulls shamelessly exposed, and a mountain of felled trees, trimmed and stacked like dead men, tidy and lifeless. She remembered that another shore faced this one and turned to see. The early greyness fell brighter on that side, and vessels of every size and shape were crowded at its edge, some as still as graves, others animated by crew and caretakers, occasionally voicing, grinding capstans, stretching sail and wrapping net. Beyond these, noble buildings and proud taverns stood, and what could have been a timbered playhouse or perhaps a rich man's hideaway loomed larger than any. She saw how the river peeled away into a broad bend, and that this was to be their watery path, carrying as it was, a mere stone's cast beyond them, a half-rigged brig nearing to the limit of its ample depth. Their tiny sculler approached it at a wide berth, but Dolly dipped lower, a new fear washing over her, as the sheer scale of its hull, floating unskirted by the rise of quayside landings, towered over them like a massive beast of burden. Suddenly the watery way beneath her offered a homely security in comparison, and once they had left the monstrous presence of the brig behind them, Dolly's whole being untightened, and she calmly wallowed in these new sights and sensations, that Moss had promised that this strange voyage would bring.

On they slid, in silence, perhaps hurried by the light of the impending dawn. How furtive this venture was supposed to be, Dolly didn't know, but the game of chance, pitting daylight discovery against sandbanks and shallow drafts, was one that had to be played with speed and dexterity, that much was evident. Dolly was at ease enough now to feel hunger in her stomach and coldness around her bare legs. Although this Sabbath morning presented few moving vessels, the nearness to the open sea meant that more and more ships were crowded at each side of them, moored and motionless. Only the occasional flag added colour to the greyness of this dawn, fluttering lazily from high riggings and tall masts. The water beneath them was greener now, with sparse patches of greasy thickness bearing witness to the river's role in relieving the townsfolk of their unwanted dross. The men with her raised their oars briefly for a breather, at which point the figure in front held up a brown bottle to his lips, which he then raised over his left shoulder, back in her direction. She glanced at Moss. He nodded at her to take it, and she dared to lean forward, take it from their fellow traveller to pass it back to her man. Moss nodded again, for her to take a drink. She swigged back a sharp draft of the sour liquid, probably some old ale that had been carried for a long way and a long while, and then handed it to him. He did the same and she passed it back to the silent stranger in front of her. The two men sat for a heartbeat, and then splashed their oars back into the dark water.

A new dread slowly drifted over her. The purpose of this silent voyage still eluded her. She fought off the distrust for these men that had begun to burrow into her being, one whom she had known for so short a time, one whose face she had yet to even see. And she herself, dressed like some ragged guiser or a gipsy harlot, shielding her womanhood from friend and foe alike, was a living travesty on this waterway of superstition and fancy. A female afloat was a curse, a stigma, a death-mark. What foolish devotion had brought her to this place?

47

The men were oaring easily now, as the current took hold of their tiny craft. Moss pulled hard on the roped rudder, and she saw him search the north bank for somewhere predetermined, it seemed, where their journey would end. The clouds of night were clearing in front of them, and a weak sun had almost cleared the horizon. The opposite bank was still thick with slumbering hulls, but the near side was more sheer, and a haven for smaller skiffs and tubs, with bigger black-tipped fisher smacks slotted at random between them.

The stranger, an arm's length in front of her, half-turned and muttered in a Scotch voice to catch Moss's attention.

"There." He pointed off towards the shore. "Hard to leeward, but guard against the current. We'll be on the Black Middens beyond, that'll finish us."

Moss leaned heavily to one side and shortened the rope.

"No!" snarled the other man, "Easy on it. This side of the buoy. The entrance to The Gut is beneath the fort. Coax it, slice it slow, back, forth, back, forth."

Moss was silent. He seemed to understand, despite the orders having no meaning to Dolly. Her eyes followed the rise of the cliff that grew high above them now, and the high walls and towers of some ancient place rose up at its peak. The river had widened beyond recognition, and had surrendered to the sea, something that Dolly hadn't seen since childhood. The distant roar and slate grey expanse entranced her for a long moment. A longer, low stone harbour wall reached out from the farther bank, tipped by a grey lighthouse whose beam had died before they had cleared the last bend of the river. Their boat was now easing towards a jetty on the nearer shore, with Moss leaning heavily on the rudder, and the stranger choosing when to work an oar here, an oar there, with practiced skill.

The boat skimmed and bumped up to the dry wooden structure and the stranger was up and scaling a set of much-weathered rungs, rope in hand, before the vessel had come to a halt. Using an oar, Moss edged it nearer to the framework and without being told, Dolly carefully rose and reached for the ladder. With little dignity, she hoisted herself up, taking the strain of her numb limbs with her good shoulder. A grimy helping hand was waiting for her at the top. The stranger hauled her up like she was a bag of ballast, and pushed her aside. It was only then that she saw that she had not been the only cargo on this journey.

The man was kneeling now, leaning unsteadily over the ladder, as Moss was pushing vertically up its sheer shafts, a sturdy wooden box, riveted and lined in brass, about the size of the bolster on her bed, but much heavier. Dolly watched with a mixture of realisation and worry, knowing that it was the awkwardness of the task and the shape of the object, rather than its bulk, that was the issue, and she knelt beside the man instinctively and tried her best to be helpful. The box was soon on the jetty at their feet and Moss rose up next to her from the boat, without looking at her. Between them, the two men picked up the box and still without a word, carried it briskly towards the land end of the jetty. Dolly followed, her insides churning. She had known from the start that there was a reason for this strange voyage, but her lack of understanding as to her own part in the enterprise had caused her to dismiss it from her mind. She now carried that confusion like a burden as cumbersome as the one being manhandled in front of her.

The mooring at which they'd arrived was a crumbling, dilapidated landscape of rotting hulks, abandoned nets and crumbling hovels, and was deserted still on this early Sunday morning. Dolly could hear the rush of the sea nearby, but nothing more. The two men made for a doorless hut that backed up on the foot of the cliff, and carried their load inside. Moss came back out alone, and smiling, came close to her. She stared at him, not returning his smile. He took her weak hand. He knew she liked this, as it broke down the barrier that she often feared her disability might raise between them. But at that moment, the barrier was of his making.

"Job is done," he said softly. She stared at him.

"What job?" she said. "What was that, what did we just do?"

"Oh, it was not a wrong thing," he said, "That's what you fear. No, no, it was a good thing, it was a help to everyone. We are..." He hesitated, searching for the words. "We are *salvatori!* We help the people!"

"I don't know what you mean", she said, staring at his face, trying to know him.

Behind him, the other man emerged from the hut, and grunted at them.

"Time we moved on," he said. "The boat secure?"

"Yes, I'm sure", said Moss. Dolly was surprised to see him not in charge, to be answering to someone else in this way.

They set off walking, along the meagre stone causeway at the foot of the cliff, past more abandoned paraphernalia of the local fishing trade, until their path widened and opened to the sea. An old woman passed them without a word, carrying an empty pannier and smoking a grey pipe. An odd figure or two were visible on the beach now, where the morning tide was lapping far beyond a clumsy scattering of brown rocks. As they walked, the sun cleared the gloom, and Dolly felt the warmth on her face. The cliff at their side had mellowed into a gentle green slope. The air was salty but fresh. The sky was wide and open, and soothed her like a song.

The men were ahead of her, talking closely as they walked. She took in the vista, the huge emptiness of sea and sky, and allowed herself a voice.

"Oh where is the boatman, my bonny hinny," she sang. "Oh where is the boatman, go bring him to me." A gull chorused back at her, and for a moment, she forgot where she was, what she was doing here. It almost felt that this was where she belonged.

They were at the top of the bank now, and Dolly could see rows of houses and bigger buildings, stretching away along the higher shore. She was silent again. There was a pump next to a low wall, and Moss was leaning down to drink from it. The other man was wiping his face with a brown rag. She sat away from him. He looked at her for the first time.

"Dolly is it?" he asked.

"Aye it is," she responded.

"I've seen you at the Horse. Heard you singin'. Ye can certainly deliver a tune, but you shouldn't be here. It's no place for a woman, river work."

"River work ye call it?" Dolly retorted. "Ill work, Ah reckon. Something crooked. There's no place for anyone in that." He didn't reply.

"So, you're an old friend of Moss?" she asked, aware that her last words had had a barb ill-suited to talk between strangers.

He stared back at her. "No, not an old friend. Maybe not a friend at all. We merely have common interests. No more than that."

"What's your name?" she asked.

He thought for a moment, and said, "Parrish. Alec Parrish. Frae the town of Leith. Ye ken where that is?"

"Scotland, Ah reckon."

He smiled to himself. "Aye, Scotland, fair Scotland. But a long time since I seen it. Huddled in poverty here below the Borders, with neither friend nor foe. Trusting no man. Nor woman..." He glanced sideways at her. "But yon Gippo," he gestured at Moss, still leaning at the pump, "Or whatever his origins might be. He has no axe to grind with the likes of me. And he knows injustice when he sees it, I reckon. More than most. More than I, maybe."

Dolly was puzzled, uncertain.

"Maybe. But all this creepin' about. And such an early hour. What was it, that box?" she said. "What was in it, to make such secrecy and dark journeyin' needed?"

Parrish spat at his feet, and rubbed the result into the dust beneath them. He stared for a moment to the ocean.

"Did you ever hear tell of the strike, the Keelmen's strike, some forty years ago?" he asked her. Her brow twisted. He answered himself. "No, you're too young, and it's never spoken of now. But it was a dreadful, woeful time. I remember. My ain father was lost to me at the cause of it."

"Your father was a keelman?" she asked. "But... how could the keelmen strike? Why, if there was work to be done, why would they choose to stop at it?"

"No, you don't grasp it," he sighed. "There's always a good reason for a stoppage like that, and usually an unjust, starving, struggling reason, and a decision not easily taken. In those days, there were those who were making money, while being far away from the work of the river, while those who were toiling and risking upon it, were sweating away for a pittance. And then lesser men, unskilled, selling themselves for smaller wages, and a danger to themselves and to others, were brought in to take the work away from those born to do it. And my father, a stranger here, a common labourer, saw fit to raise up his head, and point to those who were mistreating the river and its men. And he died for it." He looked at her slowly, sizing up her reaction. She stared back, wordless.

He continued then. "And I had to leave the river, and the town that I had no desire to even be near to in the first place. I'd been brought here as a child, and now my mother pulled me away again. I watched her choke from dust in the mustard warehouses in Durham, and so I came back alone to this. "He motioned towards the sea. "To good fresh air, tinged with a salt breeze."

He stood, stretched. "But now, it's all happening again. One man of principle, a young clerk, Turnbull by name, bore witness to the underhand schemes being played out behind official doors. The scrawl of corrupt hands on parchments, the signatures of rotten alliances and sly agreements, he saw it pass before him, and knew the smell of corruption and from whence it came. And that is what is in that chest. It's the makings of strife and hunger, the poison of greed and power."

The grand words were practised, and long thought-over. He looked down at her, as if again to gauge her reaction, her understanding. "Mere paper and ink, not gold and trinkets, but worth more than any of that, to some people. The signatories and plans and testimonials, for the building of loading staithes and wagon ways, that will mean riches to the fat and well fed, in their houses high above the river, but despair and degradation to those by the river's edge, who will be thrown out of work, their livelihoods snatched away. That's something I cannot stand by and watch again. And young Turnbull, the brave fool, has gifted it all to me, to find better use for their skulduggery and avarice. There you have it."

Dolly's mind swirled in search of meaning and significance to all this, this noble heroic talk, but as yet, none could she find. The Scotsman made to walk away, but stopped, turned towards her once more.

"I'm pleased that you know the words of Rabbie Burns," he said. "That warms my heart."

Dolly looked up. "Ah know of no such man," she said.

"You know him without knowing it," he said. "You sing his song, 'My love is like a red, red rose, that's newly

54

sprung in June', and you sing it gladly and you sing it well."

"That's a song from Willie," she said, "Blind Willie, he gave me that song. He claims it as his own!"

He laughed. "Blind Willie, the fiddler! Ha! Yes, I can hear him claiming that as his own, but I cannot see him feeling in such a manner for any woman, so as to be gifted of words like that! No, it was the work of Rabbie Burns, a fellow countryman of mine, known to many, loved by all. I saw him once mesel', astride a squat pony in the market at Dalkeith. He died not two years since, but left behind many songs that are well worth seeking, and well worth singing. Maybe if we meet again, you'll have a few you can offer me."

He walked off towards Moss, who was busy tying the string of his eyepatch, his face and hair wet from pump-water. The long night and the sour ale now drove Dolly to the back of a half-standing stone stable a few yards away, to relieve herself in a semblance of privacy. When she came back, Alec Parrish was gone, and Moss was busy with his bootstrap.

"Not such a bad bugger", he said, looking up at her. "Not as much fighting man as he looks."

"He told me what you were doing, about that box."

"Ah, good, he explains it faster than I can. And you believe him better I think". Moss was tired. Conversation was coming hard to him in this strange tongue.

Dolly stared down at him, and eventually knelt beside him and moved away his big fumbling fingers, so that she could tighten the strap for him.

"Ah still don't understand," she said. "What good will it do to steal a box full of paper, worthless letters and the like, in the face of all the trouble he says will happen? Losing ink scrawls and parchments won't stop men doing what they want to do!"

"Oh, paper, yes," said Moss, smoothing her hair, freed now from the feeble disguise of the ridiculous cap. "But worthless, no! In the box are the maps, the plans, the reckoning of money and who will spend it, who will receive it. When the Hostmen find it is gone, they will think twice about tricking the keelers and colliers out of their work. And perhaps the men from the newspaper will be interested in hearing about all these secrets too!" He smiled, nodding at her, knowingly.

"But it's only the Hostmen and the toffs that read the Chronicle!" she replied, "They won't be finding out anything that they don't already know!"

"No, no, my dear one," he said, "The newspaper is important for everyone, even you, even me. In the times ahead of us, that is how people will save themselves, through knowledge, through words on paper shared by everyone. That is why that paper," he nodded towards the hidden box, "is so like treasure. It is a box of treasure, yes, that's what it is."

Dolly stared back at him. "But it means nothing to me," she said. "Ah can't read it. Ah can't write words. How will that help the likes of me."

Moss smiled. "I will teach you. Yes, I will." He stood up. "But not today. The sun is warm now. We can sleep on the green grass by the broken church. And then I know a tavern where I have friends maybe. Come!"

56

Dolly stood, heavily, weighed down by thought as much as fatigue. The brightness of the morning sun would slowly sooth her, as they tramped steeply, towards the bare brown bones of an ancient ruin. It stood high above the river's mouth, guarded defiantly by a once-mighty edifice of battlements and broken walls, its blind windows still peering sea-ward, wary of approaching Norsemen, in their dragon-driven sailboats. As she began the climb towards it, Dolly's mind was in a dazed turmoil, with all this talk of printed words, signed documents and trust and deceit. By the time they reached the outer wall of the ruins, she was exhausted and dizzy. The pair of them lay down together in a hollow lit by sun, but hidden by tall grass. She felt his strong but gentle hand run down her face, stroke her neck, and rest easily on her chest, and then she was asleep.

CHAPTER 6

AND IF IT BE TRUE WHAT THEY'RE SAYIN'

There were certain taverns, inns and public houses thereabouts, which were seen to be forever thriving, forever bustling and busy. They seemed to boast a perpetual liveliness, spiced by the camaraderie and bonhomie of a regular, exclusive clientele. The drink on offer might vary dramatically in taste and quality, not only from house to house but from day to day, in any given establishment, and the price of it, not to mention the effect that it has on its imbiber, undoubtedly played a part in such an equation, but the sheer number of people in a city like Newcastle ensured that dry throats and loose coinage were always in evidence, as were the high-jinks and conviviality that they brought with them.

The traditions that bind one man to one alehouse, and his neighbour, or even his brother, to another, a place, perhaps situated in the same street, are unspoken and unfathomable. The trades, skills and political allegiances of certain groups of men are likely to dictate the parlours where they have congregated for years, perhaps by way of convenience or proximity. Very few men along the Tyne varied their lifetime habits in matters of the bottle or the cask, and they were enough in number to ensure that many establishments were sure of a full house on any night of the week.

For the women thereabouts, unless domestic employment excused it, choices were few, and indeed many of the female sex were content in the knowledge that it wasn't acceptable that they should even consider frequenting these places. For those that did, and who were shameless or oblivious enough to care little what it did for their reputations, only a very few houses were known to welcome, or even tolerate them.

Taverns like The Flying Horse or The Black Boy, within calling distance of the river itself, or The Swan at the corner of Pudding Chare and Collingwood Street, higher up towards the heart of the old city, were lively, enticing and entertaining places, brimming over with noise and tall tales. Occasionally fists would be raised, or even knives drawn, but those were rare and unwelcome occurrences, for men whose wit and muscle had to be keen enough to survive a day's toil at their regular labour. The flickering lights and easy talk of the public houses of Sandgate were its very heartbeat, and had been that way so for as long as memory professed it.

But there were other drinking places that crawl through a meagre existence for just as long a duration, yet for the opposite reasons. Places where men go in search of solitude and escape, where social niceties can be washed away in cheap liquor and problems quenched in tasteless, foamless ale. The darkness therein hides both incipient dirt and troubled emotion in one arc of a drinker's arm. The clientele relish the chance to be undisturbed, unpestered and anonymous. Their number is forever few, their voices invariably silent.

The Bunch of Grapes was one such a place, and by chance lay within walking distance of the house of Alec Parrish, which itself stood uncomfortably close to the ballast banks at Byker. He was wont to enter its jagged-edged door, perhaps three times a week, though never at week's end. It had been a Monday, in fact, some three weeks earlier, when he had been surprised to hear his own name being whispered, in a quiet but shamelessly quizzical tone, at the half-open hatch at which the heavyset, sullen landlord grudgingly had cause to pour his wares into unmatched and unattractive drinking vessels, as and when his attention could be summoned. Parrish himself had been sat in thought, crouched towards a reluctant fire in the back of the grate of the stone fireplace at the furthest end of the room. A tall figure, with a young man's bearing, was at the hatch, and it was from his lightly bearded lips that the whisper had emerged. The landlord, to his credit, had responded by slamming the hatch closed without a word, but Parrish's own noticeably curious response had been all the information that the young man needed. His eyes focused on Parrish, and with serious brows and a nervous pout on his lips, his head gave a cautious bow of greeting.

Alec Parrish's mind lashed out in search of a quick and suitable reaction, but he had been unprepared for it. Already the stranger was advancing towards him, passing the open-mouthed, sleeping figure of the room's only other customer, and momentarily presented himself at Parrish's side. Alec cursed for allowing himself to be caught out like this. He stared wordlessly up at the man for as long a time as he could muster. Eventually the other spoke, once more in a halting, breathless whisper.

"Mr Parrish, sir?" There was no response forthcoming. He continued despite this.

60

"My name is Turnbull, Elijah Turnbull. We have mutual…" He hesitated. "… acquaintances. They have directed me to you, in hope that I might beg of your counsel." He looked around the room, dismissing the sleeping occupant as he did so, "Concerning a certain matter, that may be of interest to you."

Still Parrish offered no acknowledgement. He continued to stare, the two beakers of ale he had quaffed earlier, refusing to relax their grip on his reactions.

"May I sit?" Turnbull asked.

Parrish told himself to play for time, and inclined his head in the direction of the nearest chair. Turnbull pulled it closer, and the rasp of its legs on the coarse floor woke the sleeper with a jolt. The man looked around briefly, picked up his cup, and discovering it to be empty, breathed heavily and stood up. He lurched towards the door with a belch and was gone. The other two watched him depart. Turnbull looked relieved, and leaned in towards Parrish.

"Elijah Turnbull, as I say, is my name," he said. "My employment, these past twenty months, has been as a clerk to the town council, with a position at the Port Office, adjacent to the Guildhall. Perhaps you are familiar with it?" Parrish looked away, feigning disinterest. In truth, these few words of introduction had piqued his curiosity somewhat.

Turnbull continued. "No matter. My responsibilities are many, and mainly laborious and mundane, but I have a facility for figures, accounting and the like. My employers are wont to tell me that I have brought a certain degree of clarity to the city's ledgers that were sadly lacking before my hiring." He allowed himself a self-satisfied smile. "But make no mistake sir, despite their carefree profferings of their inner-most financial affairs, I am not privy to their machinations, and I am my own man sir, with my own principles and standards. I take pride in my work, naturally, but I have no desire or ambition to cast my lot in with my betters for my own self-aggrandizement. I work for the city and its people, not for the privileged chambers and self-serving patrons who have found themselves in corruptible positions of advantage." He looked quickly behind him at the empty room, and leaned in further. "Yes sir, corruption, and nothing less than that, is that of which I speak."

Parrish was relaxed enough now in this man's company to observe him somewhat more thoroughly. His young face, framed in dark hair and soft whiskers, was shiny with sweat. His clothes were correct, but shabby. His boots were wet and bruised with coaly mud. In one hand he held the peak of a cleric's cap, and in the other, the handle of a hide-covered satchel, much used and long carried.

At last, Parrish felt confident enough to utter a word.

"Who?" he asked, to the other man's surprised consternation.

"You said mutual acquaintances. Who?"

In an even more earnest and quieter whisper, Turnbull mentioned a name, and then another. The sweating increased visibly as he did so. At the sound of them, Parrish was surprised and impressed, in equal measures. These were names not to be bandied about in common company, names that would mean nothing to most men in a city street, but in the dark alleys and damp cellars that led off them, these were names that invoked a potent mixture of fear and respect. Clearly this man Turnbull had gone to great lengths to bring himself to his present location.

"I was directed firstly to them, by way of lesser men, but more honest men perhaps. They in turn mentioned yourself, as one who would be most interested in what I have to say, and who could choose a most fitting course of action."

There was a certain ring of probability in these words, but Parrish remained sceptical. What information could a mere town clerk possess that would illuminate this apparent myriad of deception and intrigue, such that would ally him with villains and schemers from both sides of the law, and then ultimately seek out a stranger such as himself to act as confidante. He stared at Turnbull blankly, then allowed himself an ambivalent shrug of the shoulders. The other took that as a cue to continue.

"I take it, sir," he resumed, "That you are familiar with the methods by which the Hostmen and the council of this port manage and control the traffic of wares within and without, whether it be coal, spices, local produce, other commodities, back and forth, in order to ensure a standardised and efficient, not to say cost-effective management of what is rapidly becoming the second most important trading point in this country, second only to the Port of London?" Another mild shrug from Parrish came forth. "And are you aware sir, to what extent the commercial interests of the Hostmen, private interests I would emphasise, have become entwined with the affairs of the port and the city which it serves? Moreover, entwined with the affairs of the men, those very men, who have sworn to uphold righteousness and to act on behalf of the good fortune of this city. Those men, sir, who with regret, I have discovered to be less and less concerned with the benevolence of the people who they claim to serve, and more and more concerned with serving themselves and the weight of their own purses."

Turnbull was spitting out these words in a growing frenzy by now. Parrish watched him, and offered a loaded comment.

"Corruption amongst city officials is expected and weathered," he said mildly. "And many's the mighty empire across history that has experienced it and has paid a harsh cost for it. I for one do not condone it, but I am enough of a realist to know it is insurmountable as the curse, the plague that it is. Where there are scraps from the table, the rats congregate and grow fat as a result."

Turnbull had lost his trepidation and cautiousness by now. His voice had also outgrown the preliminary whisper.

"A realist sir, you say?" he scolded, "I would profess the same position to you myself, naturally. And as for accepting it with reluctant acquiescence, it is a regrettable necessity of my job. But if I tell you, sir, that it is a feature which has taken a new and more sinister hue in recent weeks, then perhaps you will understand why I have taken it upon myself to present the details to you, here in this place." His eyes darted around the stagnant corners about him. "And at some risk and chance of danger to myself, I assure you. I know you not, sir, and I am not in the habit of breaking bread with the men whose names I shared with you just now, and yet my feelings of disgust, and my beliefs in justice, have prevailed upon me to do so. I would ask you at last to take them seriously."

Alec Parrish by now had summed up this young man as a naïve fool, but a genuine, honest fool, with a rich earnestness that he found curiously entertaining. He was not offended by that last remark, and the instinctive wariness felt at his initial approach was already melting into curiosity. He made an open-handed gesture of compliance, and allowed Mr Turnbull to pour out the details of his position. Nothing he said was beyond belief, no detail was unfathomable, no assertion seemed preposterous or far-fetched, and the conclusions reached seemed plausible and decisive.

As Turnbull ended his soliloquy of intricacy, with much talk of underhand contracts, mutual advantages and cold-blooded profligacy, the young man sat back in near-exhaustion, as if finally unburdened of a load that had weighed him down for a long, long time. That load had now transferred itself on to new shoulders, and Alec Parrish felt invigorated and inspired by the bulk of it. A silence fell between the two men. Parrish's eyes were as unseeing as his mind was drenched in clarity. What little certainty of livelihood and ambition there was in this town was to be usurped and betrayed by the very men in whom the people had put their trust. The false gavel of injustice resonated through every strata of society, and flowed as surely and as unstoppable as the river itself. Now, thanks to a principled clerk, tainted by the underestimation of his employers, there was a slim chance that something could be done about it. But what, exactly?

Parrish spoke. "The main advantage that lies in the hands of those who are set on this scheme," he said, slowly, to the dry air between them, "Seems to be the veil of secrecy that covers their plans. That in itself is governed by timing, and appropriate placing of many separate elements in their scheme. It is on too grand a scale by this point for any individual to approach it from the outside and expose it. It is too complicated, too intricate a web to be exposed to common light." Turnbull bridled slightly at this, but Parrish continued regardless. "But if it can be made known to them that their subterfuge and long-term plan was itself known to others, even anonymously, that might give them cause to be somewhat circumspect, somewhat concerned. It would certainly slow them down a pace!"

Parrish's thoughts were rampant. The mellowness caused by the ale, the entrancing complexity of this man's tale had inspired him, stirring feelings that life had spared him for too long. He leaned forward and gripped the startled Turnbull's arm in an act of firm resolve.

"Your role is crucial in this," he said, "And it is crucial too, that your part in it is not exposed. Your knowledge and authority will undoubtedly be needed if things come to fruition as I hope."

Turnbull looked perplexed, as if regret and fear had won the day in his young heart.

"What do you propose to do?" he asked, a whisper claiming his voice once more. "Be it known I will have no part in lawlessness, violence and suchlike."

Parrish smiled thinly at him.

"No, have no fear of that," he replied. "The men themselves are not the target of my resolve. It is the plans, the contracts, the authority that they represent that we should desire possession of. You must merely make known to me the arrangement of this office of yours, and the whereabouts of these precious things that mean so much to our friends in high places. That is all. You need play no further part in it. Indeed, this is likely to be our one and only meeting, to the relief of both of us, no doubt."

"You mean to steal these documents?" Turnbull asked, his eyes widening. "But would that be enough of a recourse? The plans are already afoot, schemes are in motion."

"It would be recourse enough to delay them, to give cause for concern, that knowledge of these things has escaped beyond the elegant walls in which their spell has been cast. And if I am any judge of the character of these men, it will not be long before weak will and suspicion pokes a trembling finger in the damn of silence. These are ambitious greedy men, but weak and untrusting. Wary eyes are needed to break laws on this scale, and survival inspires betrayal. It will not be long before this castle of cards crumbles upon itself, and it will be at that point that they can be exposed, and at which time you can play your part, in all innocence, in all fidelity."

"So you don't mean that I conspire with you?" Turnbull said, in visible relief. "But you cannot do it alone, and I am wary of involving others."

"One other," Parrish replied softly. "A man of principle like yourself, with a strong heart, a knowledge of the river, and one whom I trust beyond any other. He is no stranger to just causes and has never shied away from them. It will be a trifle for him, a mere prank, but carried out with all haste and good intention."

Parrish looked at Turnbull with a firm eye. "There are details that you must make known to me before you leave. After that, go home, forget this conversation. It is not I who will next come to you, if our plan goes well. It will be the good people of this town, if such folk do indeed remain here."

CHAPTER 7

THE FOLKS O' SHEELS, THEY SAY

A heavenly choir awoke her. A fear of death froze her. She clenched her eyes shut, strange sensations of a body turned to clay gripping her, of loss and being lost, of ending at a terrifying new beginning, of guilt and regret, while voices on the wind sang in shame and sorrow all around her. Then she felt her limbs, still answering to her heart, still capable of moving, still heavy at one side. Her eyes opened. There was pale blue sky above her, there was a breeze across her face, there was the stiff collar of a dark blue coat reaching roughly up into her hair. The vivid echo of the previous night and morning became plain to her in a rush of memory. But the doleful singing remained. She sat up with a twist towards her stronger side. The singing was coming from beyond the unsteady stones that had once made a wall in front of her. She stretched up, and up again, until she saw what she saw. She was unsure still just what it was.

People, mostly old and white haired, were gathered in a small group, maybe ten in number, singing a holy song into the open air, while a parson, draped in white lace, and carrying a tall cross, looked down at their feet with his eyes closed. They stood together in that shell of what had once been a holy house, and beyond them the stone slabs of a graveyard rose at random from thick grass. All but the priest, whose eyes were closed, had their backs to her, so she dared rise up further to afford a better view.

The song creaked from aged throats, its words wandering in and out of understanding for her, but with much attention to stormy seas and redeeming skies. The tune could have been familiar, if the patchwork of voices had been stitched better together. As it ended, the holy man looked up with open eyes and Dolly pulled herself back to below his vision. Her sudden movement woke Moss, who started like a man with much to fear from such an awakening. Like many times before, his first words were foreign to Dolly, and this time lit with a new urgency. He stared at her, unsmiling, then his features softened.

"I thought it must be a wolf, but it is only a lamb," he said, smiling and lay back into the grass.

"We should go," she said. "This is a holy place. We shouldn't be here. There are folk at prayer inside these walls."

"Of course," he said, "This is a very holy place, a great church, now in pieces, but once blessed by God, so a holy place still. That does not change with the breaking of stone walls. Things that mere men build, they can easily be destroyed, but things built in God's name, they stay forever."

Dolly stared at him. She had never heard words like these from him. In a beat of a weary heart, in a voice still tight with tiredness, it was as if he had proved his goodness to her, his righteousness, his nobleness. She didn't have such words within her to know how she felt. She couldn't even tell herself that she loved him, but that is what it was. She looked down at him. His brown face was lined, scarred white on one cheek, and blue from coal dust on the other, stubbled with black whiskers flecked with grey, his ears dotted with deep dirt, his neck thick and swollen, and his one exposed eye deep and black-rimmed. It was a face that told a hundred tales, and she knew none of them, and yet here she was, here they were, once divided by age and ocean, now as close as the crumbling stones of this ancient place. And suddenly, Dolly knew that it was where she had always needed to be.

His eye was closed to her, as he said, "The day must be half done, we must find food, and then return to the Sandgate. It's far." He looked at her. "You feel strong enough?"

Dolly almost laughed, "Ah'm hungry as a cuddy. Let's make a start."

"What is cuddy?" he asked

"A horse," she explained, "And a skinny one at that."

"I once owned a horse," he began, but Dolly stopped him with a girl's giggle.

"Come by!" she laughed. "We have a mile or two today for stories like that. You said a tavern. We should find it!"

They walked directly along an empty high street, which eventually twisted and curved into high houses and merchants' buildings. The river shone in a stillness below them. Chimneys were barely smoking, but soon a meagre scattering of people was moving from street to street in an aimless Sunday fashion. A group of shabby youths were playing a gambling game with pennies on a high-kerbed corner, smoking and swearing with carefree abandon. They stared at this pair of strangers as they passed, the tall, black-haired man with an eyepatch and

71

the limping wastrel of a woman by his side, then continued in their noisy pursuits. Other locals also glanced warily in their direction as they walked the street, and Dolly began to worry that their antics of the previous night had not been as surreptitious as they'd hoped. At one point, Moss halted at a street corner, with another, shabbier row of once-grand buildings and shopfronts, all closed and shuttered, stretching away for a good distance. He looked around and about, then eventually pointed at an angle to a filthy alleyway opposite, and strode towards it. Dolly looked at it with some trepidation. The alley skirted what had once been a notable place of lodging, The Highland Hotel. A new sign below the one that heralded that name, both unreadable to Dolly, now proclaimed "Witham Wights, Grocer and General", and further on still, a dozen paces down the alley, a scratched slate above a half-open door bore the words "Cabbage Patch". It was that entrance into which they now walked.

This was no tavern. Through the smoky gloom, Dolly could see a long trestle on the far wall, with a massive man behind it, pouring beer from a pot jug into pot beakers. Various men, with river-workers gaits, sat around on wooden benches, with a group of them, all bearded, she noted, playing cards at an upturned crate in one corner. There were women there too, of the sort that Dolly recognised with wariness, and every one of them stared at her as she crossed the floor behind Moss.

She tugged at his jacket. "Ah don't want drink," she hissed. "Is there not food here?"

He raised a sly hand to quieten her, and steered her to another empty corner, and motioned for her to sit down.

She did so. Almost immediately, from a door behind her, a large woman carrying a fish pail of beer slops burst in, coughing roughly, and halted near her.

"Hew ye! Ye canna be on yer own in here," she croaked at Dolly. "Who d'ye think ye are?"

Before she could reply, from the direction of the beer trestle, Moss called over. "Hey, Anna! She's with me!"

The big woman jolted around towards him, momentarily stunned, and sneered readily at him.

"Aaah, ha ha! Mosser!" she whined, slowly. "Ye sly hound. Well, well. Stranger, a real stranger, and stranger still, that you've seen fit to make your way here. Ha!" She swaggered towards him, leaving a trail of ale splashed in her wake. "Big Mosser. Well! There's them that'll be interested in seeing you back in here. Not pleased mind, but interested. Ye know who Ah mean an' all, Ah'm guessin'!"

The eyes of the entire room were on them now, hopping back and forth between them, and occasionally in Dolly's direction. Her body tightened.

"Anna!" Moss smiled back at her. "Bella Anna! I hope you're not workin' too hard. Not livin' too late at night, every night, like you used to. Not always in the dark in places like this, I hope!" He gestured widely about him. The big man behind the beer jug snorted indignantly.

"Places like this?" the woman echoed. "Ye ungrateful sod, ye was glad of places like this, especially this place, at one time. And again now Ah reckon, seeing as you see fit to come in here on a day when decent folk are penanced and prayin'. Don't come yesel' better, all high and mighty, just due to bein' a townie. Ye're still a black rogue, Ah can tell by just lookin' at yer. Even with a dox in tow." She tilted her head in Dolly's direction.

Moss threw a glance at her. "My wife," he said calmly. "No doxy, no strump. My wife."

There was a moment of silence, where the entire company seemed to pause to absorb this. Moss had clearly used a word rarely heard within these peeling walls. The big woman called Anna stood motionless, as did Moss, facing her. The beer man turned to look at Dolly, who began to feel herself tremble from somewhere within.

"A wife!" Anna spat out the word. "You? A wife! Why, then she gets pity from me, and from half the women in Shields besides, Ah reckon. And all the other so-called wives ye've left behind across the world, ye patch-eyed, bloody..."

He stopped her. "Anna, Anna!" he said, mockingly. "Those lovely lips, do not dirty them with such bad words. Do not stain that bosom so splendid with a heart of black anger and cruel names. Come, we were friends above all else, confidantes, soothers and sharers of secrets, deep secrets..."

"Ye grease mouth bastard!" she retorted in a lower voice, plainly wracked with a hatred. She spun around and looked at Dolly. "And you, ye've nowt but gut-ache and tears to count on now, ye poor bitch!"

She pushed past Moss, banged the pail onto the table, turned and strutted back across the floor and out of the door from whence she'd come, without so much as a glance in Dolly's direction. Already, the card game had recommenced, two men were leaning towards the same girl nearest to the door, and everyone else had taken the opportunity to swig a draft from their mug. Dolly sat frozen, dulled, reliving the past few moments, though without any real desire to do so. Two more men entered from the outside door and greetings were exchanged with other regulars. An old man in a fisherman's smock suddenly began to make a commotion a few feet from Dolly, in an attempt to put paid to an unwelcome rat, though real or imagined, Dolly was reluctant to ascertain.

Moss came back to her, carrying two mugs dripping with beer, and a large beaten-metal plate, on which three shallots, two crusts of bread, some unset cheese and a large, unevenly hacked lump of ham lay like a sacrifice. He didn't look at her, merely pulled up a third chair to use as a table, and set the meal down. Dolly didn't question these actions. She took the smaller piece of bread and dipped it in the cheese, munching at the white end of the shallot first, then gnawing at the crust. Moss hesitated for a long moment, as if in thought, then did exactly the same. They ate in silence, as around them the room stuttered with curses and exclamations from the men, and giggles and sighs from the women. At one point, the big beer tender brought over, unbidden, a small round loaf dotted with chopped fruit and glazed with honey. Without thanks or question, Moss split it in his fingers and handed Dolly the larger part. She looked at it, nibbled at its crust, and realised it was the most beautiful thing she had ever tasted. It was so good that she hardly dared eat it, lest the secret of its loveliness be forgotten to her. She slowly savoured it with a delicacy uncharacteristic to her kind, and gave herself time to wonder on the events

75

of the past night, the past hours, and ultimately, the past few minutes.

They ate, drank and left that place without further incident or conversation.

"That was a queer thing to say," Dolly finally remarked, as they made an uphill climb back towards the holy ruins. "D'ye not think?" she pressed further, somewhat indignant at Moss's grim-faced silence. "Why did ye tell her that?"

"Tell her what exactly?" Moss finally responded.

"That Ah'm yer wife! Ye must've had reason to tell her that. Is she somebody ye've been with, is that it? Somebody ye were tryin' to shake off? So you used me to push her off the scent, get her off yer back?"

Moss slowed his pace, and turned to the wide view of the open sea before them. He breathed a deep sigh. The afternoon sun was still warm. The water stretched out calm and empty from somewhere below them, to somewhere far away, beyond Dolly's imagination. She knew, though, that Moss saw clearly across this untold distance to untold origins and destinations. She could almost see him slipping away, right in front of her, off across this ocean, and regretted her bold words. He stepped away from the clay pathway, and sat heavily on the rough grass. Dolly stood for a moment, then sat down at his side. The silence was a heavy one.

"This is not the path I took into this country," Moss eventually said, staring across the stretch of water, and dismissing it with a flick of his hand. "It was to Deptford I came first." He laughed and squeezed her bare leg with his hand. "No, not your Deptford," he said, "Not on your river, no, another one, near to London. That is where the merchant ships from my country would come, across the Biscay, and through the Manche to the Thames River. And that is where I came, as a young man, to escape a foreign army in my country, and the war and famine of the near countries that I could reach by land. I knew nothing of the sea. I knew nothing of England, or its people. Your generals and battles and anger with America, that meant nothing to me. But it was as far away as I dare to come, as a young man who could not forget some happier times in my own country."

He stretched his legs out in front of him, and leaned back on his hands, his face turned up to the fading sun.

"But I liked the salty wind and the games of anger and love that the sea played with me. I had many lucky seasons on barques and schooners in the Nordsee trade winds, while all around us our fishermen and colliers were swallowed by stormy waves and mountains of oceans. For me, it was like a miracle, always smooth waters, and stars to steer by." He laughed again at the thought of it. "And then by chance, returning from Holland, we caught the tail of a northerly storm and sheltered in the port of Leith, that curse of a Scottish docking. We roped three abreast with a whaler, it was so crowded on that quay, so confused, each captain trying to gain mooring, each seaman keen to find a foot on dry land. We barraged with force past a trader from Flanders, stupid fools we were, flinging lines to the quay like madmen, and a quarter rope from the trader snapped across my face from below the gunwale, and took out this eye that had been my guide and companion. "

77

He looked at Dolly, and smiled. She was soothed and warmed by his voice, as she always was, and never more so than by these intimate, hidden words. She stared at the vast sea, where a full-sailed ship had come into view, as if to majestically act out this man's story.

Moss spat into the breeze. He raised his face to the sky once more. "That man you met this day", he said.

"Alec Parrish?" said Dolly.

"Yes, Alec. It was he who brought me here to this river. He balmed my face, soothed my head, in his room near the Excise House in Leith. There was no Keelman's Hospital there to tend to me, and he had me taken to his room, I don't know why. He was a man of the river, not of the sea! Then when the time came for him to return to the Tyne, I came with him. To here, to Shields. He had a wife here then, and she was not so happy to have me stay with them of course," he chuckled at a memory, "And that is when I knew Anna, at the Highland Hotel, where I took a lodging. And where I took work, still in pain and hurt from my injuries. I could not work on the sea again, but to tend fire and sweep rooms and carry firkins, that I could do."

He turned to her again, almost in embarrassment. "Yes," he said, "That is what I had become, a sweeper of dirt and a mule for a cooper. And a strong arm to clean up the drunken sailors and hard fists fired by the anger of strong drink. That is how I made enemies. And how I made bitterness in Anna, who thought that I would be fool enough to do that forever. I never shared her affection, never mind her bed. She felt she owned me like a captain's monkey, and when I walked away, she could not drop the chain that held my neck. No surprise today then, when I come back, and she speaks to me like a lost dog."

Dolly had not expected explanation or excuse. In the months they had been together, their conversations had been light and saucy, gossip from her and knowing smiles from him, bare-skinned whispers and bar-room joking. Only when she had sung for him, either alone together or with an excuse of company, had she seen him show any hint of close emotion. And now this, a waterfall of honesty, with more detail than he had likely handed out to anyone, man or woman, before.

"It falls deep in me that you'd tell me such things," she said. "Ah didn't mean to goad you into tellin' me this, or tellin' me anythin'. Ah like that ye tell me, but Ah'd be just as happy at your side without the knowin'." She clung to his arm. "Ye might be a mystery to some, but the mystery to me is why you choose to be with a lame dillin like me in the first place, when you could choose…" Her voice trailed off, as she sensed his body tighten, and he pulled himself away from her. "What is it?" she asked, a seed of panic in her voice. "What did Ah say?"

His head was erect and pointed out to sea, fixed, as if frozen. She looked at him. Beyond, towards the abbey ruins, her eyes registered that there were others, men and women, suddenly visible, standing wordlessly, staring out to sea in the same manner. She followed their gaze, but the water was wide and empty, save for the tall-masted brig that was bringing itself to anchor a fair way off shore. It was indeed towards this that the line of folk on the clifftop were peering. The old woman that they had passed early in the day, her clay pipe still jabbed into her toothless mouth, hobbled past behind them. She seemed to be wailing quietly to herself.

She keened at Dolly as she passed. "Flee Lassie!" she cackled. "Get yer man away!" She raised a crooked finger at the yonder brig. "Here's the tender comin'!"

CHAPTER 8

DEEP AS DE'ILS

They had been away for a day, no more, yet the town that this Monday morning dawned upon seemed so different, almost a relic, a cast-off, to Dolly's newly-wide worldly eyes. She stood at the corner of the Groat Market, with Jessie Marley's basket, empty in her hands, and passed a quarter hour in watching, listening, waiting for nothing, something she hadn't done since she was an idle girl, squandering time while waiting for her sister Bertha to finish a morning's work with bristle and blade. Now, the wide street in front of her was cluttered and busy. In the meandering chares and alleys that led to it from every direction, the teetering buildings of soot-stained stone and harsh grey wood leaned towards each other, as if to squeeze out the daylight and the air from the cobbles between them. Noise, much of it from mouths, was everywhere. Women were gossiping, men were consulting.

There was much talk of John Scott, the man who had plucked local beauty Bessie Surtees from respectability at dead of night to a scandalous, unblessed marriage, in the year before Dolly and Bertha had come to town, and who now had risen to high rank in the government of London. His name was now somehow significant amid constant talk of impending war with France, and the notorious local connection skewered it with sensationalism and vividness. The lowly folk enjoyed the salaciousness of his initial renown; the more well-heeled relished any link, however slight, with someone in so high an office. Dolly barely remembered who he was, and understood less of what he had become.

Three nights previously, John Scott had addressed the great and good of the city, at the Guildhall, and it had been the social event of the year, both for those of high enough station to have been invited to it, and for the lower caste who had swarmed around the quayside that evening to observe the comings and goings of their betters. Dolly had missed the entire episode, being hard at work in a barroom, a mere six streets away. But she could now observe the immediate aftermath of the occasion, in the shape of a curious new hair arrangement that many of the local women had suddenly adopted, with varying degrees of success, in emulation of the fashionable wives and daughters who had been in attendance that night. It involved a skilled use of pins and combs that, as far as Dolly could see, shaped the hair higher on one side of the head than the other, and a smattering of ragged local girls were gathered around the troughs at the top end of the block, adjusting each other's plumes with determined nonchalance. The whole charade fascinated Dolly for a brief few moments.

The cathedral bells had barely sounded ten, when an unruly clump of watchmen pushed their way across the rising cobbles and halted briefly outside the office of the city newspaper. Several well-dressed young men followed in their wake, and a coatless grey-haired man with sheaths of cream-coloured papers emerged to consult with them. A red-coated official, with another gaggle of younger men trailing behind him, was simultaneously making his way through the market crowd from the high end of the street, and it was at this point, as the two contingents merged, that the swarms of onlookers began to take notice. Dolly melted further into the anonymous doorway where she'd been standing, her eyes dancing and flitting across the scene.

Two men, one of whom she recognised as Joseph Rowtledge, the Ratter, came to stand a yard or two away from her, both straining their necks and ears to try and catch a gist of what was going on. A few women moved away down Black Boy's Chare, and away from the scene, in a disquieted motion of concern. The Rat Man called over to another Joseph, an elderly man with a twisted foot, who moments before had been standing near the newspaper office doorway. He limped eagerly over to share his knowledge.

"It's robbery certainly!" he uttered without prompting. "Mischief, maybe murder!"

Dolly drew a sudden breath at the word.

"Murder?" hissed the third, unknown man. "Who's been murdered? And for what?"

The crippled man stretched his head in another direction.

"Why, they haven't said murder, but there's concern enough amongst the Watch. It's damn serious, by my reckonin'. Look," he pointed down towards the bottom end of the street. "Here's the Militia now. Ye canna tell me there's nowt but real badness has occurred."

A trio of young men in a semblance of uniform marched past at a steady but unwieldy pace. Another man joined the observers. Dolly averted her gaze but strained her ears.

"It's burglary at the Guildhall!" the new arrival announced with the pride of one assured of uncommon knowledge. "All the seals and yokes, the assize chains, court orders, all taken or destroyed. They got in from the fish market side, above the columns. There's no sense to it, and less sense to all the commotion they're makin' of it, in my mind."

"And who's the murdered man?" asked Rowtledge, with relish.

The informant looked perturbed. "Oh, there's no talk of murder. Not that Ah've heard." He seemed deflated now. "Did you have word of that, like?"

The conversation halted, in a confusion of momentary doubt.

"Why, it would account for all the commotion, surely", the lame man offered.

At that point, Dolly was noticed, first by one, then by all. She feigned nonchalance, and began to scratch earnestly at the empty basket she was holding, looked around her feet as if for something lost, bothered by that but unmoved by their conversation. She fussily moved off down the east side of the market, still with the sense that the men were eyeing her, and she soon melted into a gaggle of women, busily concerned with a flurry of other news.

Dolly listened easily to their talk. Tragedies like a stillborn infant, a death by falling of a young craftsman at the building of the new theatre off Mosley Street, and a beaten wife in Vine Lane, all faded into banality in her

mind, as she considered the doom-laden probabilities that yesterday's cacophony of events had cast into view. All of this, the routine, the everyday patterns, the measured pace of this town and its people would be soon jolted into a stark, painful reality with the impending arrival of The Pressers.

The way back from Shields the night before had been long and tortuous for Dolly, her weak leg losing more and more strength after the day's wanderings. By chance, a white-haired carter making his way with creels, westward from Chirton, and likely intimidated by Moss's approach, gave them a perch as far as Walker, and they were back in Sandgate before midnight, though without the opportunity to talk that Dolly needed so anxiously. Moss told the carter of the sighting of the Tender off-shore, and the man had spat and cursed roundly, but then kept his own silent counsel for the rest of the journey. It was only as Dolly and Moss had fallen together in their bed, barely touching, and open-eyed in thought for many minutes, that a conversation began between them.

"When will they come?" Dolly finally whispered into the darkness. Moss exhaled long and thoughtfully, but at first made no reply. "The pressers," she said, "Will it be soon? Should we be warning folk?"

At last she heard his voice rasp like parchment from his tired throat. "Warnings? Yes. But by tomorrow the brigs will bring news to the quayside. Warnings will already be in the ale houses and barrooms along this river. Words travel faster than you and I."

She moved towards him where he lay. "And when will they come? You must lie low and keep quiet 'til they're gone. When will they go? When will it be over?"

"Lie low? What is that?" he said, his body stirring for some comfort. "You say hide? Is that it?" He allowed a mocking laugh.

"I still have to work, I still have to walk on the street, I still have to... live! I cannot hide away forever."

Dolly drew even closer to him. "But it's not forever," she urged. "Surely, they'll come and take poor unfortunate lads and lost souls, and then be gone. I heard my own father talk of this, on the Wear, when he was a boy. There was a war..."

"There is always a war," Moss sighed. "The English, there is always a war somewhere for them. Sometimes near, sometimes far away. Jacobites or American Colonies, or Spanish, or French. Always the French, the nearest neighbour. Like now. It is to fight the French that these Tyne men must go. And I have been with Frenchmen. They are proud, fierce men. Men who would kill a king, their own king! In the name of freedom. And that freedom has only brought them war on all sides."

"Is it true they killed their own king?" Dolly whispered. It was something she had heard, but had never believed.

"Certainly!" Moss affirmed. "And many more people of power and *influenza*. Madness of blood!"

"How d'ye know these things? Who tells you this?" A fascination of terror was seeping into Dolly's tired mind.

"I have to know these things," he said. "My country lies in the centre of all wars, with many coasts to protect

us and mountains at our border to the north, but it is a rich country, a green country, for those who have chance to claim it. And it lies here," he beat hard on his chest, "Deep and strong inside. I see it in the light of the sun, always..." His voice trailed off. "Maybe one day you will see it," he said, his voice quieter now. "We will see it together..."

They slept. The next morning, he had left for his work with a dry, anxious look on his face. As he departed, he had told her to walk to the market and gather news, by listening, not asking, about the taking of the Hostmen's papers, and anything else that the womenfolk might know. He would be among the men, he'd said, but the women were the real ears and eyes of this town. Dolly had smiled at that, but he had not answered her with one of his own.

The clouds became thick and dark by the middle of the afternoon, and a heavy rain soon followed. A pile of newly washed clothes, their meagre colour, if not their dirt, having been beaten out of them at the trough in Scold's Pant many times, and again an hour previously, lay abandoned in dampness on the chair in the corner. Dolly was at the window, vainly trying to coax the wooden slats into a place that would keep most of the rain from what was left of the guttering above from leaking straight into the shabby room. The street below, she saw, was empty. The rain had brought with it a chill wind from the river. Above, there was no sign of a break in the cloud. Agitation, worry, weariness, they were all playing their part in the unease that gripped her. The chime of the cathedral clock would be unheard in such weather, so even in the knowledge that she was pointlessly early, she swung her shawl over her head and set off for the Flying Horse, and a night's work. Chances were that Moss would join her there later, but the thought of this suddenly chilled her. She froze with her hand on the door latch, her insides churning. A mere stone's throw from the river, the Flying Horse would deal rich pickings to a pressgang bent on harvesting a crop for their cruel intentions. Surely Moss would realise this, she mused, but the unease she felt showed no sign of abating. She wafted down the stairway, and scurried into the street, oblivious to the splash of coldness around her bare ankles. She searched the faces of the paltry few souls she passed on her way, to catch some sign of emotion, reassuring calm perhaps, or maybe stabbing panic, but saw only grim determination against the deluge from the heavens.

The tavern was dark when she reached it. She crept down the side alley, looked once behind her, and unbolted the tall wooden gate to the back yard. Rats scurried through a stench of slime to one side of her, but she passed them without so much as a shudder. She pushed at the back door and was inside soon enough. The building was silent. She gathered wood from behind the door, and headed for the furthest room. It was still littered with the day's pots and debris, and tobacco smoke hung like a gauze across the shred of light from the high window. She sought sanctuary in cleaning and tidying now, bringing order to the chaos of fear that had gripped her all that day.

Harrison Marley appeared, groggily, from upstairs after about a quarter of an hour. His face showed the usual signs of irritability and contempt for the world. He scratched at his behind and blinked at Dolly.

"It can't be openin' hour yet!" he said. "Ah was sleepin', with you and your clatter and crashin' about!"

"No, no," she replied, busying herself rather than looking at him. "There's ample time yet, but there was a lull in the rain, so Ah came early. Do you want a fire settin?"

"Ah do not!" he snapped. "It'll likely be quiet this night. With the rain. Square up, but then close the through door. If they come, they can bide in the 'tap."

"If *they* come?" she jolted back at him. "Who's... Who d'ye mean? Who's *they*?"

Marley stared at her. "What are you sayin' lass?" he said. "Mak' sense will ye. Ah'm not openin' this room for a pen'orth o' profit and a lout or two from the street. Now get it squared up for the 'morn and then start on the taproom. There's still warmth on the back stove so bellow it up, and boil water for herbs."

He turned on his heel and left her alone. She stared after him, deep in thought. He had shown no sign of knowing about the pressers, even though there had been river men in the place earlier in the day. Whatever talk there had been, perhaps of thievery and connivances on the quayside, it seemed that the more urgent concerns still eluded them. She went and busied herself at the stove. She sprinkled dry green shreds of leaves into a shallow pan filled with water, set it on a hinged griddle and swung it into the fire to boil.

Some years before, a seaman back from Portugese waters had brought in to the bar what he called "healing herbs", to be boiled up and imbibed as a cure-all for ailments and melancholia, and persuaded Marley to trade a bag of them for a night's ale. Who knows what promises and assertions were made, and the foulness of taste, as experienced by the coterie present at the time, had made Marley a laughing stock for a fair few days after. But perhaps in an effort to save face, he had persevered with the concoction, with claim of benefits felt and a good bargain having been made, and indeed had now developed a habit of taste for the drink. Remarkably, Moss shared in this opinion, and was known to bond with Marley over a bowl of the sweet-smelling liquid on colder nights before the ale was poured. Dolly could always smell it on his breath afterwards, and the odour of it now, as the water boiled, renewed the sense of urgency within her, for her lover and the potential danger he faced.

For an hour or more, Dolly occupied herself with familiar chores. Over a slab in the back of the scullery, where she washed out pots and jugs, she normally felt free and remote enough to let her voice rise softly into a slower song, more often than not "The Waters of Tyne", learned from a man, now dead, called Pad Ritson at the Sandhills shoe market two summers before. She had heard the song often enough previously, but Ritson's plaintiff delivery of it, despite affected by drink, had stilled the entire gathering into attention on that bright warm day, and his whole rendition had remained printed on Dolly's memory ever since. When the poor man's lifeless body had turned up floating in lonely sadness on the farther side of the Tyne a month or two later, there were others as well as Dolly, who having heard him sing that day, wondered to themselves just how deeply entrenched those words of lost love may have been within   him.

But at the sink now, Dolly remained silent, and she questioned whether she would ever return to that song again. At that moment, Harrison Marley reappeared, wordlessly poured out his herbal drink into a pewter goblet, and slurped a mouthful with an ugly grimace. He moved away, muttering. A moment later Dolly heard the bolt of the front door being pulled back, and the door creaked open for customers.

When Dolly looked into the taproom, a good half hour on, two silent old men were stood, crouched over mugs at the high end of the trestle, beneath which new barrels were wedged. The rain was still falling, more gently now, beyond the open doorway. Dolly dared to cast a glance outside into the street on the pretence of shaking a pudding cloth free of suds. No-one was in sight. The noise of a cart scraping down Armourers Chare opposite, briefly drew her attention, and a bent old woman in a sodden brown woollen shawl crept by, clinging to the wall for shelter from the wet as she passed.

Back inside, time dripped slowly by, the drudgery of it broken only by the lighting of a solitary tallow lamp, long after the deepening gloom had demanded it, by an equally glum Harrison Marley. Dolly drew water from the old tun beneath the gutter in the back yard and swilled it across the rough cobbled floor of the scullery. She swished the better of two besom brushes over it for some minutes, and then became aware of voices in the room beyond. She made her way to the through door and turned her ear in their direction. She recognised the whining bray of Anty Proud.

"They were in Cullercoats Village last night, camped at the Bell Pits," he was saying. "Ye can consider well that they'll be in Shields and Tynemouth tonight. But there's nowt to keep them there. They'll be up the river in brigs and scullers by the mornin'."

There was a silence, then Harrison Marley spoke.

"Ah'd not heard nowt of it from the quayside today," he said. "Ye'd think, if it was the case..."

"Oh, it's true enough," Anty broke in. "It's only the badness of the weather and a drear Monday night that's kept them at the coast. They have a certainty of method. Ah've seen this too many times. They'll be on that street out-by, a night hence, mark my words."

Another silence, as Marley looked beyond the open door. "The rain has ceased," he said quietly.

Dolly took this as a sign to emerge from the doorway. Anty Proud was in mid-quaff, and held his vessel still at his lips to glance in her direction for a long moment. He drained it and set it down.

"Ye should tell that gyp of yours to get low in the water with the rest of the rats," he sneered. "There's trouble on the way for the likes of him. A ripped eye won't forbid them takin' a man like that for spoils."

Dolly stared back at him with contempt. Marley pushed passed her to take Anty's mug for refilling.

"It's the press," Marley told her. "There's a tender off Tynemouth, and they'll be up here presently, looking for strong men and fit lads to haul off for recruitment. A townful of boatmen and fishers, it'll be like apple gowkin' for them 'round these streets. He's right," he added, nodding over at Anty, "Be sure to tell Moss, and anybody else ye might meet. Is he in here this night?"

She was still staring at Anty Proud. "Ah don't rightly know," she said. "But Ah'll be sure to tell him exactly what was said."

Anty shot her a glance, and almost spoke, but thought better of it. He took the ale being proffered, and turned his back to her. He was a weasel of a man, and had been known to beat all of the women that had foolishly chosen his companionship down the years, it was said. He was older and heavier than the brawler he had once been, and sought revenge for that in a caustic wit and a black temperament. He had once grabbed Dolly's weaker forearm as she had passed him in the bar, on perhaps the second or third night she had worked in the Horse. He had stared, grinning coldly into her face, as his strong fat hand had squeezed harder and harder still. She could almost still feel the grip of it now. But she had not moved nor flinched, despite the pain, and stared back at him until he released her with a spit of a smirk. Since then, she had often caught his cold stare in her direction across the room as she weaved between customers. That same stare bore into her whenever she sang from the hearth stone, and never once deigned into a clap of a hand when the song came to an end. Only since she had taken up with Moss had Anty Proud kept a whiff of a distance from her, and even that could have been merely a case of her feeling secure enough to take less notice of his presence.

Back in the dark quiet of the scullery, Dolly's resentment gave way once more to dread. If the gangs were out tonight further down the river, what if Moss had gone back in their direction, perhaps to meet up with Alec Parrish at Tynemouth to further the business of the stolen papers, or even to warn him of the danger of the pressers themselves? Even his daily work at the Walker shore held him closer to the peril they brought with them. Dolly's duties still held many hours before she could leave and seek his whereabouts. A turmoil of thoughts swirled and enveloped her. The real darkness of the hour was complete now, and she stood for a long while in the blackness, smothered by it, her imagination tormenting her like a gathering storm.

A scrape of boot on stone startled her. She twisted round in its direction. She couldn't see him, but in the silence, she heard him breathing, and knew it was him indeed.

"A gift, Dolly," he said softly. "As I promised. A special gift for you. Come."

CHAPTER 9

A SOWGERIN' AT NEWCASSEL

The next morning burst in brightly through the twisted slats of their window. As ever, Dolly was first to stir. Her body felt heavy to her where she lay. The strength of this man in the grip of passion had wrung her like wet linen, and her own responses had drawn deeply from her weak limbs, leaving them aching and drained. All this was new to her. She had been with men before Moss, but had merely watched and waited as they had taken her. Moss had taken nothing. From the start, he had given, he had coaxed, he had sculpted the pair of them into one togetherness, and she had willingly, keenly played a part in that union. He had been careful with her, but had plainly shown his desires and encouraged her to do the same. The night before had been an ecstasy, but now the morning was a reality.

As the taproom had filled that previous night, and as the evening sky had cleared, Moss had taken her by the arm and casually drawn her into the empty front parlour. He had kissed her in the darkness of the scullery earlier, but now took her full in his arms. The tightness drained from her being, and she allowed herself an audible sigh of relief. At that, he had raised his head in amused wonder, and squinted at her in the gloom.

"What is that?" he'd asked. "You do not wish me to do this? Because it is here, even though we are alone?"

"No, yes, Ah do want it," she stammered, "Ah'm just relieved that you're here. There's been talk of the pressers. Anty Proud said..."

He stopped her. "Anty? Ah, *grasso*... What did he say? I saw him go quickly when I came in tonight. What did he say to you?"

She avoided detail with a shake of her head. "No, he just brought news, that the recruiters were in Shields tonight, and Tynemouth, and were workin' the length of the river. That they would certainly be here in Sandgate, all around the town, likely tomorrow."

"Yes," he said, "I too heard this. But that was all known. But do not listen to what people say. And what they say about me. Do not fall to worry and fear. I will be safe, truly."

She shook her head again. "But not here, you should leave the town tonight. And there was Militiamen at the Groat Market this mornin', for the robbery..."

He held up his wide hand in front of her face, and it was his turn to shake his head. He stared at her, unsmiling now. She stared back. After some moments, he smiled again.

"My gift," he said. "I promised you, remember?" He let her fall away from his arms, unpegged his jacket, and reached into it. He brought out a bound-up roll of cloth. She moved closer to it immediately and he brushed it against her cheek. It felt as soft as snowfall on her skin. Her eyes widened. He pulled a tiny piece of twine, and the bundle cascaded open, like a newly born waterfall in the moonlight. It rolled down before her, and in doing so, took the form of a woman's shape, a lady's shape, a floating sark of silver cloth, shimmering slowly and perfectly, silently.

"For you," he whispered.

She reached towards it, her breath held, and remembered her soiled hands. She scrubbed them quickly against her apron, but even then, just allowed her fingertips to touch it. They ran the full length of it, and then did so again. She had seen such garments, vaulted high out of common reach, in one or two of the many pawnshops that peppered the long quayside streets, but had never felt the timid fineness of their fabric before now.

"Moss," she finally breathed. "Oh Moss, how can Ah ever be matched with somethin' so... so beautiful? How can Ah wear it and deserve it with this dillen shape and twisted body?"

He smiled broadly in the grey room. "Tonight, later tonight, you will wear it for me. It will become you and you will become and all. It will be as beautiful as you are always."He folded it lightly, and pushed it back into his coat. She stared, wordless and dazed. The noise from the other room burst between them, and she backed away, then hurried out and towards the scullery, picking up pots with feigned purpose as she went.

As the rest of the night wore on, the talk had been large and loud, and Dolly had scooped up as much of it as her duties would allow. The burglary at the Guildhall was dwarfed now, by the exaggerated antics of the pressgangs further down the river. The brother of Thomas Sharp, the watchmaker, had been taken, it was said, dropped into a scull filled with young men, chased through the streets of

Tynemouth in broad daylight. Charles Nossiter, a river pilot from Howden had escaped by burying himself in salt sacks at the fish quay, and had almost choked to death in doing so. Three lads from one family called Smart had been taken. Greaves Allen, the ropemaker, had docked at Sandgate at nine o' clock with tales of terror from down the river, for the quayside gathering, and was now being plied with free ale in the Crooked Billet, by any who had not yet heard his story, and for his descriptions of the recruiting crews.

"Two dozen men," Jim Burrows, a breathless old dockhand related upon his arrival amongst them, once he had quaffed a deep draught of new beer, "In three packs. Suited in blue, with clubs and with knives at their waists. None of them speaks the King's English!" A voice from elsewhere in the room roared, "Hoy, Moss, you'll give them good warnings for us, good lad!" The company laughed, as did Moss. Dolly caught his glance, and he pointed to his patch and smiled. She softened. It was a sign between them, that he was winking with his lost eye, a sign of reassurance and quiet intimacy.

"And a captain named Dolby, or Joply, or Jiggling, or some such. A caustic, merciless bugger in red, and a tall hat like an admiral. Tarred tails all, except him. And he's yellow haired! That's a sign of a ruthless man, I always say!"

A fair-haired creelmaker in the corner shouted out an oath of objection to this, and there was more laughter. Burrows continued, "The man who called himself my father had yellow hair, and he was a cruel bastard who whipped me for any reason, and for no reason at all.

Yellow of hair and blue of eyes is a bad combination in a man, and this Dibbling has both, they say."

"Jopling!" From the stool near the door, Moss's voice boomed over their heads. There was a sudden hush that he felt no urgency to shatter. Eventually he turned to the room. "His name is Jopling, and you are right. The man is a bastard, a ruthless..." He searched for a word, and abandoned it. "He shows no mercy, as you say. It is not just the young and strong who should fear him." He paused, and looked around. "There is fear enough here for all of us to share!"

The room dipped into silence. "How do you have knowledge of him?" Harrison Marley asked.

"Ah, a long tale," Moss sighed into himself. "A long tale from long ago. But believe in my words, he is evil, an evil man, and rightly chosen for this job we speak of."

"But how do you know of him so well?" asked somebody.

Moss looked around at the faces all turned towards him. "In Deptford dock." He paused and smiled at Dolly, motionless at the scullery door. "Not the Deptford you know, on the Wear, a place the same, but at London, on a wide, busy river. My first place of work in England. A place the same, but the people were not the same as here. The way you here have shown kindness to me and others from other lands, in Deptford it is not like that. There are so many faces, so many mouths to feed and to speak in so many different tongues. And for me, I was young and strong, but for many others, not old but also not strong, the work was hard, the wages small. And one sign of weakness and you were picked to pieces by a hundred more who will take your work, and even take the bread out of your mouth. There was much unease, much bad talk, scheming, planning. There was no trust between men. One man could not speak to another, because they knew different languages. So it was country against country on English soil. And it was also young against old, it was brother against brother. And every day there were more of us, running from war and famine and disease in our own countries. And then from close by, from Greenwich, a militia came, a troop of sailors and marines, chosen to bring order and *disciplina* to the quaysides and docksides, by whatever force, whatever action that was needed in their eyes. Men were shot, men were murdered, beaten, until the river ran red with their blood. And for me," he paused and looked down at his hands. "That was wrong. So I was among the few who fought back." He looked up at the men in the room. "And I was eventually in the very few, the very few, who escaped with a breath in their body."

Moss drank the last of his ale, and wiped his mouth with his fist. "And the man who *commanded*" (he spat out the word like a sick dog), "who gave orders to those murderers," he paused again, and smiled bitterly, "Was a yellow-haired man called Jopling." He stretched, exhausted by speaking longer than anyone, even Dolly, had heard him speak before. Shrugging, he added, "And now he is making his way here, it seems." He rose and the company parted to allow him to the bar. Marley took his beaker to refill it.

"And does he know you?" he asked Moss. "Is your face known to him?"

Moss barely moved his head. "It is a long time," he said. He laughed, "And I had two good eyes, those days! But he certainly knew me then. I was very well known to him, in fact. We became very near to each other." He smiled. "I don't plan on letting him so near a second time." He raised his mug to his mouth. Behind him, looks and furtive glances were being exchanged. Dolly noticed them all, and at that moment also noticed Anty Proud at the open doorway, lingering thoughtfully and cautiously. How much of Moss's story he had heard, she couldn't tell, but it was common knowledge now, in this room and, soon enough, beyond it.

The evening carried on in a similar fashion, with more stories and memories, many from the last bout of pressgang exploits locally, some fifteen years before. Even the coveted Keelmen hadn't been safe from recruitment then, they said, and the scars had run deep and long from that time to this. The chatter factionalised among the company, and in doing so seemed naturally to exclude Moss, who returned to his seat and busied himself with a loose hook on his jerkin. Anty Proud wisely chose a place farthest from him, at the high trestle.

The night's gathering was dwindling towards a later hour than usual, and Harrison Marley grunted to Dolly that she could leave. She was glad of it. She whipped off her apron and stuffed it between the empty barrels, tightened the knot in her hair and beckoned to Moss, smiling. He nodded and raised his mug to drain it, while she moved to the door. Then he stood and turned to follow her, and she looked back at him, noticing as she did so that every face, every eye in the room had turned to watch him leave. There was no customary word of goodnight from any of them, just a lull in every conversation, a silencing of every voice. What little trust he had known in this company, the very thing that he had just acknowledged with a glad heart, had vanished like dust in a breeze. Suddenly he was a foreigner, a stranger once again.

Later, when he lowered the silky *camicetta* over Dolly's bare body, all this was forgotten. The feel of this new cloth all around her, thrilled her like a shower of sunshine, and Moss's silent longing for her as he watched, thrilled her further. As he smoothed his hands around the softness of her, she felt herself rise and swell and straighten, as if the dillen inside of her had died, and the completed woman had emerged. Even after he had slipped the garment off her, she retained its strength and energy, and the bare room and crooked bed became a palace and a deep-piled haven, as they clung hard to each other in the rich dark.

Moss left sullenly for the chaldrons at Byker at dawn, with a promise that he would return directly at day's end. The press had rampaged in broad daylight in Tynemouth, sure enough, but would not dare do so here, he said. Dolly watched him go from their high window. A stare or two followed him as he passed, she noticed, but she told herself that this was often the case, and it was of no real concern. The looks on the faces as they had left the Flying Horse the night before, however, continued to play on her mind.

Within minutes, Dolly herself was in the street, heading for the Bigg market. It was Tuesday, and peelings day, but she also had money for mutton and perhaps fish. She cut through Dark Chare and thus avoided the quayside, squeezing her way through this poorest alley in Sandhill, with the memory of her uplifted feminine spirit of the previous night ebbing further and further away, as she stepped lightly through the black mud and thick stenches of the narrow alley. At the farther end, she emerged into the usual throng of busy lives and crackling sounds from every level of town society, and thus regained some of her new-found dignity. She had toyed with the idea of wearing the new sark like a shift under her shabby dress, and a thrill had shivered through her at the thought, but she had left it folded beneath the bolster at the head of the bed, away from the window, and as safe a place as she dared imagine.

As she pushed slowly through the rush of people and movement, her mind was elsewhere, leaping and tumbling around a swirl of thoughts, fears and desires. Gradually though, a new awareness made itself known, as it was clear that people were gathered around new concerns, enquiring, reporting to each other, wondering aloud and crossing class boundaries in the quest for information. Dolly was a stranger to panic, usually, but panic it was, that seemed plastered across every feature of every living soul that morning.

She looked about for someone to converse with. Blind Willie the fiddler was sat alone at the water pump, but she knew the loud voice of the blind man was not the best source of caution, so she guiltily passed him by in silence.

Even then, she felt he was aware of her, and she almost turned back towards him, before dismissing the thought. Across the square, the matronly form of Bella Roy was seated on a slanted cart. Bella looked wretched, as often she did in the early morning light, and was being roundly ignored by all comers. Dolly sidled up to her and offered a greeting. Bella looked up and eventually returned one of her own, though reluctantly.

"D'ye have sickliness or sadness?" Dolly asked, using words she had suddenly remembered her father repeating to her often as a weak child.

Bella smiled gently. "An equal share of each," she chuckled, and coughed painfully at that.

"Oh, that's hurt Ah can hear," Dolly replied, with true concern."That's bad fettle Ah reckon."

"It is that indeed," said Bella. "Ah tumbled on Tuthill Stair two nights past, clean sober as well! That's the joke of it. Rolled down across bosom and back, cracked me head on the post, and twisted this arm around like a sow's tail." She nodded at Dolly's loose arm. "It's weak for yer, but not pained Ah reckon, is that right?"

Dolly looked down at it herself. "At times. But not real pain, I fancy, just a sleepless ache. That looks black as thunder," she added, eyeing Bella's bruises.

"And right across me chest," she said. "Not that any man would want to find his way in that direction these days," she laughed, "But if he did, he'd liken it to a chart of sandbanks and chaldron channels. And Ah'd murder him for tryin' it!" Bella winced at the thought. "And as talk is about chaldrons and bosoms, that man o' yours. Is he still on that? Still treatin' you fondly?"

Dolly smiled, "Oh aye", she said, "Indeed he is." There was a pause between them, as each thought along their own path.

Again, Dolly became aware of the general concern smoldering across the surrounding townsfolk. She leaned into Bella.

"People look anxious this morning," she said. "Is it news of the press? They're at Tynemouth, they say."

Bella looked about her in turn. "That, certainly," she said, "But now with the Green Cuffs at camp at Leazes, well, folks have a right to shew concern. These women," she cast her eyes around the market place, "They have sons and husbands to cherish, but took for granted all this time. And now, well, there's risks on all sides."

Dolly stared at her for a moment, not grasping what she was saying, lost for a thread of meaning in it.

"Green Cuffs?" she said, puzzled? "What is that? Who is it? Ah don't…"

"Dragoons," Bella replied. "Irish layabouts in fancy braid and with a hunger for trouble. They marched from Haltwhistle yesterday and have been setting up camp positions at Leazes since evening gone. Miserable for the drawkin' they got in that rain yesterday, ye can bet."

Dolly gaped at her, her head swimming with this. "But what are they doin' here? Ah thought it was the navy who were stealin' our lads away, not the dragoons."

"No lass, they're not stealin' the men," she replied, bemused and not unmoved by the obvious fear in Dolly's young voice. "Though Ah dare say they'll be beating their drum soon enough, in a trick to lure the foolish louts amongst us to tak' a shillin' for a cocked hat and a line o'

105

buttons. No, there's no real fear of them foolin' honest men. They're on their way north to Edinburgh, it is said, to muster for deploy. That's what always happens, when the threat of war comes. We're like a step-stone, between the King's domain and the journey to battle." She chuckled, and pressed on her ribs uncomfortably. "No, it's just the press ye have to concern yoursel' with. And they'll be here soon enough, ye must have heard talk of it."

From behind them the sound of a loose skin being struck as a march, turned every head in one direction. Dolly stood and turned towards it too. At the edge of Pandon Dene a small crowd had gathered, and from within its midst soon emerged a young uniformed boy, his green sleeved arms wielding sticks in rhythm across a brightly tattooed side-drum of blue and red. Behind him, tall and erect, a line of half a dozen men walked in time to the boy's beat, all dressed in grey jackets, but with bright green edging around their wrists. Even to Dolly, it was a stirring sight. She became aware, when she eventually looked around at the crowd about her, that every man was smiling enviously, and every woman was beaming with eyes wide. Even Bella had struggled to her feet to face them, as they marched defiantly past with ear-splitting precision, heading beyond them to the river.

"Aye", Bella sighed. "There'll be a few hearts broken and more than a few heads cracked open now the army has come to town. Watch your paces, Dolly lass. There are changes a-foot."

CHAPTER 10

THE GREEN CUFFS ARE COMIN' IN

"Ale and vitals canna stay fresh forever," Harrison Marley said, to no-one in particular. Indeed, there was no-one there to hear him, save for the silent, white-haired old man they called Foster, sat nodding, as ever, over a flagon of dark beer in the corner of the taproom. Dolly, passing by the through-door with laundered dish-cloths, felt duty-bound to respond in some fashion, but struggled to find words of solace or even concern.

"How many nights of this can we be due for?" she asked.

"How can any man know?" he snapped back. "And still there's no sign of their arrival, no word from keelman or collier from down river. It's all hearsay, that's what troubles me. There's no-one in truth that's seen anything. There's nobody who's even seen sign of the tender at anchor, never mind the gangs out on the street."

Dolly's heart skipped a beat. "Maybe they won't come this far up at all", she suggested, immediately regretting the girlish stupidity of her words. Marley snorted his contempt plainly, back in her direction.

"Of course they will. From where else can they fill a Man O' War with able-bodied men with water for blood and muscle in their forearm? If they've come this far, they'll have a purpose. And every man does right in lockin' their door and avoidin' the street at night. But it's no comfort to a publican, a man of business like me. An empty barroom is an empty purse, and that's no lie." He looked sharply at her. "And it's no solace for you, lass," he said. "Your graft won't be needed and can't be paid for either. Wait a half hour, and then gan back to your man." He puffed out his cheeks in frustration. "Where is he this night?" he asked in afterthought.

Dolly leaned back on the door stanchion. "He's busyin' himself at home. There's fixin' to be done." She trusted that that was indeed the case.

His rant over, Marley ambled towards the stairway to his upstairs quarter. Jessie, his wife, had taken to her bed a week before, and hadn't been seen since, though angry words between them had been plain enough to hear in the meantime. Dolly left the white haired old man dozing in the corner and dragged herself to the back scullery. It was as tidy as she had left it the night before. She stood, pondering the uncertainties around her, for a time. There was no seat to be had, so she turned back towards the bar. As she did, she heard voices from the street, close enough suddenly to put a fear into her. Men's voices, with a strange twist to the sound of them. They were here, she thought, in a horror. The press was here. And she was alone. All she could do was to rush to the bottom of the stairs and alert Marley, and he would have to deal with it. She made a dashing move along the trestle side of the room, but had barely taken a step when they pushed themselves noisily in through the doorway. She reeled around towards them, gripped by fear and dread. There were three of them, then four, dressed in plain grey with brass buttoned tunics. And then she saw the wide green edges of their sleeves, as green as anything she'd ever seen, but stained and soiled through unknown toils and dangers. The feeling of dread eased from her, but the sensation of fear remained.

"Now then," one voice amongst them said, as the sight of her met them. "A sweet surprise for men fresh from battle!" The others laughed coarsely and almost in unison, like they were used to no other way of it. Dolly stared back dumbly.

"Surely not the woman of the house?" another, dark-haired and short of stature but handsome to his own awareness, said with a slow smile. "The daughter more likely, and lonely for company by the look of it!"

The old man Forster stirred in the corner. "Good evenin' daddy!" another of them hailed at him. "You at least have a wet before you. Would you like another for good intention?" The old man remained silent.

"Give him another one," the handsome lad said, moving closer, "And ale for each of us, as big a jug as you can manage. We have earned a taste for it this night!" More laughter, and still Dolly stood her ground, unmoving. She became aware of Harrison Marley emerging from the stairwell. Boisterously, but falsely so, he greeted them as customers.

"Now lads," he exclaimed, "You're surely welcome. It's four flagons of new ale, is it?"

"It is," the soldier replied, though without real friendliness in return. "And one for the old man, your best customer by the look of it!" Old Foster hesitated visibly, torn between making a judicious exit and the temptation of the drink. He settled for the latter.

Marley poured from the jug with nervous frivolity in his voice. Dolly stood by, each of the four men eyeing her repeatedly as they approached the bar.

"Dragoons are you?" he said, his voice already drifting into the lilt of the visitors.

"If you could call the nags that we sit astride horses, then we would be," came the reply, "But mules are mules in any country, so we reserve judgement on that." More raucous laughter ensued. Dolly edged back towards the scullery door. The dark-haired one noticed. "A small drink for the timid daughter to boot? If that's proper in this house?"

Marley looked up at him, puzzled, then followed his gaze towards Dolly. "Oh, she's the help-maid, not the daughter," he laughed. He immediately regretted the words. "Be gone Dolly!" he snapped too harshly, "You have work at back!" Dolly moved away, gladly, and hovered out of sight beyond the doorway. She heard the stumbling conversation continue.

"Well here's to ye," she heard Marley say. There was no acknowledgement. "And how long are you here for? At camp, Ah mean."

A reply came. "That is something of which we are not the best informed, my friend. Time enough I reckon. It seems like a town built for soldiers like ourselves, with castle and keep, and high walls at every turn. You must be sure of your hospitality for the likes of us. We might stay forever, you never know!" There was laughter again, though more restrained this time.

"Well, we're glad of you this night," said Marley. "We're expecting the press, that's why the streets are empty, and empty in here too. They're at anchor not four miles hence at the river's mouth, and keen to drain us of our menfolk no doubt."

There was a loud bray of false laughter now, with curses and oaths sprinkled amongst it. The same strong voice retorted.

"The pressgang, the pigtailed pirates, for the Lord's sake. Let them come and we'll see what they have to offer. We can barter with the best of them and match them, pence for pence I'd wager. Fine lads all, I'm sure of it. And they're on their way to join us, you say?"

"That's the word," said Marley. "Every able-bodied lad in the town is hidden away in anticipation of it. And who can blame them. Recruitment is one thing, press is another, I reckon."

The dark-haired soldier's voice continued cautiously. "Oh, you'd be surprised how little difference there is to choose between them," he said. "As my comrades here could attest. But we're glad of the dry land and the hillsides to shelter us from the wind. A better preference to the wild ocean and the churning belly, I dare say you agree."

"Ah have knowledge of neither," Marley replied. "Ah'm an inn-keeper from a family of the same. My mother was well-known in these parts, and further afield, for her convivial house and her fine ales, and Ah saw no reason to stray from her path."

The conversation stumbled on, with another round of drinks being poured. The reassuring clatter of pennies on the table, punctuated talk of a home in the northern part of Ireland, of a long month in the port of Bristol, and of

111

Colonel Fullerton, their commander, who had seen fit to recruit these Irish lads little more than a year before. When talk of past campaigns was raised by Marley, they were noticeably reticent, and the cordiality of the gathering waned correspondingly. The voice of the short, dark-haired one cut through the increasing din.

"And have ye heard tell of our wayward discipline?" he asked. "Or of our rambunctious behaviour? Our trepidation in battle perhaps?"

"Ah've heard no such thing," Marley responded, sounding ruffled. "Ah know nowt of ye. Ye have an Irish brogue, and the thirst of a soldier, and only that matters to me, as long as ye've the money to pay for it." A sudden clatter of tin cups across a floor, a thump of falling chair-legs, with more laughter, sent the old man Foster out of the front door at a pace. Calls for more ale rang out. Harrison Marley would earn his pence this night, Dolly thought.

Suddenly, in the midst of this, the silhouetted figure of the dark-haired dragoon lumbered into the doorway before her. She saw his black outline sway slightly, and lean lazily against the jamb.

"Dolly, is it?" he said softly.

"Aye it is." She stiffened as he held out his hand to her. "Come and join us," he said. "You'll get no invitation from your landlord, but ye surely can't begrudge me mine, and nor can he. It's a joyous time for us. Our very first night in our new home, so a special occasion, ye can't doubt it"

Dolly's curiosity spoke up for her. "Your new home?" she said. "But I thought you were on the march to

Edinburgh, and on to..." She halted. He was laughing to himself, and at her, and lurched forward, taking her stronger arm in his grip to pull her into the pale light of the main room. His comrades saw them reel in together, and a low cheer raised from them. Dolly looked at Marley, who returned her stare without moving or speaking.

"Dolly, my girl!" the soldier announced to the room. "Let me introduce me noble brothers in arms, newly mobilised and now stationed at the calling of your good self and the fine people of Newcastle. Privates Mullholland, Favor and Stapleton, and myself, Andrew Carmichael, corporal, at your service. He bowed deeply, tightening his grip on her wrist as he did so. Dolly watched him, knowing that the fear must be plain in her eyes. He stared into them now, a fixed smile creasing his face. There was a twisted scar on his cheekbone, she saw, and his hair was pressed into a vain curl on his forehead. He was handsome, undoubtedly, but the knowledge of it had driven an unpleasant, ruthless streak into his heart. And skilled too, she realised, as the space between them shrank slowly, and his other hand found a place at her waist.

"Dolly!" It was Marley's turn to call her name. "If ye value your job, you'll take your hands off the man, ye loose wench, and get back below. And your own man not two streets away. Back off, Ah tell ye!"

The smile remained on the Corporal's mouth, but any trace of it faded from his eyes. But still he didn't let her loose. He looked down from her face, her woman's form still apparent under the shapeless pinny she wore, and in

113

doing so, saw her weaker arm and slighter hand, hanging as ever, a breath behind the rest of her. His eyebrows raised involuntarily. He hadn't registered her deformity up to that point. Indeed, the changes in her life in recent times, were coaxing her further and further away from her weaknesses, as she had less and less cause to dwell on them, and more cause to forget them. But at that moment, the cripple inside her forced its way to a prominence once more, perhaps by way of self-preservation at what she feared might happen. Not since she was a child, in the face of physical torment by stronger, mocking children, had she used her weakness in such a way. Her reaction now had been automatic. Only the weak eye resisted it, retaining its determination and steadiness.

Marley, meanwhile, had decided on a different tack. "What's that ye say? Ye see yourselves here for a good spell? We thought ye were here to catch yer wind on the march across the borders, that's the usual arrangement."

Corporal Carmichael turned to face him, his hand still gripping Dolly's wrist, and with a trace of irritation in his voice.

"Ah, the man who claimed to know nothing, knows even less than he thought!" he said. A chuckle or two rose from the others. "Well, truth be told," he said, all the while casting his eyes across the length and breadth of the woman in his grip, "Those tepid Yorkshiremen who have been at your service these last years have earned a calling to more active duties. Militiamen in a rested river town a day's ride from the border, such a posting has cast few demands in their direction, and they've grown fat and lazy on the strength of it." He turned and smirked at

114

Marley. "So, come Saturday, they'll be skewed in rank and file, and marching north to whatever fate awaits them. And it will be our good fortune, the notorious twenty third, to have occasion to sit back and keep the sheep farmers and coal hewers from squabbling over the last slice of pigmeat and the last cup o' sour gin. Assuming we've had our fill of them ourselves in the meantime of course, is that right lads?" Once again, the hounds bayed in response.

"So, there's new rules to be cleared, and new claims to be staked," he said, wrenching Dolly towards him suddenly, so that she felt her head crack on her shoulders, and the sharpness of his tunic at her breast. "And I make the first claim Dolly, my dear. What d'ye think o' that now?"

There was silence. A new voice broke it.

"I think it is many tall words from so small a man."

It was a voice deep, soft, and it came from the street door, still open behind them. Every ear heard it, and every face turned towards it. Moss was coatless, his torn shirt tied at one side. He towered in the doorway, as he always did, but never quite so noticeably before. The silence hung for a beat or two of Dolly's heart. Carmichael released a long, loud breath, and tilted his head upwards, as if by instinct. She didn't look, but Dolly sensed his smile had returned. His grip had certainly tightened.

Moss barely moved. "Come," he said to her. She looked at him, looked down at the grip her wrist was in, and looked back at him once more. "Come," he repeated, "He will let go."

Carmichael chuckled softly. "And why will he do that?" he said.

"Because he is unarmed, he is drunk, his friends are also drunk, and I am not yet angry. He does not want to see me angry. And because he has a hand upon my woman. There is no honour in that, and for a soldier, even an Irishman soldier, honour should be an important thing. I know it always was for me."

There was another silence. Dolly felt a softening of the grip. She waited, then pulled herself free. Carmichael was still, his head tilted as if puzzled, his eyes fixed upon the tall, patch-eyed man across the room. Dolly moved towards Moss, and he tenderly eased her past him and through the door behind him. He backed out after her, turned with her and they both slipped into the shadows that led down Dark Chare towards a sort of safety. The blackness swallowed them immediately.

A new peril faced them now. A man on the street with the chance of a pressgang at any corner, in any doorway. Dolly almost pulled at Moss to hurry him. The Chare was pitch black, the meagre moonlight blocked by the tumble of overhangs and sloped roofs above them, the windows blind and lifeless. The alley veered off slightly partway, and as they turned, the narrow greyness of a street beyond provided their only beacon. There were noises at every dreadful step, lifeless objects, living objects, obstacles that seemed to slide out to obstruct them, a spoken word from a black oblivion above them, or a terrible death throe from a lost soul below them, no awareness of a force following behind them, and nothing of what might be ahead of them, and always the terror

116

that the hand that Dolly held so tight might slip away and be lost forever. At last, they reached the broken wood of their familiar door, and fell together into sanctuary.

CHAPTER 11

PRESSING ALL THE MEN

The next night, they finally came. Any element of surprise had been long since lost, and discussion was rife among the men of the town that day, as to why that should be, why such hesitation had occurred. It was generally agreed that there would be still further delay now, to convince the hapless prey that normality had returned, and they had nothing to fear. Then suddenly, they would pounce, it was said, and the smirk of blithe smugness would be wiped off the faces of the sons of this town forever. So ironically, it did come as something of a surprise that night, when the tumble of feet on cobbles was heard, as the grey gloaming descended on the chares and alleys of Sandgate, and breathless brutes of men, not hitherto known for their timidity, were observed loping full pelt from entry to entry, keen to put the smell of the quay firmly behind them. A louder, and eerily more regular pace was set in their wake, by a tight pack of uniformed men, strikingly similar in features to one another, when seen from a safe distance, moving as one up the steep new stones of Broad Garth, with a limb of them occasionally peeling off to throw cursory glances in doorways and entries, while showing no intention to act upon a result. It was merely a display, it seemed; a show of efficiency of a kind not often seen in a civil street. And at the rear, determined and unflinching, a tall, starched officer in marine red, a curious black hat perched atop his yellow hair, and a formidable cutlass at his belt. He barked orders, he snarled directions, and occasionally chanted a marching rhythm in a rasp from somewhere beyond his throat. Those who dared, watched them head in a direct line into the heart of the city, ignoring the shabby hovels and tumbledown public houses within earshot of the river, for richer pickings in the higher streets.

The populace below, nearer to the river, waited indoors, as if sheltering from a pestilence. Men feigned nonchalance and irritation at this incarceration, yet surely knowing in their hearts that it was the wise option. Sons scorned their mothers, husbands scolded wives, but budged not a muscle, nonetheless.

Dolly had known not to return to the Flying Horse, for that night at least, and was turning over in her mind what future arrangements would have to be made to avoid certain confrontation with Corporal Carmichael in the future. And how too, she could give thanks to the old man known as Foster, who had made it his business to reach and inform Moss of the antics being meted out at The Flying Horse that night. Moss himself had laughed off these events as a young man's misplaced bravado, but for Dolly it was yet another knot of impending trouble in what had almost threatened to be a smooth, fruitful, well-lit line through life, only a matter of days before. She sat in the thin chair at the foot of the bed, watching the low candle lead its shadow dance across the stained ceiling, and tried to bring order to her mind. Moss squatted on the floor beyond, and leaned into the meagre light, his boot stretched over his hand. He peered at it, examining it

119

for wear and damage, his eye squinting in a twist of angle and direction.

His sudden movement startled her. He had sensed a commotion, even before it was in earshot. His head jerked up and he flung the boot onto the mattress, and in a stride was at the window, having blinded the candle as he passed. The noise of confusion and fear reached them soon enough. Moss peered out of the best corner of their window, gently blowing the smoke and tallow from his finger and thumb. Dolly could hear the mad pounding of running feet below, a raised and breathless voice close by and another, pitched higher, at some distance away. She stared into the new darkness, not moving, trying not to let her imagination be sucked in by the sound of this night.

"They have come," he murmured to the gloom. There was more sudden, shuffling on stone close by, and confusion of steps at speed to be heard. Moss twisted his head around to source it.

"Ah, Lucas, the fool, what is he doing out there this night? The boy, it is not a sport! I warned him, I warned them all..." His voice trailed off into despair.

"Don't you go to them," Dolly said. "Don't. You can't help them. Ye have to stay here, with me." There was an angry determination in her voice. There was no answer from him. Then a new sound took to the night; a more orderly foot, with ordered companions, a curious calling out, regular, but meaningless, and base, as if from an animal that was unknown to them. Dolly's blood ran cold. The sound stopped, then came back once more. It got closer, then drifted away, all within moments.

"Yes, I hear them," Moss was saying, "But I do not see. They climb to the heart of the town. Yes, they know their business very well."

Dolly joined him at the window. The mad dance had taken on a curious echo on such a still night, through the crazy, snaking alleyways and entries. She sensed other faces at other windows, but saw none. No light shone from any of them. A plague was moving amongst them, she felt, and an angel of death followed in its wake. She clung on to Moss's arm. Still he squinted into the gloom. He was still there, a long time after, when the rowdiness of the returning pack stirred Dolly from sleep. No orderly step now, but the herding and scolding of a gaggle of unfortunates, voices raised in a mix of anger and pleading, of pain and resignation. She came sleepily back to where Moss stood, and now the glow of torches and flame could plainly be seen from the direction of the river. She thought she heard women weeping in full voice. But it could just as easily have been the sound of young men and boys.

Moss left early the next morning, and Dolly herself took to the street minutes after him. She avoided Dark Chare, rather than face the day-lit reality of their flight of two nights ago, and wheeled past the quayside. It was crowded, perhaps more than usual. She pulled back into Kirk Chare almost immediately, rattled by the sight of three green-cuffed soldiers in conversation by the rope store. She soon determined that the short stature of Corporal Carmichael was not amongst them, and she pulled her shawl higher and tried to blend in with the passing crowds.

121

She took the Castle Stairs up towards the Bigg Market, purposely avoiding Broad Garth, the scene in her head of last night's horrors. In doing so, she was faced at their summit by scores of Green Cuffs, loading baskets and tied bundles on to carts, in the shadow of the ancient keep. She sidled nervously away from them and crossed the cathedral square by way of the Amen Corner. Twice, she was greeted by people of her acquaintance, and twice she pretended not to hear. At the foot of the market, May, the weekend barmaid from the Horse, was selling pegs, made by her mother, from a pannier. May was a dim girl, whose tackling of chores in the Flying Horse often gave Dolly more work than she already had, but in the bleak times in the cold scullery in winter, the two women had bonded to some extent, and Dolly greeted her warmly on this morning. May gave her dim reaction in response.

"Ee, Dolly, have ye heard?" she said, her eyes wide. "The Militia's away! Leavin'! Them canny lads, shipped out to somewhere foreign, without a by-your-leave. Them with wives and bairns hereabouts, no choice given to them. It's a terrible state of affairs."

Dolly's thoughts struggled to adjust to this conversation. "Oh, aye, Ah did, Ah had heard, indeed" she stammered. "It's a shock, ye canna doubt it. They've been here a lifetime. It's not right. All this change, the Green Cuffs comin' in, and the pressers! On this very street last night, Ah hear."

May perked up somewhat. "Aye, that's true enough," she said. "There's talk o' that, there's no mistakin' it. Some high town lads carted away, from up by Pandon, and from the Colliers on Pink Lane. They were chasin' them down Puddin' Lane an' all. That's where Lanky Dodds got taken, ye know Lanky, his mother made pies. And a man called Wrightson, old enough to be yer father, they reckon, and several young lads from the Gowerley's Raw end…"

On she went, sending Dolly into the distraction of watching drawn features and stooped heads across the length and breadth of the square. What she really needed to know was not the roll call of last night's victims, but whether the culprits would be back. A customer for pegs gave her the opportunity to take her leave, and she scoured the street for familiar faces. It was still early. The church bells had peeled long and loud moments earlier, but Dolly had missed the count. Two well dressed women padded gingerly by, and were greeted by a parson. Dolly watched them for a moment. She had not even wet her face that morning. Her skirts were stained to her knees with salted damp and mud, and her feet still bore a muddy memory of the sprint down Dark Chare. It was almost that she had never noticed such things before.

Blind Willie the fiddler had reached his usual morning perch at the pump, and perhaps comforted by the knowledge that he wouldn't see the grime of her appearance, she resolved to join him.

"Good day Willie," she greeted him, and stationed herself within hearing of the old man. He hesitated and pointed vaguely with a bent finger, his head raised in wonderment. "A comfort to see you here as usual, in such mixed-up times," she said.

"Dolly!" he exclaimed in triumph. "Dolly, Dolly, Dillen Dolly, Fine lass. Sit near for a spell. Yer voice Ah hear clearly, but yer way of speech is altered Ah reckon?"

Dolly was taken aback by this. "Ah think not," she replied with no little indignation. "Ah'm ever the lassie ye've known for almost me lifetime."

"Nah, nah," he cackled, "Trust a sightless body with ears to hear. Ye've a proper slant to your words these days, and Ah know rightly what it is. Two aspects," he said, leaning into her. The crooked finger was raised again. "Firstly, Ah hear ye have a man, and a foreign man at that. The patch-eyed gypsy, is that right?"

"Aye it is," she agreed, "But he's no gypsy, he's from noble Roman stock!"

Willie threw back his head and laughed loudly. "Roman stock is it?" he cackled. "Why, where's he been hidin' all these years? Or is he back for his wall?" She smiled at this. She had little knowledge of this history, and considered stories of Romans and Norsemen to be nothing more than bedtime tales and backstreet myth. "Well, Ah've heard him talk," Willie went on, "And his stumbles and silences must count for somethin'. And now Ah hear you've learned to talk to him in his way. What use is there to speak of love and fancy stuff, if the man next to you is short of understandin'! That's one thing Ah hear in yer."

Dolly was amused by this. She could hear herself in conversation with Moss, choosing her words, rounding off the roll of them, avoiding some that she knew he wouldn't catch the meaning of. Her language had indeed taken on a different gait because of it. But it went deeper

124

than that. Willie leaned further in, and put a second finger across her arm.

"And more," he said. "The songs ye have. The poetry of them songs. Never let them tell yer they're ought but poetry, as good as anything these stiff-necked scribes in the Indian Kings scrape on to paper. Better by a long way, in fact. All them lovely words, neat and exactin', spread like honey on bread, full o' life and sunlight. Them's the words for you, lass. Ye've undoubted got the voice for it, but Ah trow ye've got the wit for it an' all. Cling to them lass, tighter than ye cling to the gyp!" He roared another laugh. Two women passing with tied sheets glowered in their direction, and Dolly felt her face flush.

It was hard to get serious talk out of Willie, and Dolly had never really had occasion to do so, but now, when pressed for opinion on other recent events, his face grew stern and clouded. It would continue, he told her. He'd been around long enough to recall similar events on the quayside thirty years before, when scores of men had been rounded up and carted to the coast, never to return. The single gang from the previous night was, in his experience, merely a forward guard for a more widespread assault yet to come. The nights ahead, he told her, would bring grim telling for the wives and mothers of the Tyne.

"What of the Militia," she asked at length? "Ye know the Black Cuffs are awa' and the Green Cuffs are comin' in?"

"Oh yes," he said. "Ah've heard the Irishmen, this very morning, and Ah've heard of their reputation. Bad buggers, cruel men, that answer sparin'ly to their commanders. Bad episodes in the cities of Liverpool and Bristol, they reckon, so they've sent them here, a long way from London. And London, that's where their colonel bides, Fullerton, an old man weary from wars in the Chinas and the mountains of India, still playin' at soldiers, and no firm hold over man nor horse. Aye," he sighed, "Ah sit with me fiddle and me Spanish juice, bein' poked and made josh of, but Ah soak it all up, Dolly. And ye know what? Nobody ever asks 'us for knowledge or wisdoms. And Ah could tell them all they want to know, if only they would ask. But what can a blind man know? He can barely find his lodgin' at day's end. But Ah ken it all, lass. If only they'd bother to act quizzical."

It was still too early for him to find his way to the barroom, so she patted his hand and left him with a fond word. There were people gathered in cautious talk all around her, pale drawn faces with clenched hands. Dolly found herself within sight of the Flying Horse, its door pulled shut and windows dark. There was noise from the yard echoing up the side alley, so she slid along it cautiously. Harrison Marley, in a coat over a bare torso, was breaking a barrel for firewood. His head turned as she entered the yard.

"Ah hate destroyin' the cooper's work," he said, "But it's beyond mendin'. Probably one of auld Elsie's from Harraton or Fatfield." He looked defeated in that dim place.

"Did you open last night?" she asked. "With all the trouble?"

"Oh aye," he scoffed, "Ah opened the doors. For about a quarter hour! Then it was like Hades in the street out yonder. There was Foster and me and Charlie Rust in there, so Ah bolted back and nipped the candles. There was a rattlin' of the door at one point, but the rest of the time it was folks fleein' up and down the lonnens, shoutin' and hollerin', and up they came from the quay, swingin' a bloody lantern like it was the bishop's procession. We sat for nearly an hour, more very likely, then back they came, by way of Pandon and the town wall, a bundle of poor lads roped up and hollerin'. The bastards! It was an awful sight, even with just a lick of moonlight. Well," he considered, "If that's the end of it..."

Dolly burst out, "No, they'll be back, there's no doubt, they say. Tonight, and in greater numbers!"

"Who told yer that?" he snapped. She hesitated, anticipating his ridicule.

"Willie Purvis," she murmured, "Blind Willie, in the Bigg Market, not a minute past. He's certain of it!" She waited for the scorn that never came.

"Aye, if Willie says it, Ah believe it," Marley replied, much to her astonishment. "He's better than the Journal for tidings and news. He's the cuddy's gob, as me mother used to say, though it was another blind man she was talkin' of. Aye, there's something in that, if Willie speaks of it. Ah've no doubt."

"So what of work for me tonight?" she said. "There's no cause for me to be locked up in an empty taproom with the work of the devil gannin' on outside." She added cautiously, "And then there's the other matter, of the Cuffs and the anger of that corporal."

"Aye, Moss made himself a foe that night, and Ah reckon he knows it." Marley looked back at her. "But there's others, local folk, that Ah'm not sure he's abreast of, that don't hold him in much regard either. Take me meanin' as ye will, and he's a man Ah'd trust, if it came to it, and Ah know also that he treats ye well yersel', Ah've no cause to doubt it, but he's used his foreign ways in the past, strange ways to the likes of us, and that's marked him out. There's them that resent him for that, and only for that! A black-haired foreigner with a way of his own." He splintered the last of the barrel, and continued. "Now that there's new importances in town, new bodies to reckon with, on one side or another, there's them who'll be seekin' favours, and measurin' out favours in return. And Moss is lit like a beacon by any account. He should watch his back. Ah'll tell him it meself! That young lad's only a corporal, but he's got ideas higher than that, and a means to hoist for them an' all."

There was silence between them, as Marley caught his breath. Finally, he said, "Bide at home tonight. All this uncertainty, there's no sense in temptin' it. And tell Moss what ye will, but mind to leave in the good intention of what Ah say. And Ah'll speak to him mesel', as Ah say, when the chance permits it."

"How's Jessie?" she said as she turned away.

"Bitter," he said, as he walked back to the door. "Bitter and ailin' from it." He closed the door without looking back.

CHAPTER 12

MY GOOD DAYS ARE DONE

With a low, rushing grey cloud and a howling wind to cover the sound of the church bells, Dolly had no means to know what time it was when she finally heard Moss's boots scrape up the stairway that evening. She had paced the cramped width of that sparse room for a lifetime, it seemed, washing her hands in her own worry, examining every crack and crease in wall and floor, and speaking out loud to the mother of Jesus, a skim away from desperation, hoping that Moss would return in safety. And then, he lurched in, with a weary smile on his face, which dropped to hunted stare when he saw the look of anguish on hers. She felt the stew of relief, anger and embarrassment boil within her, and turned from his gaze.

"What?" he asked, with an urgency. "There is news?"

She turned back to him, weighing up what her answer should be. She felt like beating him with a fist, or perhaps pulling him to her like a lost child; she could not decide which, in such a short moment. She flung up her hands in frustration.

"There's no news, except that Ah'm... Ah was anxious for your safety," she said. "It feels late. It's dark! Look, out there." She turned her back to him and moved to the window, pulling the rag of curtain hopelessly down to no purpose. She heard his coat being thrown to the floor behind her.

129

"No, it is not late," he said. "Well, a little late, perhaps, but the dark is due with the seasons, and the weather, that is all. I'm sorry you worry, but I'm glad of it too. It means..." He hesitated. "It means that things are strong between us. And that is why I make sure I come back, straight to you." He was beside her now. She made no answer. "The men, the colliers, they have hidden for two nights, and now they talk like they are better men, and can take back their foolish ways. They will be in the public houses tonight, gathered together. A crowd. Together, strong together they say, they have no fear of the pressgang. Perhaps they are right."

She turned to him, urgency in her voice. "But you're not like them," she said. "Look at you! You stand apart, you're different. Do you understand what Ah'm sayin'? If they see anybody in a crowd, the one man they'll see is you! Just look at yer!"

He looked with mock surprise, and then laughed a true, deep laugh. "Am I so different?" he said, his eyes wide, his hands held out in false supplication. Then she burst out laughing herself, with a sudden force that released all the hours of emotion, and flung herself at him in mock anger. "Ye bloody scoundrel!" she hissed at him, and he grabbed her by her hips and mockingly ground her body against his. Her next insults were lost in a rough kiss, and he lifted her off the ground like an infant. She squealed in a flash of playful pain, and he let her down gently. She buried her face in his chest. He smelled of sweat, of salt, of soot, and she clung to it. Moments passed.

"Ah spoke to Harrison," she said into his clothes. "Ah went by the Horse, and saw him. He doesn't want me there tonight. There's been nobody in these past evenin's. The doors were bolted last night. He heard all the commotion." She looked up at him. "He said it was an awful thing to hear, those men bein' took off like that. And Ah spoke with Willie, ye know, Blind Willie, and he reckons it'll continue. Harrison reckons that Willie knows these things."

"Yes," Moss agreed. "The ears of the blind are strong. Yes, he is right I think."

Relief eased its way through her. She ploughed on ahead. "And Harrison said you had to be more careful than most." She looked up at him again. "Just that he was keen to be helpful, ye see, and for me to tell you what he thought. Advice from a friend, like. That ye were not to trust people, because everybody now was afeared for their own skin, and they were liable to put others out into harm's way, in a hope to save themselves. Like ye were a bit of a prize, a special catch, with ye bein' un-English, and that un-English things were not being trusted in these times." She stopped. He was looking over her head, still, thoughtful. "There's talk of war, that's what it is, and nobody's sure of who we're meant to be at war with, not yet." She felt herself go red in her face. "D'ye hear what Ah'm sayin'? Do ye understand?"

He took a long breath, and she felt his hand in her hair. "Yes, I hear it," he said. "I understand it all. I am the coloured moth that the grey moths fear, and so must destroy. There is a story that I heard as a small boy. I remember it. I always remember it. And you yourself,

131

you have chosen to fly with the coloured moth, so afterwards they look to destroy you also." He raised her face towards his. "You too, you must be careful. Remember not to trust people. Marley speaks to you like a friend, like a father, today, but tomorrow, he sells you like a *schiavi*. Not a servant, worse than that! A slave! Trust no-one. No-one. Except maybe the blind man."

Sometime later, a round boom echoed from the river, and bounced through the narrow streets in a sly, soft manner. It was said later that several separate gangs had come ashore at Byker, and positioned themselves at points around the lower end of town. A shot had been fired in mid-stream at a marked moment, to send them all at once into the maze of alleys, flushing out their quarry from wherever they had gathered, and herding and funnelling them into the snares of pressmen, working in small groups from corner ends. To flee from one meant being trapped by another, and within half an hour this brutal efficiency had resulted in a tidy bag of human trophies for service to the king. The wind mercifully cushioned the horror of plaintive voices and merciless recriminations that had so enraged the populace on the previous night, and the torches at the quayside were soon fading into mid-stream and away to the river's mouth, where the tender lay like a queen bee off the easter bar.

Dolly witnessed none of this, lying coiled in silent terror on the bed, but Moss kept watch, however fruitless, once more at the window, and even considered braving the streets afterwards, to gain account for the evening's happenings, but reconsidered, the tone of Dolly's earlier entreaties still fresh in his ears.

132

Another dose of fitful sleep ensued, drenched in dreams and half-conscious fantasies, for both of them. During one of many wakeful interludes, Dolly heard Moss whimper like a child, and then speak a three-horned word in his own language. She was fearful of it, but he was silent after that, and she drifted back into sleep. The wind howled on into the night.

He left as usual in the grey morning, with only a word or two exchanged between them. The wind had dropped. Dolly took a wooden pail from the vinegar store below, and walked sleepily to fill it with fresh water at the pump on the quay. There were people about, black-wrapped dockmen, a group of yellow-breasted keelmen in intense conversation, and a few women also drawing at the pump. There was a lingering smell of burnt pitch in the air that caught Dolly in the throat. She remembered the torch-lit fury of the night before, filled the pail to the deepest split in the rim, and carried it back carelessly to the room. She washed herself slowly and carefully, resolving to do this more often and just as thoroughly. Afterwards, she eased the silken sark from under her pillow and slipped into it. There was no looking glass in the room, but she could see her own reflection vividly in her mind's eye, mirrored by the luxury of touch she was feeling across her body. The sour smell of the chunk of harsh yellow soap she'd used, found in the back of the downstairs store last spring, almost broke the spell. She longed for the day that it was worn away to nothing, and she could take the chance to buy a new piece, coloured lilac or lemon, like the ones she'd seen on the apothecary's bench in the Bigg Market. She looked around the dismal room. Bertha had found this place, long ago, and they paid a farthing a fortnight for it to a gin-soaked brewer's widow in the hovel next door. The old woman never asked for it, and Dolly admitted that she herself had been liberal with her obligation in the more recent past. But since Moss had been there, the rent was paid more regularly now. But the reality of the room's appearance, the broken window, the stained plaster, the crumbling skirtings, were making more of an impression on Dolly's awareness these days. Nothing she could do, no amount of cleaning and sweeping, could ever improve it, and the realisation of that depressed her deeply at times like this. She pulled off the sark hurriedly, lest the very atmosphere of the place might soil it, and dressed again in her long thick pleats and shabby bodice. She pulled at her wet hair with her fingers, teased the wool-comb through it painfully, and then tied it with the same length of cloth that Bertha had left behind for her, years before. She sat on the bed and stared at nothing, a tumble of woman's confusion rattling around inside her.

She started suddenly at the sound of feet on the stairs. She knew they belonged to Moss, but knew also that it couldn't be, or at least shouldn't be. Then he was in the room. He raised his head in distracted greeting, and stood rubbing his hand across his head.

"What's happened?" she pleaded, her voice risen in a fear. "What are you doin' back?"

He sat next to her, his eyes to the floor.

"Two of the men are gone," he said, "We think taken last night. And the horses. The pressers came by way of our landing, and must have taken them. Or loosed them.

They are gone anyway. I must go to the Hostmen's depot, by the Long Stairs. Do you know of it?"

She shrugged. "I know those steps. There are many buildin's at that spot, where the old bridge-end lies."

"I must tell them," he said. "No work can be done. And the blame must be placed somewhere." He fell into silence.

"Come then," she said, "The sooner ye tell them, then the more honest ye'll be in their eyes. They must know that men have been taken. The names will be common knowledge by now, I'd bet."

"Perhaps," he said. "The stableman, he said that the pressers must report names of recruits at the Militia Hall, but it seems strange to me. They do not care about names and families, I think. They have their crews, they will leave now."

"Truly?" Dolly exclaimed, grasping for relief, and immediately was seized with a guilt at the misfortunes that she was overlooking. "They'll go off, just like that?"

"Almost certainly," he said. "Last night was the big catch, their nets are full, they will haul them in and be gone. Everyone agrees. Men are riding to the coast this morning, to get more news."

Dolly sank back. Another broth of emotions reeled around inside her. At length, she and Moss rose together and set off for the Hostmen's Hall. Every corner, every informal public place was peppered with groups of people, deep in candid conference. Angry voices, though few of them raised, were soothed by tones of resignation from others. No work was being done on the quayside. Even the river itself was still, and the vessels at mooring

135

swayed gently, as if in deep respect. A true disaster had been dealt out by uncaring hands that last night, and the new day was in mourning.

At the Guildhall, Green Cuffs were gathered in clumps at the fish stall end. Moss and Dolly instinctively veered to the other side of the street. A brief, but ear-splitting rattle of the recruiting drum cut into the air, causing Dolly to grab Moss's arm. It was followed by laughter from the soldiers, and an indistinct barrage of abuse from an old woman close by. The sneering corporal could have been amongst those gathered, but neither Moss nor Dolly looked in that direction. A friend of Moss, a thin man called Longstaff, was coming towards them, and a brief conversation struck up, with the latter leading it. He'd seen it all, he claimed, the manoeuvring of the separate gangs through the chares and entries, the violent outbursts from both sides, the brutal herding and binding of the captured, and the enviable precision of the entire exercise. There had been collusion, certainly, he said, as witnessed by the familiarity of the layout of the town, plainly utilised by the hunters. The account went on for some minutes, and Dolly's attention strayed. She twisted her head back to the group of Green Cuffs. Anyone of them could have been Corporal Carmichael. She looked back at the tall, patch-eyed countenance of the man beside her. A hat, perhaps, she thought, might go some way as a disguise, but so many other aspects of the man were impossible to hide. Absent-mindedly she glanced around them, seeing the strangeness, the individualities of the townsfolk more clearly than ever before. Each one of them had tales and tragedies to bear, she thought. Then her eyes caught sight of one familiar face, that of Anty Proud, his neck straining in their direction momentarily from the corner of Side. Their eyes met, and he pulled back into a cut and was gone. Moss had a soothing hand on Longstaff's arm, and they parted. The Hostmen's office was close by.

There were written words and script of authority above every door. Neither Moss nor Dolly could tell which door was the one they were seeking. A thin man in a threadbare powdered wig, looking somewhat ridiculous, hurried out of a doorway guarded by cherubs carved into stone. Moss stared at him, and then signalled to Dolly to confront him. She was momentarily dumbfounded, and then called at his back, "Sir, can I ask of ye, where is the Hostmen's Hall?"

The man halted and spun round, viewing Dolly with a look of distaste. After a moment's hesitation, he pointed across the street, directly opposite the entry to the Long Stairs, at a tall double doorway in a grey stone-block building with cream-framed windows. It looked like a prison. Dolly followed his hand, and turned to thank him, but he was already on his way down the street. Dolly advanced to the tall kerb, with a view to crossing, but Moss pulled her back, and coaxed her to the wall behind them.

"What is it?" she asked, wide-eyed.

"It is difficult," he said, "I don't know how to tell these things. You must come with me to speak for me." He was staring intensely at her now.

"Me?" she responded, almost in horror. "I can't come with you. They won't let a woman speak. They likely won't give me entry! You must just tell them what you have told me."

Moss looked away, and pulled his hand dryly across his chin, a look of worry and hesitation on his face. Dolly was taken aback. In the months since they met, her world had come to revolve around the strength of this man, and now here he was, timid and reticent, asking her to step up to speak on his behalf. The feeling this gave her, though a surprise, thrilled her deeply.

"Just explain," she said to him, "How you came to the chaldron, and the horses were gone, and the men were gone. Ask for guidance as to what to do next. There's still plenty of work on isn't there, while the weather holds?"

Moss turned back to her and smiled weakly. "Yes, you are right. We have come to do this, so let us go in and speak."

They turned to cross the street. A cart full of mustard flagons rattled past, steadied by a tall blind man. Loud voices were rolling in meaningless argument from Potter's Pawnshop, just behind them, and a bright hammering on metal was ringing loudly from the dockside beyond. Some children were chasing a limping dog at an angle across the road, and a group of sailmakers were arguing over the folding process, on a straw verge covered in canvas, at the fork in the track. People chattered, and clattered across the scene, their heads bowed in the drudgery of mid-morning, with only the smell of bad fish to make them raise their noses in interest. As the mustard cart passed, Moss led Dolly across its wake towards the building opposite.

They were in mid-stride across the rutted road, when a red-coated figure, hatless, his hand pulling back a stain of yellow hair, emerged blinking into the daylight, from the entrance of that very building, not four yards in front of them. Moss saw him immediately, and the suddenness of his halting was what gave notice to the man, who even then, turned away momentarily, to get bearings for his departure. Then the grains of recognition ignited in his mind, and he jerked his face directly at Moss. He stared in a moment of surprised silence, while the look on his face whipped through a list of reactions, his jaw dropping to let loose words that did not come. His head stooped towards them, as one hand steadied his belt, and the other reached for the handle of a sword hanging from it. Moss was already in motion. With one arm, he swept Dolly behind him, and with the other he reached for the rear of the cart to his right, in a single motion dislodging a jar of the mustard, like a child's hoop and toy, from the open back. The jar spun once in mid-air, bounced on the kerb and then its base burst open at the feet of the red-coated man. A thick yellow cloud belched up from it, like an explosion, and greedily enveloped him. The crash alerted passers-by, who saw the man reel back, his hands now rearing up at his own face, his feet sliding from underneath him, and a choking scream of a shout escaping from somewhere amidst it all. Perhaps some of them saw Moss, still holding on to Dolly, scrambling back to the other side of the street, and be hidden by the base wall of the Long Stairs, but by then the carter's horse was dragging the cart crookedly across the road in fright, the blind man at the side of it had lost his grip and was noisily reaching out for guidance. People were calling out, coughing, warning those nearby, closing windows and banging doors, and a scene of stinging chaos had overtaken the whole corner-end.

Two dozen steps higher, on the Long Stairs, there was a flat patch of ash, where Moss pulled Dolly to his side, breathlessly. They stared at each other in a split-second tumble of confusion. Dolly started to speak in a panic but Moss held up his hand.

"That man, it is Jopling," he hissed, "From the pressgang. He saw me, he knew me. I have to get away. Go to the Bunch of Grapes, near the Ballast Hills, in Byker, and get word to Parrish. To Alec. He will help!"

"But you! Where can ye go?" Dolly barked out at him, her face a mask of fright.

"Not far!" he said. "And you, do not go back to our room! They will find it, and there is nothing there for us now. Find Parrish. Tell him this." His hand chopped a word at her, "Balilla!" he spat. "Balilla! Can you remember it? Balilla! Parrish will know! Here," he said, pulling at a clump of weeds topped by pale mauve flowers, and pressing a ragged bunch of them into her hand. "Raise your shawl and carry these, as if to market, and walk slowly back. They did not see you, and they won't look at you now. Balilla! Say it to Parrish!" He kissed her roughly, and turned, and was gone.

140

CHAPTER 13

ALL THE WAY TO WALKER SHORE

The street that swooped round from the edge of the quay, at the point where the last bones of the old bridge lay crumbling by the river, was known as Side. The foot of the Long Stairs paid into Side, and Dolly lowered herself off the last step, the purple weeds in her hand and her heart in her mouth, her figure concealed by the abandoned mustard cart. The horse was calm and tethered outside the pawnbrokers, a sharp contrast to the rest of the scene, in which Green Cuffs and regular watchmen dodged to and fro, while local people tried to attend to their usual business, amid the general commotion. Dolly kept her head low until she reached a chare entrance fifty yards along the block, into which she backed, allowing herself a glance around her.

There was a stretch of sail-cloth on the ground, covering the spill of mustard, and the red-coated figure of Jopling was seated, a soaked cloth buried into his face, on the steps of the Hostmen's offices. A group of Green Cuffs stood over him, along with a well-dressed man and a tall lady in a day-pinafore, who now and then lent over him, a second damp cloth in her hand. The blind man from the cart was also sat, alone, on the kerb nearby. The driver was talking earnestly to an officer. Soldiers and watchmen were busy in a bewildered fashion, as if searching for something that they didn't know the nature of. Three of them, belatedly, disappeared up the Long Stairs in cautious pursuit of the same.

There were onlookers too, drinkers from the Flying Horse amongst them, and Anty Proud prominent in their midst, talking rapidly to a bemused audience of onlookers. Dolly pulled her shawl higher and slipped away. Moss's instructions had been quick but clear, though one of them she now chose to ignore. She still had time, she felt, to head back to their room above the vinegar store and retrieve her one and only possession from beneath their pillow, the delicate sark that Moss had given her a few nights before.

She was moving too rapidly not to attract attention, and realising it suddenly, she dodged into another entrance from where she could look back at the way of her footsteps. There were people around, but only the usual faces and figures. She moved on, more carefully now, and peered up the street towards their building, for the sight of watchmen or militiamen. There were none. She crossed at the last moment and was inside the old door in a second. She stopped and cocked an ear for any sign of life. Again, there was none. She was already up the stairs and into the room, her hand feeling under the bolster for the soft cloth, when she heard a voice of authority barking in the street below. She took a glance through the curtain, and saw a flash of grey uniform. In a panic, she grabbed the sark, pushed it beneath her smock and sped out of the room. At the foot of the stairs, she heard a rattle at the door latch in front of her. She pulled back against the dark wall, and her hand felt the narrow opening alongside her, which led into the pot store. If there was another way out of it, she was unaware of it, but it was the sole option. She stuffed herself into the tiny space and stood frozen. The passage in front of her was suddenly lit up by daylight from the opening door. Almost at once, a uniformed man was a breath away from her, but he saw nothing in the gloom.

"Stairs!" someone grunted and the man moved back, and a bump of booted feet banged out an untidy rhythm, up and then above her. There was little commotion, save the grinding of the bedstead across the floor, a clang of pans and a bounce of tin cups. Then the feet tumbled back down towards her. There was a voice.

"No-one here Corporal", it said.

"No, I dare say," came the twang of a reply. Dolly knew the sound of it, the lilt of it, the arrogance of it. "There's little for them to come back to a midden like this for, but we had to check it. That sluttery of a barroom, that's all we can try…" Carmichael's voice trailed off as he and his men moved outside. Dolly exhaled a long, measured breath. The door was still shedding a dull light into the passage beside her. Her heart began to drum, her mouth was dry as tinder. She was still as a grave. She stayed there for a long time. No stranger to panic by now, at some point in this tomb of desperation, Dolly realised she couldn't remember the word that Moss had so desperately shared with her. What was it?

The street was empty when she finally slipped out of the door, and slid a stride or two away from it, before veering into a slim alleyway called Grinding Chare. It was long and mostly empty, made up largely of the bare backs of commercial buildings situated on cheaper back-lanes away from the quay. Dolly paced down its full length, and was at the far end of Sandgate before she knew it. She had no idea of the hour of the day. Her weaker leg offered an aching numbness from being standing and still for so long, and the churning of fretting within her since Moss had departed, had left her feverish with worry.

She followed the river, as best she could, for a long time, by way of empty lanes, a good half mile before branching away to where she believed the ballast banks lay. The landscape was bare, save for a cottage or two, dotted at curious angles, with heavily smoking chimneys atop each one. Men were ending their day's work, and passed her in groups, looking weary and unfriendly. A young woman with a deep basket piled with charcoal, and soot staining her face and clothes, struggled past her, and Dolly asked for the whereabouts of the Bunch Of Grapes. The girl stared at her, then flung her head to one side, as if to indicate that a further climb of the hill was necessary. Dolly marched on, and over a slight rise saw a short terrace of dwellings, with a taller building at one end. As she reached it, she saw the blue and white sign, showing faded fruit that could easily be grapes, she thought, creaking painfully in the light wind.

The door opened as she approached and two men came out, turning away from her and making to somewhere further up the hill.

"Sirs!" she called. One of them turned briefly back, but showed no inclination to respond. "Sir!" she called again, "A bit of help if ye please!" This time he stopped and squinted back at her. "I'm looking for Alec Parrish. A Scotsman. A dear friend, a relative in fact. Known around

144

these parts, I believe." Both men had stopped now and looked at each other. One blew his nose noisily with his finger and thumb, and shook his head. They turned away. "Do you know him at all, then?" she called after them. One responded into the distance. "Forgive me," Dolly pleaded, "I didn't hear ye. Is he known to ye?" Her words came out rounder, her voice more shrill, as if in some vain attempt at respectability.

"Aye!" came the reply. "He'll likely be about, presently!" He pointed a dismissive finger at the public house. Dolly sank back on a broken mile stone within sight of its door and pulled her shawl tighter. There was a dampness in the air. Minutes later, a male head appeared at the door and looked at her for several moments, then the door was pulled closed. She sat, her thoughts dancing a bewildering pace around the day's events, and the turmoil that seemed to go hand in hand with this man in her life. One of the many things that dragged her into confusion, was Moss's unqualified reference to his being a soldier, when in confrontation with Carmichael two nights previously. This was an unexpected twist on the unwieldy details of what she knew of his life. It had sounded more than bluff to her ears. The many years difference in their ages seemed to hold a bottomless pit of adventures and journeys that made little sense to her. She relived their parting moments of hours before, and knew the heartfelt gaze of love he shared with her was genuine enough, and at that point she heard his voice pronounce the word again in her memory.

"Balilla!" she announced, loudly to no-one. She looked about. The path she'd taken was empty, but behind her, a sole figure was advancing across the parched roughness of the scorched meadow. She looked away. Eventually, she heard the scrub of his boots nearby, and she glanced at him. Alec Parrish recognised her immediately, and needed no telling that she brought trouble.

"Lass," he said, as if in begrudged greeting. He stood away from her, and caught his breath.

"Moss sent me," she said meekly. "He told me to tell you, something. He told me to tell you, 'Balilla'."

He stared at her, then nodded his head once and looked thoughtfully at the roadside. "I've earned a drink with a climb through briars like that," he said. "Come!" She followed him to the door, and into the near-darkness of the pub opposite.

She had sat near the entrance. He had drunk quickly and silently, and had not asked her to join him. No-one else but a stout man behind a hatch into another room had been present, and as they had left, she'd heard the door being bolted behind them. It was dusk when they reached a line of stone cottages within sight of the river. Nothing had been said, and she had walked a good step behind him all the way.

Inside, the walls glowed red from a good fire in the grate. It was warm, almost cosy, with a pile of rugs on the floor, topped by a ragged fleece. Dolly noticed a small, framed portrait propped on the tall mantle, but she could make out no detail from where she stood. There was a table and two chairs, a ripped sailcloth hooked to the stone wall, and a shuttered window. There were books too, in an unsteady stack on a split log next to the fire.

There was a stump of a candle, but no attempt to light it was made. She stood, feeling safe for the first time that day. Parrish wedged a black metal pot into the fire, and secured it among the cinders with a poker. He pushed a chair across the stone floor towards her and said "Sit ye," in a husk of a growl. She sat. He put a white clay bowl on the table, and rummaged in a wooden box beneath it, out of which he took out another, which he wiped with the edge of his jacket. He placed it, along with a dull metal spoon and a scorched wooden spatula, on the table too. The pot bubbled into life, and then from it, he ladled two generous portions of thick soup, and signalled for Dolly to eat. She tasted potatoes, onion, and coarse lumps of spiced rabbit meat, and it was delicious.

Parrish finished quickly, and wiped his mouth on his sleeve. "Balilla," he said quietly. "Do you know what that is?"

Dolly shook her head. Parrish leaned back, half-closed his eyes, and told his tale in the flickering firelight.

"Your man, Moss," he said, "When I first knew him, when I first saw him, that eye had just been slashed out of him, with a pulley line from a trader he was working on. The sort of thing that happens on a quayside any day of a year. But that day, that moment, I was walking along that very quay, with much of my own business to keep me occupied. And all I did was to lend a hand to carry the man to the mooring side, and staunch the wound with a meal-sack. I didn't think he would survive it, looking down on that face. But he gave not a groan in pain, not a whimper, from a wound that would have another man keenin' like a bairn. And there was another man, a

147

companion to him, there with him, an older man from the same city in that foreign land, showin' a grand amount of concern for the lad. Talking to him in the same language, I suppose, easing him. And the name the man was calling him, soothing him, that name was Balilla."

He rose, cracked a length of dry branch across his thigh and pushed the bigger piece into the fire. He toyed with the result for a moment or two, rearranging the glowing cinders and white ash as if arranging thoughts in his head.

He went on, "And it was the older man, the comrade, who told me, as best he could, who this lad was, and where they'd come from, and why he was concerned with this state of affairs. And when I heard it, I knew it was up to me to help him, if it was in my capability to do that. So I did." He smiled to himself, and closed his eyes again.

"Forty years before, the older man told me, their country had been under the rule of a foreign army, from the country of Austria, on the other side of the mountains to the north. And this army, naturally, treated the people of this country badly, like slaves, like cattle. Sucking them dry, working them to death, starving them, using their men, abusing their women. And this was the life that the future had in store for them, with nobody strong enough to stand up and fight against it. And then one day, a transport of soldiers was passing through a village, with weapons and supplies and plunder, no doubt. Not knowing the lie of the land in those parts, they let their horses pull their wagons into flooded ground near the river, and they became lodged there, not able to budge. So, the soldiers rounded up the men from the village to make them pull the carts free from this mud and sodden ground, and herded them into this rank and stinking swamp of a place, ordering them, scolding and scourging them, whipping them. And on the dry bank yonder, a young boy was watching this going on, very likely his own father amongst those being driven in this manner. And this child, he was disgusted and angered by the sight of all this, so he picked up a stone from the river bed, and he threw it at one of these soldiers. It struck him smartly, I dare say. And then he took up another stone, and another, and then someone else nearby picked up a stone and hurled it, and then someone else, until the townspeople came and picked up their own stones, and pelted this platoon of armed bastards, relentless, until they withdrew, leaving their weapons, their supplies, just fleeing like the cowards they were. And so began an uprising, inspired by the actions of this one small boy, that eventually led to the overthrowing of these invaders, and the liberation of the whole country. All due to the action of this small boy. And he became a hero, a legend, known throughout the land, by everyone, and the name they gave him was Balilla."

Parrish stood up, and took a cup from the hearth, reached into the box beneath the table for another, and poured measures of liquor into them from a brown bottle he took from beneath the fleece on the pile. He pushed one cup towards Dolly. She took it without drinking from it.

"Balilla became the symbol of freedom throughout the land," he continued, "Known to everyone, including, of course, the enemy oppressors. And naturally they hunted him, sought after him, to destroy him, to cut him down. They found his family, but not him. They destroyed everyone known to him, anyone who was associated with him, but not the boy. He was sheltered and hidden from them by everyone who met him. And the boy became a man, and fought alongside his people in vanquishing the enemy, but by then he was a marked man. He couldn't stay to enjoy their new-found freedom. He had to flee, with just a few comrades as his companions. And everywhere they went, they found the same oppression, whether from armies and soldiers, or from landowners, or from company bosses, and Balilla stood up to each and every one of them, until his infamy and legend caught up with him. It always did, wherever he went. So eventually, he left behind the name, the man that he'd been, and sought a new life, just so he could survive, far away from everything that he'd known before. And that is the man that I helped that day on the quayside, and the man who you have come to share your bed with."

He turned to her, his eyebrows raised. "Did you know any of this?" he asked. She shook her head. "No, I thought not," he said. "It is not through lack of trust, I'm sure. It was to protect you. He has lost everything else that he has held dear to him, so he needed to save you from that." He paused. "But now, he sends you here to me, with that hidden name on your lips. There is serious trouble I fancy. What do you have to tell me?"

Dolly looked into the cup she held in her hand, and drank from it. She began to speak, slowly, drained from what she had just heard from him.

150

"By unlucky coincidence," she said, trying hard to match the eloquence of his own tale, "Moss was recognised in the street by the Hostmen's Hall this morning. It was a soldier, a captain, dressed in the red coat, that he had had dealings with, bad dealings, when he first came to this country. The same man was here in charge of the pressers. It was the devil's own chance that brought them face to face. Moss managed to flee, but there was much uproar with it. There were many who must've seen it. He took off past the old keep, away up the river Ah think. Ah know he's spoken of acquaintances there. But they'll be chasin' him, and he's on foot." She paused, and then added, "There was another soldier, an Irish lad, in the barroom a night ago. He was..." She hesitated again. "He had his hands upon me, and Moss threatened him. It has left further scores to settle Ah fear. And Marley, the landlord, he warned me too, not to trust any that know us, not with the way things are, with all that's uncertain in the town. And as for me, if Ah go back to our dwellings, they're sure to take me for being with him, for knowing what Ah might know." Her voice trailed away, and then she said, "He told me to come to you, to tell you. Ah don't know where Ah should go otherwise."

Alec Parrish stared into the fire for a very few moments. "You must stay here," he said. "I'll go tonight to the Sandgate, and find out what I can. It's not late yet, there is time."

"But the press is still out," Dolly said, "No-one is venturing to the streets at night. And you, even you will be in danger from it!"

"No," he said, "They have ceased. I have word of it from Tynemouth today. The tender is to weigh anchor with the first tide. Jopling was surely at the assize to register names of those taken. They must include keelers, if he was at the Hostmen's office. Anyway, I will have word of it later, no doubt. You must stay here regardless. Moses and Annie are the people yonder." He pointed off, towards the fireside wall. "They are honest folk. Speak to them tomorrow if I haven't returned by then. Tell them it all."

Within moments, he had gone, and she bolted the door behind him as he had instructed. She edged a chair nearer to the dying fire, and dared to lay the other half of the cracked branch across the brightest part. She watched it smoke, then bubble into flame. The heat felt good on her face. How warm and safe was Moss at that moment, she wondered, and juggled in her mind the details of the story she'd heard. The young boy, stone in hand, that she pictured, with thick black hair and dark eyes, was impossibly beautiful, his eyes shining with bravery and solidarity. And soon, she was a young girl beside him, encouraging his fortitude, standing boldly with him against a common foe, in a land she'd never even seen. And she too was beautiful, strong, unblemished, untainted by physical weakness. Later, as she slid into sleep before the last gasp of the fireside, these were the swirling, tumbling images in her mind.

CHAPTER 14

STYLISH AT THE RACES – O

At the head of the Long Stairs, Moss had looked west, and had seen the river snake away beyond the ford across the river that linked the north bank to the Blaydon wagon way opposite. He knew well the feelings that the hunted feel, and resented that they had a grip on him once more. He knew too, that if he headed north out of the city, he would have to avoid the Green Cuffs encampment on the moor, and also negotiate the still-mustering Black Cuffs, who were due to leave for Berwick two days hence. His only option was to wheel back across the Tyne, and seek shelter with the Scots miners he knew of old, at the Speculation pit at Low Shibdon. There at least he could hide for a while, anonymous among the coal-stained faces and strong limbs.

It was a distance, to be sure, and he had started at a pace. He tore off the eyepatch that would mark him out as much as anything would, and kept his good eye on the river whenever a break in the warehouses and workers' hovels allowed it. They would soon peter out and he would be on open land as far as Scotswood. There was no sign of pursuit. His dark coat was dusted green at the flank with mustard. His body was cold with the sweat beneath it. It was the body of an older man, he thought, slower and heavier than when he had last taken flight from Jopling, through the streets of Greenwich, a dozen years ago.

There had always been men like Jopling, starched into uniform, with a sneer of authority and a coldness of heart. The man had relished the brutal treatment he administered on those voiceless foreign workers at Deptford, their breath barely caught from an exodus through a warring continent, thinking themselves finally secure across a calm channel, in a land of prosperity and opportunity. But the greed of man knows no channels or boundaries, and there are always those willing to encourage and execute the mistreatment of the disposable poor. Moss had watched it all happen; the flood of hungry workers, with silent wives and pale children, the gleeful reduction of already meagre wages, the queues of hungry men at dockside lines, the regular eruptions of violence, the factionalising of nationalities, until a veritable war of nations boiled up on the brown banks of that wide English river. And now, that is what was on the horizon again, here on the Tyne, with the scheming of the greedy Hostmen and the faceless merchants of this northern city. That is why he and Parrish had acted, by hijacking the plans and warrants that would bring such clouds of despair. It was a meagre delay in the grand scale of things, nothing but a grain of a tactic, to lay bare such dealings to the eyes of the ignorant populace, and avoid a repetition of the bloodbath that had taken place three hundred miles and twenty years away.

How ironic then, that Jopling should appear at that moment, albeit with a different task to achieve. He had shown no hesitation back then, when the Greenwich barracks was asked to provide a unit of peacekeepers on the Deptford dock. They arrived with their old flintlock muskets primed as if for target practice, the yellow haired commander with his arm raised and ready for the order to fire. What he had not expected though, was the unity of force that had responded. These were men who had seen war and conflict in their own back streets, and despite their lack of uniforms and weapons, were prepared to fight back. All they needed was a leader, and that was a role that Moss had always resisted. But when the true identity of this Genoan seaman was proclaimed, all eyes turned to him. Little good it had done them, in the event, but he had risen to it, and gripped tight on the responsibility until the bitter end. When all was lost, Moss could still remember lying bleeding on the deck of a collier brig sliding towards the mouth of that river, with the sound of musket shot still crackling through the streets behind him.

The name of Balilla was not one of his making. His own strength and sense of justice had created this character, but it had been for others to christen it. It had echoed through the streets of Deptford like it had through the alleys of Genoa, and into the earshot of Jopling soon enough. That had been the word on Jopling's lips just now, as their eyes met once more, and the sense of recognition dawned upon him. Balilla was manifest again, and here, as large as life, in this distant northern town, just when both men, Jopling and even Moss himself, had least expected him.

Moss strode onward. How different the people were on this part of the river, he thought now. There was a vagueness about them, a lack of purpose, plain to behold in the blank eyes of the clumps of silent men standing at street corners or hunched low on broken walls, wherever he looked. The road on which he walked was rough and unused, paying out into untidy strips of clay tracks every few hundred yards. He was well away from the river at this point, with no obvious way to pick up its path again. He looked back. No-one followed, but those he had passed had, to a man, turned to gaze at his retreating figure. His only means of bearing was the stone pithead, far ahead on the farther bank, which he had yet to see. At Scotswood he left the road and squelched through marshy ground behind the stretch of cottages that lay ahead. This slowed him dramatically. His way ahead was hindered by a wide burn that flowed into the main river from the north side, which he would have to pass at a higher place, and then trace his way back to the ford. How different it had all looked from the south bank, where he'd worked, soused in coal dust, two years before.

His head jerked around suddenly, to feed his one seeing eye. The wind in his ears had masked the rumble of hooves, growing in volume now, from whence he'd come. He sank into the dampness and rested on his bent knees, his head down among the high grass. Grey coated men, four or five in number, high on horseback, riding with a purpose. They disappeared from his view into the main street beyond, and the sharp sound of hoof on stone told him they had slowed. He turned directly towards the river, intending to cross the burn wherever he could, and hopefully reach the dry main bank in time to reach the ford before them. But he knew immediately that this wouldn't happen. The burn could be crossed on horseback a mere stone's throw from the main current, whereas he would have to risk wading it at the point of joining. At that moment, two dragoons appeared high to his left, straining their necks in his general direction. He crawled through the stench of the reeds, slithering towards the river, and straight into a nesting waterhen, who reared up noisily as he walloped into her. He didn't look back. They were surely alerted by now. He stood up and loped as best he could towards the river, still a good length in front of him. A rapid glance back told him that the two horsemen were finding the going no firmer or faster, and he was already gauging his chances at swimming the full width of the water ahead, when three riders advanced strongly and easily to his right, trotting over firmer ground on the edge of the bank. One already had a musket raised at him. Moss stood still, his palms open on slightly raised arms. They had him. The men sat easy in their saddles for a moment, then watched the fugitive slowly stride towards them, his head bowed. A single rider dismounted and approached him wordlessly, gesturing with his weapon to make him advance.

They marched him along the bank, emerging at the mid-way point in the main street, where a handful of people had gathered, to witness the excitement. One of the mounted men had barked words at him, but Moss was of no mind to try to understand him. They stopped him there, and one of the other riders pulled out a flourish of twine, and lashed his hands to a gate-post. He addressed him as "Frenchie" and laughed at his twisted form. Another one urged a villager to fetch a pail of water, and when she did, the soldier snatched it from her and flung the whole of it over the prisoner, telling him,

"You're stankin' Frenchie!" His fellow dragoons laughed along with him at this.

Moss seemed apart from it all, his mind turning over at a frantic pace. Much of what had brought him to this place remained unclear to him. Where he would go from here, that would be determined later, no doubt.

With a breeze and intermittent sun, Moss was almost dry by the time more soldiers arrived, three dragoons, and a short wagon, probably a converted gun-carriage, driven by a Black Cuff infantryman. Moss saw immediately that the largest of the horses was ridden by Corporal Carmichael, who alighted with style and took a stone bottle of ale from one of the capturers. He swigged, spat, and walked squinting over to Moss.

He stared at him, closely and for a long time. "Didn't you talk to me of honour?" he asked, after a while. He stepped back and theatrically looked the filthy, twisted figure of his prisoner up and down a number of times. "Not much in the way of honour from you, my friend," he said. "A spy, indeed. The impudence of it. A treacherous, scheming, rat in the nest. The lowest of the very low." Moss made no reply. "All is known, feller," Carmichael continued. "The whole tale, plain as day. The game is truly up. There'll be people who want to talk to you. It's just a question of finding which language you talk best in, that is all." He stared at him for a time, in silence. "Let's get him back then lads," he said at last, "And keep a ball trained on him at all times. He's a sly one, make no mistake."

A dozen locals stood by, watching the dark-haired man be hoist into the cart, tied face down to the flat-board, and be rattled away to his fate.

By the time Alec Parrish reached the Black Boy tavern at ten that evening, news of Moss's capture was common knowledge. The place was noisy and full, and even the dark streets were busy with relieved drinkers, cautiously celebrating the withdrawal of the pressers. Parrish feigned good spirits too, and rummaged his way to the bar. He peered over the mug of ale at his mouth. He knew no-one here by name, but recognised a few faces. He filled his pipe beneath a tired candle, and walked to the fireplace to light his spill from an ember. Two men were seated nearby, and he struck up a conversation with them about the press. Yes, they said, the tender had sailed north to Berwick at noon, leaving a lot of bitterness, especially at Shields and Tynemouth, from where two score men had been taken. That was many more than Parrish had heard himself, but he made no comment. He changed the subject somewhat.

"What about this man who was taken today," he ventured. "Here in town was it?"

"No, no," replied one of the pair, "He'd been makin' for somewhere to the west, away from the Watch. Hexham, it was said. A spy, no less, a French spy. Can ye imagine it, here in Newcastle! He knew him well," he said, pointing at his companion.

"Really?" Parrish said, looking impressed.

"He was well-known by many in these parts," said the other, lest he be damned by association, "But yes, I've

159

supped here with him many times. Mosserello, or some such, by name. Foreign. French, it turns out. Watchin' us here all the while, getting' to know the area, getting' bearin's for an invasion force they say. He was in here, stood where you are now, a week ago, no more. Can ye believe it!"

"And how did they take him today?" Parrish wondered. "I mean, how was he discovered?"

"He was recognised, they say," came the reply. "The adjutant of the press saw him on the quay this mornin' and picked him out as a marked man, known in the city of London. There was a skirmish, they reckon, right down by the Guildhall, and the military man was hurt. The Frenchman escaped. They're a sly breed, a ruthless bunch. Goes to prove if he can overcome a military man with trainin' and that! Anyway, he's taken now. And God help him."

"He's alive then?" said Parrish.

"Aye, he's at the barracks of the Old and Bold, at Fenham. They're not long back from facing the French. They'll have his story out of him. They'll know the ways of them, and the tongue they use. He'd sit here at nights, I recall, smilin' away, not sayin' hardly a word. But listenin'. Listenin', ye see. That's the sign of a spy, ye can't deny it."

"Right here amongst us," Parrish added thoughtfully. "What with the press, and now this. The back streets aren't safe for a man."

So it continued. Moss's guilt was plain, his allegiance proven, his fate decided. One more detail sparked up later in the conversation. Compliments were reserved for a local man, whose observances had paved the way to Moss's capture.

"Aye, it was a lucky thing," said one of the drinkers, "Anty Proud had had his suspicions, and lo and behold, was on the scene of the skirmish this mornin'. He was able to point the way for the Militia, as he was familiar with the man's past, that he'd worked on the wagons at Blaydon. It was plain that that was the direction he'd head, by way of the ford there. He's an arse of a man, Anty, but he's proved his worth this day. He'll be lordin' it up tonight down at the Horse, I'd bet."

"He had a woman there, the Frenchman," said someone at the bar. "The lass with the cast, and the short of limb. They get her to sing there."

"That's right," said another, "Dolly, gentle in the head a bit. A dillen, Dolly Coxon! Bonny sisters she had, and a rare singer herself, but simplified. Standin' around at corner ends, gawpin', by the Groat Market, often as not. Dillen Dolly, the women at the wash call her. She wouldn't have known him for what he was. Not enough of her to realise it."

"Don't ye mean Wool Maggie?" someone else piped up. "Moss, the spy, he was with Maggie, the flax man's sister. I've seen them in here, times past."

"No," said Parrish's original informant. "She's been off to the markets these last months, Alston way. They head off every summer season."

"Well, she's back now," another man said. "She was in the Old George Yard two nights since with a young Green Cuffs officer, I can tell ye. Soon as the men of the town have to keep their head down, there's women like Wool

Maggie on the look-out for a young fool with wages and a yearnin' for sport. She's a fierce one. I wouldn't like to handle her."

"Oh I could give her a try, and bear the bruises!" cracked another voice, to general laughter.

Parrish knew Wool Maggie, and he knew Anty Proud too. He stared thoughtfully at the black crack in his mug, and saw how settled the fate of Moss was likely to be, and saw too how the spite of those around him would help to seal it. And Dolly, there was nothing simple or wanting about her, he knew that as a certainty. He knew too that her heart would be broken if events led in the direction that he suspected they would.

CHAPTER 15

TOGETHER THEY SOUND SO SWEETLY O

Moss had undoubtedly done away with Dolly, it was generally agreed, in the knowledge that his deceit was about to be uncovered, and that in her simpleness, she could have incriminated him sooner and deeper. The hood of domesticity she had given him was of no further use to him. The fact that she had not been seen by anyone of consequence since her conversation with Harrison Marley in the backyard of the Flying Horse three days previously was all the proof that the folk in Sandgate needed. Dillen Dolly was dead, her weak body no doubt swallowed by the Tyne in the dark of night.

Anty Proud could have contradicted this, of course, having spotted her in Moss's company moments before the mustard-stained incident with Commander Jopling the day before, and would also, no doubt, have disputed the general consensus surrounding her lack of wit to boot. But in truth, no-one had seen Anty Proud since he'd staggered heroically out of the door of the Flying Horse the previous night, having been plied with enough free drink to have rendered a lesser man senseless. Imagine the surprise on the faces of those who, believing that Dolly was surely soon to be discovered, weighed down by a missing creeler's anchor, at low water mark before the week was out, instead came across poor Anty's corpse, kneeling as if in penitence, beneath the props of the old bridge, early on Sunday morning. Strong drink and a poor sense of balance were blamed; the gash in his forehead having been surely sustained in the fall that sent him to his doom.

Friday morning, meanwhile, saw Dolly in solemn conference with Alec Parrish, who had returned home in the small hours, and had disclosed to her all that he had heard. His own knowledge of the fate of Anty Proud, yet to be discovered, he kept to himself.

"But why say he's a French spy?" she quizzed Parrish, her face a mask of worry. "I thought he was from Genoa, beneath the Alpine Mountains. He's talked of it many times. That's surely not French lands, is it?"

Parrish held up his hands. "He's not a Frenchman, no, but his land is governed by the French. They haven't invaded it, but they rule over it to protect it from invasion, as they themselves say. That's what I understand, from what he himself has told me. So he has no allegiance to the French, or anyone else, but he could be seen as being allied to them. That's what could be held against him, especially now at this time of threatened war with them. He's different from the Englishman, he looks different, he sounds different, that's a bad start for him. What's to say he's not a Frenchman, born and bred?"

"The coloured moth," she said. Parrish looked at her, and understood. She returned his gaze, her eyes widening. "Is there ought we can do for him?" she asked.

Parrish looked away and sighed heavily. "He's at the barracks. He'll be well guarded. They'll be questioning him. That'll be hard to bear, but he can take it. Ye can rest with that. It's the next move, that's what we have to get tidings of. They could take him back to London, where he's known and wanted, but that would be a big undertaking. They'd more likely keep him here, with the Fifth Northumberlands, in their custody. The Green Cuffs haven't the wherewithal as yet, being newly arrived, and the Black Cuffs leave tomorrow for Berwick, so they wouldn't want the responsibility." He paused. "Unless, of course, the man Jopling has a say in it." He thought on.

"But what authority does he have?" asked Dolly. "He's a sea-going man, not a dragoon or a fusilier or anything of that sort, surely?"

"Well, that's the quandary," he said, fingering the dust on the sill in contemplation. "Just what is he? What authority does he have, indeed? He sports the uniform of a soldier, but he does his work on behalf of the navy. There's a company known as His Majesty's Marine Force, of which little is known here in our own country, because they operate only in foreign lands, transported to the theatres of war by ship. I hear they've had much success on that front. They must be based somewhere, mind you, probably in London, for voyaging from the Thames river. And that is where Jopling first became known to Moss."

"At Greenwich, I heard him say," said Dolly. "Where is Greenwich?"

"Certainly London or thereabouts, though I know not exactly where," he said. "It matters not, but points to the assumption that Jopling will try to extend his claim on Moss, both in terms of what occurred in past times in London, and more particularly the humiliation of what occurred yesterday. If only there was a way by which we could determine his next move."

A silence fell between them. Dolly studied the man, trying to gauge the level of his concern. His sincerity she did not doubt, but his sense of hope seemed to be weakening.

"I could go to him," she said at last. "As his... his wife! Surely they wouldn't begrudge a man a visit from his own wife. He himself might be able to shed a light. Or at least they may tell me of their intention."

"No, no," Parrish waved away the suggestion. "One advantage that we have, is that you are dead to them. That is the rumour among those on the street. I don't know what advantage it is at this point, but it's a card that may indeed be useful at a later point in the game. And I cannot go. My association with him, should it be known, might echo widely, and interfere with other matters of importance. He wouldn't thank me for that. At any rate, he's a spy by their telling of it. They would be wary of letting anyone see him at this time, for that reason alone."

Dolly looked up at him, suddenly thoughtful. "See him?" she said. "See him yes, but what if someone were to visit him, but couldn't see him. Would that stand, if a reason could be handed to them? A valid reason?"

Parrish stared back at her, and shook his head, confused. "I don't grasp your meaning, lass. There's no sense to it."

Dolly came forward to him, and looked up into his face. "Someone who had reason to visit him, to come face to face with him, but could not see him. What threat could that be. Someone whose concern was me, and what had become of me, but was plainly no aid to his escape." She paused meaningfully. "A blind man, perhaps?" she said, in a soft, urgent whisper.

Alec Parrish looked back at her. He smiled. "Simple Dolly. Well, well, well. The Dillen Doll, they call you," he said. "Ha! If only they knew in truth! My God, woman, Moss chose you well."

Friday always began early at the markets. It was all a noisy blur to Alec Parrish; the bustling women, the harassed men, the wary stallholders, the brusque merchants, the trestles and tables and unsteady carts, some piled high with fruits and greens, some with breads and cheeses, many strewn with the same style of brown tableware and wooden boardings, smooth bowls and rough-edged vessels, pewter mugs and misshapen glassware, broken tools and poisoned lace, damp-ended rolls of cloth, used shoes strung in pairs or in friendless solidarity, and everywhere the wide-eyed stare of the hungry, their few coins held tightly or hidden under stained aprons.

Parrish bought a short twist of black tobacco, and carried it like a customer, in a wrap of rustled cream paper. He edged his way through the crowd, feigning interest here and there at the wares on offer. The blind man sat where Dolly said he would be sitting, on a low wall near the water trough. Willie Purvis was known by everyone of course, but at that moment, he was alone and silent at the edge of this great throng. Parrish sat next to him, just as a flat-hatted fish monger pushed his way with loud authority into the melee, a rough and bloodied board of gutted herring held high above all heads. Willie was well aware that someone was close, and shifted slightly on his perch, pulling his leather fiddle bag firmly behind his bent legs. He said nothing, a rare thing indeed.

Parrish leaned sideways towards him. "A message for you," he said quietly. "From a lassie." Willie could barely stop himself from offering some comic retort, but he did so.

"What might that be?" he wheezed, a smile on his mouth.

"She said, "When Ah was young and lusty, I could lope a dyke, but now I'm auld and stiff and I can hardly step a syke." She said you'd know her from that, when I saw her this very mornin'."

"Ah!". Willie smiled broader than ever, and tilted his head slowly back. "Now, ye bring me good news, and Ah thank ye for it. Due to hearin' bad news in that regard, not a day since."

Willie couldn't have seen it, and many more were without the ability to read it, even with the advantage of full sight, but the details of Moss's situation were to be found, in official print, in the morning's Journal. Parrish had peered at it, displayed in the office window of the news service, and scanned over the accusations of treachery, the assault on one of His Majesty's officers, the flight along the river, and the suspected murder of a local woman, with whom the accused was known to associate. The story, now it was in writing, was damnation itself. Parrish's confidence had ebbed away as he read.

He looked around, and turned again to the blind man.

"She has a favour to ask. You'll know the man is innocent," he said. "Of all charges against him. She can vouch for him, as I can myself. But neither of us are in a place where we can even attempt to reach him, to offer our support, and moreover, find out what the future has in store for him. But we thought perhaps…"

Willie tossed his body back and forth, and clapped his knees with his hands in mock delight. "Tarum tickle, tan dum, tarum tickle tan dum," he chanted, his face crackling with smiles. "Yash, yash, a shang ye want. Yash, yash, just tell me what ye want me ta do!" A few people around them looked over, some smiling knowingly. Parrish forced a smile, to go along with the ruse, while thinking all the while that the man was mad, and that he was just about to enter into a bargain with a maniac.

"A visit to the man perhaps," he said, when Willie had paused for a moment, "to demand from him the whereabouts of the poor lass, so that she be granted a Christian burial, for perhaps she was kin to ye. It's a lucky shot, by any means, but you're a wily man yer'sel'. If you feel you could manage a trek to the barracks, on a path that isn't known to ye?"

"Oh aye, I know it, I can sing that for ye, this very day. My pal, Bold Archie, he can help me wi' the way of it, if his ma will let him out of her sight for a minute!" He cackled alarmingly. Parrish regretted inviting Willie's involvement with his whole heart. "And Captain Ben Starkey, a man o' breeding and rank, short o' stature, big o' heart. He'll tell ye that hissel'!"

"It's likely time we're to be short of," he said. "Would ye be back in time to join me in a glass at the Trader by the brewery this evenin'? There's a fear the man could be elsewhere by miles by morning."

"Ah'll have parlance nee doubt with these Worthies this very noontime, and we can discuss the talents and the verses you request. It's still early in this day, but rest assured, ye'll have the sangs lifted sound and clear by it is done."

Parrish looked at the man. His wrinkled face and hooded eyes gave nothing away. A squat fellow in a long coat arrived and sat on the other side of him. "Cuckoo Jack!" Willie exclaimed, as if he had seen him approach, "The lost terrier still not found, Ah hear!"

"Oh, Willie," the man groaned, "Ah feel Ah've lost a best marrah. Ah'm that cut up!"

Parrish stood carefully, and slipped away.

He was back at his home at the distant chime of the half hour. Dolly was mending her wool stocking by the window with a bone-needle and thread she'd found on the mantle. Parrish entered without a word and caught sight of her. He stared at her fingers, and stood still in thought. She looked up at him.

"I found it on the shelf," she said, apologetically. "I won't use much of it, it's just to bind it."

He turned and closed the door, and drew off his coat with his back to her. "No matter," he said, "There's more in the chest. You should have it. I've little use for it."

Dolly almost enquired further, to sooth the silence between them, but veered to more immediate concerns. "Did ye see Willie? Is he to help?"

Parrish hesitated. He resolved to put a bolder slant on things than his own heart was wont to do.

"Aye, I believe so," he said. "It's hard to tell as a certainty, but he's to meet me tonight by the Brewery. His

170

cronies are to take him to the barracks and he's to bluff his way in, if he can." Parrish poured water from a jug and drank. "You're listed as missing," he added, "With Moss blamed for it."

Dolly stood. "Then I must show mysel'" she exclaimed. "I must be seen to be unharmed, and standin' at his word, that he's wronged, that he's innocent!"

Parrish held up his hand. "No, ye must hold back for that! They will have ye for his accomplice sooner than his champion. And then there'll be a pair of ye to worry for. Ye have to bide, at least until we get more word."

"But it might be too late!" she pleaded, her voice rising. "When Cully Robinson got murdered for the goose, the culprit was hung by the second day! We don't have cause to wait, surely!"

Parrish faced her squarely. "This is more detailed, more complicated than that. There's still no proof that he's harmed ye, and they have him for deceiving, by way of espionage, as they're callin' it. It's a French word for God sake, and they have him as a Frenchman. That's going to involve much in the way examination and probing. It will all take time. We have to bide ours, and think deeply. Haste will be of no benefit, for him or for you. Believe me."

"But what can I do?" she said. "Hidin' away like a rat, a prisoner no less than himself. Ah can't even venture outside."

Parrish laughed to himself. She had never heard that from him before. Strange that it was now.

"You'd be a ghost, a spectre. You would scare the daylights out of the townsfolk! I'd pay to see it." He

171

stared into the near distance. "Even disguised and covered, the weakness of your walk would give you away. You can't hide that from God himself." Dolly considered that, and said nothing.

"I have food," he said, going to his coat and pulling out a packet. "And tobacco, but I haven't seen you smoke." She shook her head. "My wife, she would share my pipe at evening. Her own mother had led her to it. I don't like to see it of a woman, but she was headstrong. I was happy for that mostly."

"Where is she now?" Dolly asked.

"The plague took her, as a young woman, here in this very town. We'd missed the scything epidemic of earlier times, but pestilence always comes back to its places of origin. And she was unlucky, as were many. We could well have stayed south of here, but I brought her back. Just at the time of its rekindlin'. Well," he sighed. "A long time ago, it was." He busied himself with a fire. Dolly slowly moved nearer, and scraped boiled oats from the black pan and shaped them on to a girdle-plate for baking. He went for more water. She crouched and blew gently at the kindling. He knelt by her, and gently laid wood. The flame crackled into life and warmed both their faces. She became lost in thought. As did he.

CHAPTER 16

SOME HAD HARNESS

Stretched face-down on the cart, there had been nothing for Moss to do but close his one good eye and brace himself bodily against the punishing pounding of high wheels on stone and the merciless wood of the flat boards, as the ramshackle vehicle jostled its way in the direction from which he had just come.

At one point, the whole frame of it leapt cruelly from that road to another, carelessly crossing the high grassy verge that divided them, and tossing him up and back down with a painful jolt. He felt like he had been kicked squarely in the ribs as it settled. He cursed loudly in his own language, and heard answering rebukes from a voice close by, but the noise of the wheels and the pounding that his head was taking meant that any meaning was lost to him. He could however make out the harsh laughter that ensued, presumably from another of his mounted escorts, at the opposite side. He tensed himself as much as he could. Inevitably, every time he relaxed his muscles, another sharp jolt would pierce his torso. All the while, he could see nothing but a sliver of track through a meagre gap between the wooden slats where his head had come to rest.

The journey took an age, and then he felt his body lean as the cart cornered into another direction. It came to a brief halt, and there was a smattering of voices, calling out, military style, mentioning ranks and obeying orders.

The cart started forward again, and then finally stopped. Someone climbed on and stood, legs stretched out over him, and proceeded to cut Moss's bindings with a keen blade. The man snarled some indistinct threat as he did so, and then Moss felt himself hauled up by his armpits, cast to his knees on hard ground. He reeled into the dust, unbalanced and disorientated, his neck twisted into pain, his limbs like broken cornstalks. Fingers gripped his cheek and chin, and jerked them up into the sun, the owner just a blind black shape in its dazzle. When the grip relaxed, Moss was able to look around. He had no idea where he was. There were military men, most dressed informally, with loose braces and undershirts, with others in full uniform, all to a man staring at him, bemused, mildly curious, resentful.

An officer appeared from a building to Moss's side, and marched smartly towards him. Moss was amused by this ridiculous display of soldiery and may have allowed himself a sardonic smile. Whatever, he was rewarded with a hefty kick from a guard next to him. He rolled over and clutched at his thigh where the boot had struck. When he looked up, he saw his captor, Corporal Carmichael, speaking to the officer, with characteristic bravado. Moss's grasp of English had somehow deserted him in his exhaustion, but then he heard the officer snarl at the guards, "Tether him!" He added, "Not in the guardroom, in the tack, in sight of the door." The guard aimed another kick, which Moss anticipated, and avoided, rolling to his knees in a half-crouch. From behind him, two men grabbed him and twisted him backwards, and dragged him through an open doorway.

A smart fist to the side of his face stunned him, and he tasted blood. He was left seated on the ground, his wrists bound together in front of and above him, fastened securely to a rusted iron ring hanging from the wall.

"A drink!" he croaked as loud as his dry throat would let him. There was no response, and no drink.

The sky, he saw, was darkening. Moss struggled to make sense of his plight. Gradually things slid into a semblance of order in his mind. He had attacked an officer of the King, certainly. He and that officer were known to each other, as he was also known to the young corporal who had delivered him here, but surely that was nothing more than coincidence, that Carmichael had been the one to attend his capture. His vague grasp of time at this point, suggested that all of Jopling's information had surely not been delivered to this place where he now found himself, and yet he was being treated with undue harshness, and moreover a surprising amount of attention, given his initial infringement. He had almost come to the wild conclusion that Jopling had perhaps succumbed to the raw mustard that had enveloped him, and that he was now in serious trouble, when a group of horses turned noisily into the compound where he was, and on one of which, his head bare and a white cloth tied across his lower face, sat the red-coated figure of the man himself. He dismounted clumsily and then bent slightly, a harsh cough taking his breath away. The man next to him had noticed Moss across the way, and pointed in his direction. Jopling swerved around, and strutted immediately towards him, swishing a short riding crop into the air angrily as he walked. As he reached Moss, the swishing continued, and met its mark with relish.

Sometime later, long after darkness had fallen, Moss was aware of someone approaching him. There was a tepid lantern hoisted on to a wall beyond, and the man unhooked it as he came forward.

"Well me lad," said Corporal Carmichael, a mock-friendly tone in his voice, "You're quite the renegade, are you not?"

Moss glanced up at him briefly, instinctively, then looked away. The Irishman continued.

"We've been hearin' all about you, from yon red-coated captain. You and he go back a spell, he reckons. To London city! London city indeed. Now that's a place I'd love to see, and plan to, one day. You never know, do ye. And I'd never have guessed, when we made each other's acquaintance the other night, that I was in such distinguished company as yourself. A freedom fighter, a soldier of the people, and now a spy in our very midst, just as this noble country is facing up to a foreign foe once more."

Moss looked up at him again, this time in genuine puzzlement. He made to speak, but his dry throat and bloodied mouth trapped the words into silence. He tried once more.

"I am no spy," he rasped. "Whatever that man has told you, it is through his own bitterness and evil ways. You would be well to watch him, and not rely on his words. Or his promises."

At that, Carmichael looked interested in the pale light of the flame.

"Indeed," he said, slowly. He smiled. "In fact, my heart tells me that you have the right measure of the man. Lads like him are not uncommon in this business of ours, and I can recognise it in a trice, and did so in him, I have to say. But that is no advantage to you my friend. I also recognise you for what you are. And even overlooking our little…" He paused meaningfully. "…confrontation the other night, I can spot a man of wilfulness and cunning. And no man has attributes of that sort without just cause. Though again, it would depend on what you mean by just, I suppose."

Moss was weary. The corporal surely liked the sound of his own voice, and much of the meaning in what he was saying was washing over Moss like a droning irritation. A silence fell between them.

Eventually Carmichael straightened and breathed heavily.

"They'll be wantin' to know who your friends are," he said, "And how you get your secret words back to your command. And what you've told them. And… well, you know as well as I do what they'll be after. And the means by which they'll discover it. Then that'll be the end of ye! Justice. Retribution. All of that. I'll get word to that lass of yours that we had this little chat. Is it Dolly? That's right, Dolly, at the sign of the Flying Horse." He chuckled. "Now there's a thing!" he said, in friendly, buoyant tones. "A flyin' horse. Imagine that! Think of what a lovely thing that would be to have at your beckonin'. Ye'd be out of here in no time. Out there across that sea, over the mountains, and away to freedom. I'd envy you that, believe me. We're both bound by duty, by oath too, I've no doubt. But at least I myself have a bed to sleep in tonight, at the pleasure of this company here. Then back to my own tomorrow."

He turned to go. "I'll give your good wishes to our mutual friend, the red-coated captain," he said. "And to young Dolly too, when I catch up with her."

Moss watched the light fade away across the compound. There was no moon. The darkness was complete.

His bound wrists felt raw when he woke. The dawn had risen behind thick cloud. Almost immediately, a young lad with straps hanging low from his waist, came over and held a grey tin cup towards him. He paused momentarily, staring at the sightless socket of the prisoner, then allowed him a gulp or two of water. Neither men spoke. The soldier withdrew out of sight once more.

There were various comings and goings over the next long while, with little attention being paid by anyone to the shackled man slumped in the doorway. Eventually, Moss heard the approaching rattle of regimental boots and buckles, and the figures of Jopling, Carmichael, and the officer from the day before, accompanied by an infantryman with a musket, came into view. They all halted and stared with distaste at Moss.

"Do you understand the King's English? said the officer, curtly. Moss stared back wordlessly.

"He does, sir," snapped Jopling. "Only too well."

"Very good," the officer continued. "Your past is known to us, thanks to the good counsel of Captain Jopling here, and it is plain you are guilty of treasonous behaviour, seemingly over a long period of time. Such behaviour has now come to a smart and justified end. I would be done with you in a manner that you justly deserve, have no question, but there is undoubtedly information that you hold, that it would be advantageous for us to be familiar with."

The officer creased his face in irritation. "Your capture, though welcome and long overdue, could not have come at a worse time for this company and my command. We are under orders to re-establish ourselves some distance from here, and that as soon as we can muster. Therefore, to the intense irritation of all concerned, you must be taken with us, and these gentlemen to whom we owe our thanks for your incarceration, must be put upon to accompany us also. This is highly burdensome, but unavoidable."

He turned to the soldier next to him. "Secure the prisoner in the drop-cart," he ordered. "Block the windows, and batten the door with slats as well as locks. He'll join the second advance. Choose three men and take charge until you reach congress. Bread and water. Shackles at hand and foot throughout. Get to it." The man saluted and spun on his boot-heel. They all followed him, except Jopling. He stood motionless, his face a blank mask, and stared down at Moss. How familiar he looked, how unchanged and inscrutable, Moss thought, and looked away.

Eventually, the soldier spoke, in quiet, measured tones.

"There are men who would rejoice to see you now, strung like the animal that you are, helpless, friendless, and no spurious cause to stand behind." There was no anger now in the man's voice, but the hate in it was plain enough. "This is what you deserve," he said. "You're nothing but cast-off filth from a lost kingdom, with no right or reason to be in this country, never mind to be telling us how to keep it in order. No-one invited you here, no-one wanted you. Not even your own country wanted you. You're chaff. Do you know what that means? Something that is thrown away, not even fit for pigs, something not even the hungriest could ever swallow."

Jopling moved closer, and closer still. Moss could smell the mustard on his tunic, and saw the yellowness of the stains on his hands. He spoke again, quietly with menace.

"It is short payment to see you here now, after the long days of shivering through Deptford's streets in pursuit of you and your kind, and now the smart of the burning spice you dared to fling at me. Nothing but to see you bled white like a sow would compensate for all that. This long journey that I'm forced to make on your account, it will be worth it at its end to see you skewered like the worthless meat you are." Jopling pulled back, as if to regain dignity. "Nothing to say now?" he mocked. "No dockside step to stand high upon and preach in your pretty tongue, to wild eyed patriots and foolish old men? Well, they'll grease that tongue for you where we're going, I promise you. You'll have a plenty to say, mark my words."

Jopling backed away, his eyes blazing, his hand wiping his mouth thoughtfully. He turned and disappeared from sight.

Moss's thoughts churned inside his weary head, and brought him to a murky, confused conclusion. Whatever Jopling had reported to the officer in charge of this place, had caused a charge of treason to be levelled at him, and it all stemmed from actions in another place, not here. The stealing of the Hostmen's documents played no part in this. There was some comfort to be had from that knowledge, in that Alec Parrish's involvement and connection evidently remained unknown to all, and sending Dolly to seek shelter and advice from him had not been such a foolish move. All his troubles, he felt certain, had stemmed from and lay at the hands of Jopling, and were due to his combative endeavours in Deptford, years before. It was only too obvious how fresh and open the wounds remained beneath that ludicrous red coat and tall black hat.

At the same time, his own predicament seemed a hopeless and pitiful situation. He had no idea where he was, or to where he was to be taken, and any means of escape, or deliverance, seemed beyond the grasp of all. There was purpose and resolve in the intentions of his captors, despite his presence being an admitted inconvenience at a time when, if he understood correctly, the entire company was about to uproot itself and make for a new location. Had he been in such hopelessness before, he kept asking himself, as if some solace would emerge from the answer? He concluded that he had not. He tried to measure his own strength, of mind if not of body. Desperation and despondency were still a distance off. Remorse, anguish, for himself and for others, Dolly foremost, were all equally absent. Moreover, he still had the presence of mind to banish Dolly from his immediate thoughts and concerns, in the hope that Parrish would accept responsibility for her wellbeing, at this time at least.

He felt weak though. He suddenly recognised the defeated posture that his body had slipped into. His thoughts were racing, jumping from one place to another. The sparsely melodic voice of an old man drifted into his consciousness, like some forgotten lullaby from a past he barely recognised. Emotion rose into his throat, and he shook it away angrily. He looked up and listened. The voice he had heard was real enough. It came from three ragged figures, standing in the near distance, in conversation with a uniformed infantryman. Moss peered at them, trying to pick out a single detail. One of the trio suddenly looked at him, and cautiously raised a hand, as if in gentle greeting. Suddenly the door of his makeshift jail was scraped shut, and he found himself in blind solitude. He was suddenly alert, but puzzled nevertheless. From somewhere beyond, an old man's voice wafted through the blackness.

"Dolly the Dillen doll," it sang, "Dol Li A"

CHAPTER 17

THE TOWN MOOR TO SPEND THE DAY

The two guards at the crossed oak limbs that was all that barred entry to the Fenham Barracks, were hardly on their mettle. There was more of their company and stock on the outside of the perimeter than on the inside, all meshed in the confusion of a pre-departure muster, with weaponry and supplies being brought to point, only to be returned to store rooms and stables a short while later, in a crossing of commands that was to the bewilderment of all. Much of what was to be transported was yet to be unpacked from their previous move, six months before. At that time, they'd been uprooted from the tented encampment on the other side of the Town Moor, where the Green Cuffs were now in residence, into this other, wide parcel of barren land. It had been negotiated for the construction of permanent stabling and housing for a domestic regiment, but up to now, it boasted nothing but a line of rough wooden huts for the use of both horses and men, with little to distinguish between them, to show which was for which. The completed barracks would now be for the Ulstermen to eventually enjoy. The Yorkshire Militiamen were headed to an uncertain future, north of the border.

The two Black Cuffed lads rested on their muskets. Any sly, idle chat between them had long since petered out. There was a prisoner of some importance to consider, that much was true, but he was locked in the only stone

183

building on the site, a relic of the farm that had stood on this spot since ancient times, built, it was said, from stone that the Roman armies of old had quarried into their walls and mile forts, long ago. The few belongings that these two sentries had were already in packs at their feet, and tomorrow those feet would be marching off to glory.

Both men, as one, then noticed the three beggars, as they believed them to be, marching in single file to a sharp command of "Left! Left! Left!" across the pale brown scrub of the moor. Their path took them wide of the Green Cuffs' lines, and directly towards where the two sentries stood. After a long while, the sight of them became clearer. A straight-backed toff in faded tunic led the way, and kept the tempo with a sure, shrill voice. A twisted shape of a bandy-legged balding man followed, a gnarled stick held out straight in front of him, held at the loose end by the leading man. Some steps behind both, and rarely holding a firm line, a tall rake of a figure, wearing a battered hat and gaiters, brought up the rear. One of this pair was humming a tuneless air, loudly and persistently. The sentries were intrigued, but not overly so. The trio stopped at last, not three yards away from the guards. The leader halted his ragged command in loose military fashion, and the humming, coming it seemed from the bare-headed, central man, ceased.

"God blish the king!" he spluttered, to no-one in particular.

"Gentlemen," spoke up the leading man, "Soldiers of the realm. Allow an old campaigner to salute you and beg your indulgence" He gave a flamboyant wave from the rim of his hat, and smiled. "Can I présent my comrade,

184

Mr William Purvis, a balladeer and music hall artist of some renown, who has recently suffered a bereavement, the details of which you may already be aware, and who craves information regarding the details of the tragedy. We suspect your commanding officer, or whoever is in charge of the situation regarding the French traitor in our midst, could and should be of assistance." He smiled politely. "Forgive me," he added quickly, "I am Captain Benjamin Starkey, retired, at your service."

Both sentries stared at the men for a long while, without word or movement. No sign of interest or comprehension registered on their faces. From behind the miscreants, a sweating Lieutenant, his tunic unbuttoned, wiping grimy hands on a cloth, approached and glanced at the gathering.

"What's this, soldier?" he snarled. "No charity hereabouts. Clear the entry, make haste!"

One of the sentries made to respond, but before he could, the leader of the small pack re-introduced himself, and launched once more, almost word for word, into his entreaty. The Lieutenant stared at him, looked him up and down in puzzled disbelief.

"Captain, you say?" he said at last, his face twisted in distaste. "What regiment?"

"Alas, Sir," came the reply, "Long-since disbanded and dispersed, and not in your lifetime I suspect. Perhaps your commander could be more of an ally, both in years and experience, for me, with every respect to you, Sir, if I would only be allowed to have a word with him." Behind him, Willie took the opportunity to fire up a wordless melody of support.

"You have information about the Frenchman then?" the Lieutenant demanded.

"Ah, quite possibly, quite possibly, and keen to impart it, given the right direction and encouragement. We know little of his case, but some detail of the man." Starkey smiled again. Willie keened ever more lustily behind him.

The Lieutenant huffed, wiped his nose on the cloth and broke into a stride. "Well then," he said, "Come with me. But not you, bag o'bones!" he snapped, pointing at Bold Archie, much to the latter's relief. Starkey offered words of thanks and pulled at Willie's stick to lead him onwards. They clumsily negotiated the wooden rails and toddled after the officer, in the direction of the stone office. He ordered them to hold their station, well away from the entrance. The door of the adjacent stable for the officers' mounts was open, and Starkey glanced in, almost casually. Immediately, he caught sight of a tall man, standing but leaning at a strange angle, tethered, he guessed, and head bowed. Starkey was not so familiar with him, but he sensed that this was the man himself, though his distinctive eyepatch was not in evidence. Starkey skewed his head around and about, and then hissed at the blind man, "Sing up Willie, sing up!"

Willie obliged with a rare softness. "Sair field, Hinny," he crooned, "Sair field noo! Sair field Hinny, sin I saw you!"

Starkey watched the man in the stable rouse himself, and peer groggily about him, his single eye scanning wildly for the source of the song. At last he caught sight of them, and stared in confusion. Starkey stared back, and raised a hand in silent greeting. Moss nodded slowly back

186

once, at which point an older officer appeared at the other door. Starkey jolted himself back into his role of choice.

"Colonel, sir," he exclaimed with joy, "Excuse this interruption into your busy day, but may I present the esteemed poet and minstrel, Mr William Purvis of the All Saints House of Domesticity for Distinguished Residents of this fair city. If I can explain…"

The officer interrupted. "I know who you are, or claim to be, and though I'm far from clear as to what you are doing here, I have to inform you that under no circumstances can you see or talk to the person of whom you so blithely make mention!" To their left, the door of the stable was slammed shut at this point. "This is a military enquiry, and any civil ramifications that are involved will be dealt with by the local courts and authorities. It is to them that you must direct your attention, not here. Lieutenant, escort these men from the barracks immediately!" The soldier strode forward and reached for Starkey's arm. The latter pulled it away before he could touch it. He spoke up boldly as he did so.

"But sir, can we thus count on your prisoner being available for civil justice, at the Assize here in town, as is customary?"

The colonel was taken aback. "The prisoner will be escorted to Berwick in our custody, as befits an individual faced with a charge of such severity. He will remain in our charge, naturally. This is not a question of a mere midnight tip from a Tyne bridge for a mouthy doxy, sir! This is a crime against the King! No less than that! Be away with you."

"Dolly, the Dillen Doll!" Willie sang out with relish. "Dolly, Dolly! Dolly the Dillen Doll! Dol Li A!" The strange melody of the dark-skinned barrel organ player, so enchanting to Dolly that day in the Groat Market, had found a new guise, and stopped the colonel in his tracks. He glowered at Willie with undisguised contempt. On and again Willie sang, louder, as the Lieutenant pulled Starkey off by his sleeve, and marched them past the gated stable, the stick still gripped between them, wherein Moss would clearly have heard the song, and out beyond the raking clatter of the entrance barrier.

All the way back across the Town Moor, Willie sang on, chorus after chorus, then a verse, then another, its words lifted from other songs, though some new, some immediately forgotten. And it was to its beat that they marched back to town that day, and the ditty was complete and etched into their hearts and minds by the time they reached the city wall.

Willie was still enchanted by the song, now with a wayward fiddle accompaniment, in the taproom of the Trader that evening. Alec Parrish heard it as a lament, and tried to push it from his consciousness. Willie sat, bowing and scraping, in the corner near the fireplace, chuntering verses that meandered in and out of his own exclusive amusement. Parrish took his mug of ale and stood near the door. The room was busy, but he knew no-one, and none knew him. He passed a polite word with an aproned serving-man, collecting pots at random, and became aware at last of a straight-backed individual in a curious coat, standing at his elbow.

"And a new visage in our midst," said Captain Starkey, his eyes fixed ahead of him. "The perfect foil to hear of our strange adventure on the Town Moor this very afternoon, Master Purvis, Bold Archie, and myself."

Parrish hesitated, took a quick glance sideways at his new companion, and decided to go along with the charade. "I'm a weak man for a tale of hi-jinks, accompanied by a tankard of ale and a warm fire." He could quickly tire of this, he thought to himself. Starkey sensed it.

"To the point then," he replied. "Our friend will be taken to Berwick tomorrow, with the departing regiment. These are serious charges, have no doubt. Justice, as they see fit, will be swift and decisive, of that there is little doubt."

"Did you get the chance to see him then?"

"See him, yes, speak to him, no. This information was gleaned in anger from the commander himself. Probably more than he intended to reveal, I fancy. But convey to the lady, we did manage to communicate to our friend that there were those still labouring on his behalf. I am sure we left him in no doubt that there were machinations in place for his benefit. Hopefully, that will be of some consolation. To both of them."

"She'll be very grateful," Parrish said. "As am I. Tell the blind man as much, will ye?"

Starkey finally turned to look at him, and smiled. He moved away. Parrish pondered over his drink. Blind Willie changed his tune at last. The man known as Cuckoo Jack, with whom Willie had been speaking earlier in the day, suddenly burst in, the lost terrier in his arms.

The room cheered. The dog barked loudly. Cuckoo Jack wept unashamedly. Willie made up a song on the spot, about loyal dogs and stormy nights. Events raced around them as they stood. The tender had sailed that morning, its new recruits sullenly stored below decks. The Black Cuffs would march north at dawn. Moss, the only man that Parrish had ever trusted, would go with them. Parrish drained his cup, and left the taproom.

A rich, persistent stench greeted him as he entered the cottage. He hoped desperately that it was not from something he was expected to eat. It was bad enough that it came from a pot that he would have to use for meal-making in the future. Dolly had been leaning over it, her face lit by the flames of the fire, as he entered, and her head jerked up, in his direction, startled, guilty. He suddenly saw her as womanly, attractive in face and in form. The thought of it unsteadied him.

"What news?" she asked.

"What is that you're doin'?" he said, his face twisted against the smell.

"It's of no matter," she replied. "What news from Blind Willie?"

He closed the door, sat stiffly at the table, and told her what Starkey had said. She showed little reaction. She had plainly wanted to hear more, and better. She stared into the cooking pot.

"What *is* that?" he persisted.

"I mean to go to him," she said, "Follow him perhaps, and do it in disguise. Change the colouring in my hair to begin with. This is a dye from the woodbark and the root of the blackberry bush opposite. I have seen them do this

190

at the soap factory on Wrangham's Entry. It will be a dark brown, near black when boiled and cooled."

Parrish came to her and stared warily into the bubbling mush, his eyes squinting in the odour.

"Ye cannot put that on yoursel', lass, for pity's sake," he said. "You'll look like a nest o' crows! And smell like a midden besides. Clear it off the hearth, and let me put it outdoors!" He took a poker and hooked the pot at the handle, carrying it at arm's length towards the door. A glance at her showed a flush of embarrassed anger on her face. "At least let it set to cool outside," he said.

She was sat, defeated, at the table when he came back in. He rummaged at the fireplace, opened a window shutter and hung his jacket by the door, thinking on. She was silent.

"So, you mean to follow him?" he asked at last.

"What else can Ah do?" she replied. "Ah cannot stay here forever, and me face is known on the quayside, so Ah can't return there. And how will it serve Moss if Ah just watch him go with the Militia in the morning? He has been given a sliver of hope, as you say. To abandon him now would be cruelty, and nothing less."

Parrish knew all of this. No words came readily to his mind, or to hers. There was silence between them. Eventually, she felt his eyes upon her, and she looked over uneasily.

"Why do you stare so?" she asked.

He wiped his hand dryly across his mouth. "Did you ever hear tell of a woman named Hannah Snell?" he asked. Dolly shook her head. "She might well live to this day," he continued, "and her tale is a weird one, but true

191

enough, as I'm led to believe. It tells that as a young woman, she was deserted by her husband. He left the county, so she resolved to follow after him. She did this by assuming the name of her own brother, James Gray, and dressing as a man, in order to travel unmolested. She travelled widely like this, by all accounts. She even enlisted as a soldier, and fought as such with the English army. Her story is known well in the Highlands, as she claimed to have fought against the Scots who followed Bonny Prince Charlie, and much taunting from the English has resulted from it, though it's hardly credible to me. But a woman she surely was, with children, and several husbands, though with a good portion of her life spent in man's clothing and in the company of other men who knew nothing of her true identity."

Dolly's eyes were wide in the fading firelight. Her heart beat hard within her. Parrish did not look at her, but continued.

"Now I wouldn't suggest that you could follow such outlandish paths, but it sows a seed of possibility in my mind, as to how you could venture once more into the world without fear of discovery. And it would open more opportunity of movement and decision, to me at least." He finally looked at her. "And no need for that rank slop you've concocted. If you were prepared to coat your hair in that filth, then taking a sharp knife to it would seem a softer option." He smiled.

"I would gladly do it!" she said firmly. "And the rest, the guise of a man, the company of men, certainly that I am used to, from time spent in the taprooms of Sandgate. But the style and gait of a man, the voice of a man, surely

192

that is a harder task. And what of the clothes of a man? I have no convenient brother to willingly share his livery."

"There is ample in pawn in the scattering of shops along the quay," Parrish shot back at her. "But we are short of money for the venture. I have nothing to match in pawn, and I doubt that your own clothes would fetch enough."

Dolly looked down at her stained, ragged skirt, her harsh linsey-woolsey bodice, and her threadbare shift. She hesitated. Inside it, long nestled against her skin, she could feel her only treasure. Slowly, she clutched at it, and drew it out into the air.

"There's this," she said softly, holding up her cherished memory of Moss's love for her. "This could be worth a good few pence in pawn. Here, take it." The hand she held out towards him clutched something tightly. He stared at it, as she let it tumble like a waterfall from her fingers. It was the soft, silken sark, the one thing that she valued most of all.

CHAPTER 18

FOLLOW THE HORSES

The North Yorkshire Militia had begun their long trek north even before daylight had reached the Town Moor. There had been no ceremony, no drum to step out to, just a weary, haphazard shuffling into line in the damp gloaming, and a paltry gathering of sad, silent women, elderly men and curious children, watching and wondering, as carts, mounted officers, sullen infantrymen and scurrying supply masters wandered away in untidy rankings. An official meeting of colonels, where rights of deed had been handed over, had ended in wine-soaked disarray the night before. The Black Cuffs were done with Newcastle. The Green Cuffs were now the official watchers.

Some hours later, there was still much to do. Three quarters of the thousand-strong regiment were on the march, but the rest were still hauling boxes and packs from the camp, securing loads, checking off names and belongings from ledgers, and accounting for muskets and ammunition. Alec Parrish took all of this in, as he walked cautiously up the chalky track from Pandon, accompanied by a limping, ragged youth wearing a blue oarsman's cap, pulled firmly down, and a brown, speckled jacket and trousers.

As they reached the barracks entrance, Parrish nudged his companion, and a high wheeled carriage pulled by a single horse, manned by two soldiers, one holding a musket, edged its way through the gate and swept precariously on to the north road. Another armed guard sat awkwardly on top of it, holding on grimly to a chattel-hook. The opening at the rear had been clumsily and hastily secured by ropes and nailed slats. The cargo it carried was meant to be hidden, meant to be tethered.

Dolly stared at it, but felt no sense of affiliation to what it might contain. She was overwhelmed by what was happening in front of her, and suddenly felt hopeless in her strange, masculine garb, with this moody stranger who was now her only companion. She had felt weak since watching the clumps of her hair that he had sliced from her head, smoke, crackle and then burn like stinking weeds on the fire, the night before. Now she was cold, lost and tired from lack of sleep, with no idea where she was to lay her head, if she even lived to see another moon. As they watched, the wagon picked up pace, and bobbed and bounced off into an uncertain distance. Parrish felt deflated, defeated, and strained to shake off the sensation.

The unlikely pair of misshapen wastrels walked on, and approached a white-shirted quartermaster, stood by a stack of plain boxes at the side of the track, with a charcoal stick in one hand, and board in the other. Parrish assumed a servile attitude.

"Captain," he said, "Is there a place in your ranks for an old soldier and his lad, willing to do heavy work for a bite of food and safe company on their long journey across the Marches? I hear that you're fairly stretched for helping hands and fit manpower. And we're passing along the same road as yourselves, by coincidence."

The soldier stared at them with obvious distaste. "There's no place for Jacobite blood in this company," he said, "Make your own way, the route is plain enough."

Parrish laughed. "No, no sir, don't let my way of talking unsettle ye," he said. "I'm an Englishman, and loyal to King George, and my own father fought under Cope, against the Pretender, I might add. The burr in my tongue comes from being forced to live with the heathen Scot as a boy. And I'm reluctant to return, believe me, if it wasn't for the death of my brother in Leith, and the settling of his estate."

The other man spat lustily, and stared back at them. "Ah, Cope," he said, "A wronged man!" and considered them further. "It's true we're short-handed," he acknowledged, with disgust. "Why they're so keen to get idle infantrymen to their destination, without thought for the attendant support, only shows how incompetent this command is, after years on their arses in this town." He turned and gazed around him. "That's the last of the baggage carts yonder," he said, pointing. "Now, all the wares are accounted for and annotated, so don't even consider filching or playing anything underhand, or you'll pay for it with your skins. Tell the reins-man that I've appointed ye both, and fill from that set over there. The train needs to be clear of the moor by noon. Ye'll get meat at supper at Morpeth if we reach it before dark, at the Earl's table no doubt." The man looked at Dolly, who lowered her head to his gaze. "Is the lad strong enough?" he said. "He looks workshy to me!"

Parrish laughed again. "Not at all, not at all," he said, "Cursed by a want, I admit, but fit for whatever toil I direct him to. Have no fear." At that he pushed Dolly roughly with a curse towards the objects of their labour. "Get to it!" he ordered, "Ye heard the captain!"

For the longest of times, they lugged and stacked without a word between them. Dolly was exhausted, but strove to hide it. Parrish kept a keen eye about him, and engaged several men with blithe conversation as they worked, with limited success. Eventually, the last cart was ready to move off. The rest of the train was well advanced up the sloping track by then, and only a handful of servicemen were still occupied amongst the smoking rubbish fires and splintered boxwood that was all that remained of the camp. There was room for one body on the tail of the cart, and Parrish nodded to Dolly to take the place. She did so with some difficulty, and Parrish was relieved to see that no-one had noticed her clumsy attempt at it. Then they were away.

Parrish walked, one hand on a low slat by the rear wheel, his eyes on the road. There was one man on the riser at the front with the reins, and a group of half a dozen straggling servicemen about twenty yards behind them. Dolly watched their weariness. The years domiciled in one town had knocked the soldier out of each of them, it seemed. Dolly stared beyond them, at the town she was leaving behind. It was unrecognizable to her from this vantage. The river was hidden, the steeples were low pinpoints amongst the warren of smoky structures. The windmill at Spittaltongues was barely known to her, yet it was the only familiar friend she had now, as she was jogged and rattled away, from everything that she'd known and lived alongside in her few adult years. She tried hard to picture Moss in her mind's eye, but at this point in her journey, she seemed to see only a confused, fleeting image of him.

The city took a long time to disappear from view, but the road soon faded into a worn and rutted track, hemmed in by trees on all sides. Dolly sat faced backward, and knew nothing of the approaching fields and farmlands until they were upon her. The cart shook unsteadily past a dark inn, and on into a hamlet of meagre size, where they stopped briefly to aid another bigger transport with a snapped rung on its front wheel. Parrish too busied himself with this, but Dolly didn't alight, given the struggle she'd had to get up there.

All sight of the city was left behind now. When the journey began again, they passed lines of ragged workers toiling in bare fields, then the landscape became untended and wild, stretching out across barren emptiness, hoisted into jagged hills, then hidden by untethered woodlands. On and on they went. Occasional groups of travellers, headed in the opposite direction, stood aside as they passed. The sea came briefly into view, far off to the east, grey and lonely, with odd buildings pitched against it remotely. Nothing was familiar to her, the trees, the earth, even the distant water, seemed to be from another place, a far-off country. The bigness of it overwhelmed her. The hours crushed her.

After a slow struggle uphill, they suddenly sped to a free jog down into a lush valley, with houses scattered off to both sides. Parrish stood now, balanced by one foot on the rear step of the speeding cart, but hadn't looked at her since they started out. Dolly gripped the long siding with cramping fingers. Her back was aching from her crouched position, her legs and behind felt tender and bruised. Then all at once they turned across a wide stone bridge over a brown, peaty river, and they were surrounded by town buildings, leaning into an empty marketplace with a castle ridged by round, hefty earthworks beyond it. They slowed but still they did not stop. Servicemen and horses were in abundance.

They were shouted at, somewhere to the front, ordered to find off-road refuge further ahead and await instruction. They lurched into movement again. Suddenly, around another corner, Dolly was confronted by a group of beautifully dressed ladies and men, climbing into a double-drawn carriage outside a coaching inn. Their satins and reds and blues took Dolly's breath away, their powdered hair and yellow plumes dazzled her. Their faces were painted. Even one of the men had the same effect on his face. A footman, in quaint old-style attire, vaulted to the footplate, an arm-length away from Dolly as they passed. Dolly had seen thin sketches of scenes like this, pinned for display in the window of the Guildhall, and in the Journal office. To see such a scene acted out at her feet in this way was a dreamlike swoon for her. The carriage floated off, the way she herself had come, and Dolly watched it until it crossed the bridge and disappeared.

All at once, a jarring knock from Parrish's fist against her calf brought her back to reality. She turned sharply towards him, and followed his nodding gaze, diagonally across the road to a tall, many-windowed official building, secured on both sides by an old-fashioned bar gate. Standing outside its door, in smiling conversation with a Black Cuffs officer, stood the red-coated, tall-hatted figure of Captain Jopling, in amused observance of the disorderly scattering of horse and men that had overpowered this unsuspecting town. Both were granted a salute by passing infantrymen as Dolly watched. They were a distance away, but Jopling's bright uniform singled him out unmistakably. Dolly noticed too, what seemed like a scarlet rash on one lower side of his face, at which he dabbed with the back of his hand more than once. The mustard had indeed left its mark. At that he turned towards where she was seated on the cart, and she dropped her gaze at once. The cart bounced on, and Jopling turned his back on it nonchalantly.

"Distinguished company on this journey of ours," Parrish muttered, and eased himself off the step of the cart and resumed a walking pace beside it.

At length, the cart ran to rest on a verge of scrub beyond a dingy public house, with a bold portrait of a dragoon hanging from an eave. Real soldiers, muskets propped against walls or lain at their sides, were everywhere. Dolly smelt food cooking, and Parrish signalled at her to remain in her position atop the cart. He wandered off, and came back in a moment, with two tin plates of stew and a single piece of thin bread, which he divided. Dolly was glad to get down from her perch, and settle on the ground by the wheel, where she ate with her fingers.

As he finished, Parrish threw down the plate and looked around him with a wary eye.

"We'll sleep outdoors tonight," he said, confidentially, without looking at her. "Be aware that there'll be sentries, guards, all manner of things, that are of no concern to us, or us to them. There's a high wall beyond the church that will be all the shelter to us." He looked skywards. "It'll be dry this night at any rate. There's a blanket beneath the rein-hook. If it's not in use later, I'll sly it out for our sharing. We'll smell of ripe horse, but no matter."

"Where is this?" Dolly asked.

"The town of Morpeth," Parrish said. "A cold, cautious town, ruled over by greedy merchants. The coaches and hauliers take a bigger road to the west, to avoid a levy, and follow a wide valley that comes east much farther north beyond the Cheviot. They say this is the path that the priests took from the Holy Island, when they first came into England. We'll see saints and pilgrims tomorrow, no doubt. That would have been a guise for us, maybe, but I've no stomach for them, the hypocrites." He fell silent as a pair of uniformed men rattled past with loose bridles and buckles. He continued after they had passed.

"The redcoat," he said, "I'm surprised that he is with the company. It's easy to consider why he's here, is it not?"

"Moss?" she whispered.

"Aye, no doubt," he replied. "Hanging on like a polecat for his share of retribution. He's easy to spot, so keep out of his sight. It's better that he's here with us, I reckon." His voice trailed off, his last statement left hanging. Dolly glanced at him. His face gave nothing away.

"Is Moss here, d'ye think?" she asked him.

"I've seen no sign of him," he replied. "If he was in that boarded wagon this mornin', it will be a good few hours ahead of us. As it is, there's only a fraction of the brigade hereabouts. The bulk can't have made it much further, but there are fortified towns ahead that would house them. Harbottle is too far, I fear, Felton a good day's march more. Mitford has flat land to the west of it, and a strong-walled lodge. That's my guess as to where they're garrisoned tonight, and where your man will be in safe keeping."

He gathered himself up, looking squarely around him. Night was not far away.

"We should find that stretch of shelter. I'll return for the blanket. Ye'll be cold from sleep in the night, so stay close to me." He added, his eyes pointed determinedly away in bluff embarrassment, "And don't be fearful of advances or suchlike." Dolly shook her head, uncertainly. He went on quickly, "Tomorrow we'll be lagging to the rear, but that's probably best. There's little sense in changing allegiance now. We can move for'ard as we get nearer the coast. Remember, if you're spoken to, wave a hand from side to side below your chin. The soldiers will see that as a dumb sign. They'll laugh at ye, no doubt, but there'd be worse if the truth was known to them."

Parrish led off towards a church-like building, where a muffled curfew bell was ringing like a sob. The sheltering wall was barely that, and other non-uniformed men were already in place against it. Dolly found herself at the windiest, most sparse point of it, at the rise of a mound. It was dry, and it was quiet, but there was little warmth to be had. Parrish pulled out a cloth bag from under his jacket, and pointed with it to where they would sit. There was a round, metal flask inside the bag, which he uncorked and handed to her with a flick of his head. She swigged half a mouthful. It burned, and she choked back a spluttering cough, that would surely have alerted all to the fact that there was a woman amongst them. Parrish watched her, and once she had swallowed, he took a drink himself. She lay back against the wall. She was weak with exhaustion. She felt his limbs touch her own, and heard his breath close to the back of her head.

It seemed like the strong smell of the rough blanket had awoken her. It was damp with dew, as was everything else, and it covered the sleeping top half of Alec Parrish, while his long legs stretched out at a keen angle beyond the hem. She hadn't seen him go for it, or return. Sleep had claimed her, almost immediately. There was noise from the town, voices and horse movement. Already, most of their fellow slumberers along the wall were moving, stretching and gathering themselves to leave. She moved to stand herself. Parrish's arms emerged, stiff and clenched, and he sat upright with a start. In a moment, he edged his head sideways and bade her follow him. Their cart was still where they had left it, horseless and driverless. An iron pot of water stood nearby, and Parrish dipped a cupful out for himself, then refilled it for Dolly. He replaced the blanket at the front of the cart.

At length, the sturdy driver returned, leading the nag, and acknowledged them with a grunt. Alec eagerly went forward to help with harness and straps, and then made an extravagant show of testing ropes and shackles around the contraption, for tightness and solidity. As Dolly watched, a parade of horsemen emerged from the marketplace, and trotted past them in file. They looked grand and disciplined, their tunics fastened and hats firm. The horses seemed high and strong, but their form faded towards the rear, which she suddenly realised, was being brought up by a clumsy, red-coated rider on a grey mare, looking warily down at the head of his mount. Jopling passed within a few yards of her, all sign of dignity and superiority being bounced out of him in a ridiculous absence of horsemanship, that was not unnoticed by the infantrymen around about. Dolly cowered into her jacket, but Jopling stared now only straight ahead, not least to appear impassive to the ribald remarks and rumbling jeers of those of lower ranks at every turn. But the steely resolve of the captain's face made a strong impression upon her, and on Parrish too, as he came up beside her, looking grim and disturbed by this near encounter with the perpetrator of their woeful situation.

As the long day, and the twelve miles of monotonous tramping wore on, the pale snarl of superiority that had been cast in iron across the face of Jopling, stayed as vivid in Dolly's mind as any of the real sights and sounds that barely punctuated the tedium. This was barren country that they were passing through, and even the thick forest to the west seemed grey and lifeless, matching the colourless scrub of tired grass on the other side of the track. Progress was evidently slow ahead, and there were many delays in a biting wind, as the baggage train waited for the ranks ahead to stretch into marching order. The militiamen would squat down immediately, whenever the column halted, and complained in low voices to each other, until a weary young officer arrived from the front file and ordered them to continue marching. The driver of the cart had angrily ordered Dolly off the back at the first slope, and she was finding it hard going, with her weak leg trailing noticeably. Parrish walked alongside the driver, with whom he could be heard indulging in stilted conversation. Dolly felt isolated and lost, almost angry with Moss for leading her, however unwittingly, into this situation. The country around her was wild and unknown, and the options ahead of her equally so. A dampness in the air gave way to rain after a while. The pace was slow and infuriatingly hesitant.

At a place called Felton, there was a bridge that had to be crossed over the Coquet river. This narrowness was the cause of their frustration, as it turned out. They were in sight of it before noon, and Dolly caught a glimpse ahead of the line of dispirited men stretching down the road, firmer now, as carts and wagons negotiated the old structure and climbed at a slant on the opposite bank. The troopers halted once more. This time, the driver of the cart also climbed down, and Parrish came back to join her. His voice was low beside her when he approached.

"We shall reach Alnwick by dark," he said. "There's much disquiet amongst these ranks. They're as hungry as we are, I've no doubt. There was no church service this morning, and they appear to resent that as their due. The priest was tending to high ranking officers at Mitford. That's where their French prisoner would also have been, because no-one here has any knowledge of him. It's hard to gather information without arousing suspicion, but it's clear these men know nothing of it anyway."

"Can we be certain that this is the direction that he's being taken?" Dolly asked, her face turning to him anxiously.

He looked down at her. "No, we cannot. But what other choices there may be, elude me at this moment. And the red-coat is travelling this road, is he not? That means something. But it is a curious, directionless company, this pack of uniformed buffoons. Three years at rest in Newcastle have drained the discipline out of them, and replaced it with resentment. Certainly, amongst this rear-guard of storekeepers and cart-drivers that we have latched ourselves on to." He peered around at them with distaste. "I'll go in search of food," he said, "But don't cling to hope too much."

He returned in a while, with a pouch full of cooked vegetables, mostly cabbage, and some potatoes in scorched skins, still hot from the fire. In one pocket he had some small, hard green apples and in the other a slice of salted fat from meat. They sat together and he fed her like a lapdog, piece by piece. She let him do it. At once their eyes met, and they exchanged an awkward smile. He looked thoughtfully over at the militiamen, sitting in brooding clumps across from them.

"Would they know you?" he murmured. "If they paid a moment's attention to you, would they recognise you, from the music-halls and suchlike?"

Dolly stared back at him. "Music-halls?" she retorted, indignantly. "I've never stepped inside a music hall in my life. What do you mean?"

It was his turn to look indignant. "I heard you sing," he said, "But only in the taproom of the Flying Horse. I assumed you were used to a more public stage. You certainly sounded good enough for one, as I recall!"

"No," she said, feeling her face redden at his sudden compliment. "I only sang at the Horse, and at a couple of other places where Moss took me. There were never Militiamen there."

"They'd have remembered if they'd heard ye," he said. "There's little joy for a man in these times. A woman's tender voice wrapped around a loving word and a plaintive air is something to savour." He looked at her. "There'll be other times to sing, lass, of that I'm sure. It's a fast and slippery task we've set ourselves, but we'll get a hand on it, don't ye fret."

Dolly's mind rattled with uncertainties and questions. The cowl of disguise she'd adopted had no outlet for such things, and they were bottling up inside her, eating away at her resolve. These words from Parrish were surely meant to sooth such feelings, as she now realised, and she was glad of it. This was a man that Moss had trusted and relied on, and even with such little choice open to her, she was determined to share that trust.

As they sat, the usual young officer strolled past and addressed the men opposite. None stood for him, and some didn't even look at him as he spoke.

"The road ahead is clear, we can cross by the bridge at our convenience," he said, stiffly. "There are provisions at Alnwick, where the castle is unoccupied, so billets inside are plenty. The sooner we reach it, the choicer these will be. There will be a gospel and blessing for Evensong, for which all duties will be laxed. Now, file in and we can make good pace until dusk."

He turned and walked away, as the men slowly stirred and pulled themselves to their feet. None spoke. The driver remounted without responding to Parrish's smile of acknowledgement. Dolly made no attempt to ride, but clung on to a side strut when the cart lurched forward. The rain began again as they crossed the bridge. Some local women were sheltering under a pull of canvas with a pitiful array of withered root vegetables, laid out as if for sale, in front of them. Dolly glanced at the women and took in their bewildered, haunted eyes, and weathered faces. More than one stared meaningfully in her direction, as if her masculine disguise fooled none of them. She turned away uneasily, fully expecting to hear a shout of betrayal at any moment. None came, and the company tramped on, the rain heavier, the sky laden with cloud, the road beneath their feet muddy and uncertain, and the country around them untamed and unfriendly. Dolly sang into the racket of the cart, low, breathlessly, "Ha ye seen ma bonny lad, alang the waggon way?" But the song didn't distract her or take her attention, and she slipped back into her own shadow of loss and uncertainty almost immediately. She stumbled, she shivered, her feet dragged themselves back and forth to the coarse grinding of the cartwheel, and whenever she looked up, the road ahead stretched on forever.

CHAPTER 19

A GOWN ON LIKE A PREEST

The sound of a tuneless, breathless voice, wavering without attention to melody or meter, then soaring in loudness and pitch into the night, swung gradually towards them. It was matched to the unpredictability of the weak light of an advancing lantern, searching for a straight path in the drenching darkness. Dolly hadn't been asleep. The underside of the cart offered little respite from the wind-blown rain, and what little dryness there'd been, when she and Parrish had climbed beneath the wooden boards, was now sodden and cold. But they'd been turned away at the gate of the fortified wall, and had drifted back along the Bailiffgate to this sole familiarity, their transportation, before it was lost to the encroaching night. They had sensed that there were other lost souls out there in the blackness, but none had come forward to offer them shelter, so here they were, like scorned dogs shunned by cause of stench and bad temperament. The promise of food had not applied to their sort either, any more than that of shelter. Parrish worried for the girl, weak as she was, and now cast out in such foul weather. Curiously though, he noticed, the longer she had walked that day the stronger her infirm leg seemed to have become. She had strode firmly and surely, on and on, and he had eyed her curiously from the other side of this wagon. His expectations, when they had departed the day before, had been less optimistic, and more concerning.

He too now heard the voice in the darkness, and felt the girl sit up abruptly at it. He held her back with a firm hand, as he peered through the rain at who this might be, by now almost upon them.

"Jesu Christi," he heard. "Domine omni potente." The culprit was suddenly there, and clattered against the wheel of the cart with a sharp oath that shamed the holiness of his song. Down he fell in front of them, with a groan of pain and a splash of weight in a gutter awash. The lamp slid off away from him, but remained lit. Parrish slid out easily from beneath the cart.

"Careful, Pilgrim!" he shouted. There was a flurry of confused language, which made plain that the fallen man took the other for a robber or an assailant of some kind.

"Unhand me, bastard!" he snarled, flailing with limbs of one sort or the other, whelping in pain, cursing in anger, lashing out in defence, with Parrish gradually losing any signs of sympathy in his responses.

"Stay still Pilgrim," he snarled at last, "Lest I crack you on the head to add to your trouble. I'm offering assistance, not thieving or assaulting you, can ye not tell the difference."

"Do what you will," the other sighed at last, "I'm done for here, drenched with mud or blood, I care not which."

"Then get up!" Parrish wheezed, hauling the body to its feet, "And be on your way to leave us in peace in our own misery. No shelter and now no gratitude, even from a singer of God's songs, on a night like this!"

Dolly had scurried out from her place, and retrieved the lamp, which flared brighter for a moment when she righted it, lighting up the strange scene in dank gloom.

The fallen man, now upright, was bare-headed, hair shorn to his grey skull, his tunic buttoned high to his neck, with knee-britches and grey leggings now muddied and wet. He lookéd dazed, more, she thought, than he ought to, from such a meagre misadventure as had just happened. He blinked at her and shielded his eyes from the light with a hand holding a thick black book. He squinted at Parrish, who was bent over in a vain effort to slap away dirt from his own clothes, and then planted a wide-brimmed hat on his head with a gesture of distaste.

"Forgive me," he said, quietly, and repeated it louder. "I cannot be chastised for my fear at being surprised by silent strangers loitering at a gate in darkness, though I see now that I have misplaced the path, and that this is not the gate as I surmised. Nevertheless, you surely concede my right to anxiety, on such a night as foul as this."

"Enough then," Parrish replied, with obvious disdain. "Be free to find your way, and leave us to our own equal anxieties, now that we are all as wet as each other. Perhaps you have more opportunity elsewhere to recover from that, while we do not, so please, continue on your way."

The man nodded and took the lantern from Dolly. He looked at her for a moment, and then at Parrish.

"Well," he said, "Despite the poorness of this lamp, I can see plainly your plight, and feel duty-bound to offer you something better in the way of shelter, if you have in mind to follow me. There's much of this night still remaining, and much rain in God's heaven yet to fall. My house is only a short distance from here, and you're welcome to take refuge there, if you have a care to." There was no answer forthcoming. He added, "I am a man of God, not seen or heard at my best this night, but my sin of a weakness for strong drink is one for me to discuss with my maker, and shouldn't hinder you in your acceptance of my offer of sanctuary from this sour weather."

Dolly hoped that Parrish could see the look of keen anticipation on her face, and accept such a welcome invitation. He did so.

"Lead us, preacher," he said, and held out an arm of encouragement. "The gratitude will be ours to display, and gladly."

The three of them moved as one behind the flickering lantern, all wavering as uncertainly as he who's hand extended it into the night. Twice a sharp turn was taken in something less than confidence, but then an audible exclamation of triumph assured them that success was imminent. There was a low gate, and some tall bushes, and the sound of wind above them gave the impression of high branches. They reached a door, which the holy man opened with a kick, but without a key, and they were immediately out of the rain and inside a wide room, which the dancing light of the lantern revealed to be hung with holy pictures and thick drapes. A strong smell of something at once both sweet and bitter filled Dolly's nostrils. A spill from the lantern was used to light tall candles on a high wooden stand. There was no fire in the grate. The preacher left through a further door, and Dolly looked over at Parrish, who glanced blankly back at her.

"Don't remove your wet jacket lass," he hissed. "No matter how damp ye be, just rest gladly in the dry." She nodded. But just then, the preacher returned with two thick rolls of speckled coverlets, and said, "Get out of those wet garments, and wrap in these. I can't afford to waste dry tinder at such a late hour on a fire, but these should suffice." He handed one to Dolly, who hesitated. "Come lad," he said, "The dust of it is holy dust." Dolly took it reluctantly. He tossed the other at Parrish. Dolly and he stared at each other. Parrish nodded slowly, meaningfully. Dolly turned to the wall and stooped over as she unbuttoned the coat. She kept the hat where it was. She slid out of the coat, as Parrish struck up a conversation with the other man. She pulled the harsh blanket around her and sat on the floor where two walls met.

"So, you are the local priest?" Parrish asked, mainly by way of distraction.

"Not priest, no," the other replied, with a cautious tone. "The candles, the images, the burnt spice you might have smelled, it's all but a relic of past times. And my fondness for the papal liturgy of which I might have sung a line or two prior to our meeting, it's purely out of a love of rolling the Latin poetry on an English tongue. I'm Clerk of this parish, that is my position. It's one which was formerly assigned to the castle and its incumbents, but as that hideous edifice is vacant at this moment, I am saved from such duties. That is, until occurrences such as this very night, foist themselves upon me, and I am called upon to give service to the King's troops. It is their solemn due, to be allowed a Sabbath's spiritual exercise, and it is one they grasp with a sickly determination that only men of war could muster. It is from that bitter duty that I was returning just now." He stared back at Parrish, as if he suddenly knew he had spoken rashly and with too much candour. "And what of you and the boy?" he said. "What is your position in this sorryness?"

Parrish's mind raced. His distrust of authority in uniform and high office regalia was matched only by his disdain for the haughty trappings of the church and its hierarchy of sanctimonious hypocrites. Too often had he seen the trust of common folk be manipulated and betrayed by those claiming to act in God's name. Their power and influence was a blight on this country, and its hold over king and commoner alike was a callous, evil grip, that preached misery and suffering to those who already had more than enough of their own to burden their lives. Yet here he was in the bosom of it, and glad of its succour, despite all his deep misgivings. If the soul was the core of a man's character, as their religion professed, Parrish let his eyes bore deep into that of the man before him in search of a trace of it. He saw nothing within, only a looming contradiction, which mirrored his own, not least his distrust and wariness.

Parrish offered a wary response. "We are travellers, nothing more," he said. "We left Newcastle by coincidence, yesterday morning, just as the Black Cuffs were taking to the road. We had no choice but to ask if we could travel with them, or else delay our journey north. Nothing is passing this way without their leave."

"So you have no affiliation with them, other than that?" the Clerk asked, his eyes cast down.

"None," came the reply. "I have little time for them, or for their allegiances. I'm a working man, my own man.

214

Not God-fearing, nor King-fearing, though more respect for the former than the latter, if pressed for it."

There was a silence. The holy-man reached to a stained-wood cupboard and pulled hard on the door to open it. He took out a long green bottle from it, and turned back to Parrish.

"A drink, to honesty between men?" he asked.

Parrish smiled, nodded, and smiled again.

"And the boy?" asked the cleric. "The brew is corpulent, but will warm rather than burn its way into a young heart!"

"Oh, he's not been sheltered from it," Parrish said. "He'll sip and stay at his own pace with it. We're grateful. Such kindness. It's unexpected, believe me. Things have lain heavy for us of late"

The Clerk poured a deep red liquid into three small glasses. He held out one to Dolly, which Parrish took and reached to hand to her, saving her the need to move from the shadows.

The cleric drank first, and savoured it. He looked back at Parrish. "Your trouble is your own affair, and my concern is with the people of this town, not men of war or wanderers between borders drenched in too many tears. But I'm a man of God, and if you need to share a burden of anguish or worry, then this sanctuary could be two-fold, for heavy heart as well as drenched head."

Parrish looked back at him, then dropped his gaze. He sipped sparingly, and held the glass up to the candlelight. He was not used to drinking from a glass vessel like this, and the red glow it cast warmed him as much as the liquid itself. In the corner, Dolly felt what he was about to say, and was glad of it.

"It is true there is more to our presence hereabouts," he said slowly. "There is a man of our acquaintance, who is also travelling with this regiment, though not due to his own desires. He's a good man, a remarkable man, whose life and deeds have made a deal of difference to many others, as well as ourselves. But as often is the case, for every man that has benefited and has been grateful for his guidance, there have been those who took exception to it." Parrish leaned forward and looked hard at the Clerk. The rich liquor loosened his tongue. "Do I exaggerate it, the importance of what this man represents? No, I don't think so. And much of what I speak was achieved before I had knowledge of him, so it could be that even I don't know the full breadth of it. And it wasn't even something he chose to do, it was something that fell to him to deliver. It's hard to explain it, without being more overt than discretion demands." Parrish leaned back in the chair.

The Clerk stared back at him, his face ghastly in the gloom. "Do you wish to make a fool out of me?" he said quietly, "Speaking that way about some reluctant conscript, collared through drink or running from justice perhaps, as if he is some sort of..." The Clerk breathed hard down his nose in distaste. "Saviour!" He spat out the word.

Parrish raised his hand. "No, forgive me," he said, "I did not intend to draw a comparison in such a way. I merely spoke factually. And in truth. And now if I tell you that this man is wrongfully in bondage, and is likely condemned, you are going to consider me a blasphemer and a trickster, when, I repeat, I merely state the truth, the case as it stands."

Dolly watched the two men. This was a deeper slice of Alec Parrish than she had hitherto witnessed, steeped in honesty and respect for another, and to see it rejected churlishly by the other man was unnerving. A Holy Man he might be, but it was plain that he was a man of strong opinion and not to be played for a fool by anyone. The drink, for which he'd confessed a weakness, only poured fuel on an inbuilt belligerence. Dolly saw the spirit of hospitality run the risk of draining from his temperament if this conversation was to continue.

"Then explain yourself sir!" he barked, and drained the glass. "Convince me that you are not merely foisting ridicule rather than gratitude. There are holy orders that have passed on this breath, but I am by nature a man of short temper and consider forgiveness to be one of the Lord's most over-indulged foibles."

Dolly saw Parrish smile again, and lean back in his chair. "You are indeed a curiosity sir," he said, almost warmly. "A veritable wolf in shepherd's clothing!"

The other man smiled back. "I like that!" he said. "It catches an abundance of elements in my nature, all of which I battle with constantly. But I am still waiting to hear your rebuttal, am I not?"

"Then you shall have it," came the reply, and Parrish poured out his tale, more than the bare bones of it, but omitting the role that Dolly played in its unfolding. She herself listened to the telling of it, at once fascinated as if hearing it for the first time, and yet also breathless at the audacity of its detail being laid bare before a stranger. The Clerk sat steady in his chair, occasionally raising his head minutely at some detail or other. But then, sharply, it was the mention of a single word, the name by which Moss had once been known, that caused the Clerk to stiffen visibly where he sat, and raise his eyes upward, unseeing, but suddenly as if something had been revealed. Dolly had melted into the story's telling, and had struggled again to mould the flawed flesh of the man she knew, into the myth that Parrish's portrayal conjured. The image of him in chains that the story ended with was equally intangible to her. The silence of finality with which the tale died away was broken by a barely audible whisper from the lips of the Clerk.

"Balilla!" he said, into the stillness of the room. "And I threw the word "saviour" back at you as an insult. So much for faith, so much for humanity!"

Parrish stared back at him. "You know this name?" he asked.

"Oh yes," came the reply. "Most certainly. And it is of much wonder to me that I hear it now, within my own four walls." He now stared at Parrish, as if peering into his very soul. "A wondrous, sinister turn of events," he said, with breathless incredulity in his voice.

Parrish's face looked unearthly in the light of the candle. Dolly was suddenly aware of the heady effect of this rich, sweet liquid that she had swallowed, as Alec's features melted into tight lines of pain, concern, anguish, all of these things, in reaction to the Clerk's words. The Holy Man was standing now, the bottle in his hand, and moved to pour more drink into Parrish's glass. He

218

glanced over at Dolly, but seemed to know that she needed no more. He drained the last of it into his own glass.

"I have travelled widely," he said, "both as a young man, and later as part of my spiritual quest. Borders aren't quite so formidable to men of the cloth, and I have crossed many, freely and safely. I had in mind to visit that holiest of lands, by way of a pilgrimage, but sickness prevented it." He looked reflective at these words and sank further into his chair. "I doubt whether such a journey can ever be achieved at this point in my life, but I still dream of it." He drank, and thought for a moment, before clearing his mind once more. "Even then, thirty years ago, winter was as cruelly determined to exert its power on a young man as it was upon an elderly one. It certainly halted me in my tracks." He smiled ruefully at the thought. "So I was forced to convalesce in a town called Bergamo, at the foot of the Alpine mountains, a border town not unlike the one where you now find me, forever changing hands between warring neighbours and transient invaders. It had learned to survive as such, and hid within itself a wide range of factions, each as passionate as the other. Again, my cloth and bible opened many a conflicting door to me, and I learned much of mankind and its spirit in those winter months, warmed by the simmering passions of angry men, greedy men, and righteous men. Some even harboured equal shares of each trait, and clung to them for sheer survival. It was a turbulent time for those people, and likely remains so to this day. But they made me welcome and nurtured me in a time of need, much as I try to do for you this night." He smiled at Parrish, and glanced at Dolly, her eyes wide and shining in the gloom.

"And it was there that I heard that name, the one you mention in much the same way as those shivering peasants did, so very long ago, in the hovels of a snow-bound town that still haunts my dreams."

The thought of it, as well as the intoxicating drink, brought a rumble of a laugh from him. "I do believe that until this very moment, I had considered it a mere myth, this tale of a hero, risen from within their midst, and then spirited away before any breath of failure could sully his reputation. How cynical of me! And how blessed this night, to hear that name again, and to have the opportunity to even consider it to be a reality. Yes, however preposterous it strikes me, coming from the lips of a bedraggled stranger and his changeling daughter. Or wife, is it?"

Dolly pulled in a sudden breath at this. How had he seen through her disguise in the face of falling rain and the confusion of night? And how could she deny it now, and be damned as a liar to a man of God? Parrish stared back at the other man, his dry face expressionless. Finally, he spoke.

"A mere trifling piece of subterfuge on our part," he said, "And an understandable one, don't you think, in the face of the company we were forced to keep? One woman of decency in the midst of a thousand marching soldiers. I did not rate my chances as her sole defender if it came to it."

"I surmised as much," the Clerk said. "But you still do not qualify it with the nature of her relationship to you.

And she herself is silent on the matter, I notice." Both men looked at Dolly. She gaped back at them, feeling very exposed and vulnerable. The emotion slipped easily into anger within her. Her voice rose in liberated frustration. It felt like she had been silent for a month.

"I am neither!" she said, firmly. "I am the wife of this man of whom you speak, so... so heroically, and I consider him dearly in a very different light to either of you!" There was more that she wanted to say, needed to say, but she stopped herself. The enormity of repeating the matrimonial lie, out loud, directly to a man of God and indeed in his own house, weighed heavily upon her at once. The sin of the deed was nothing to her, but the presumption that the word "wife" laid open, smarted like an open wound. It had been Moss himself who had used it first, and the knowledge of that was some comfort to her, but Alec Parrish had not been party to this, and she wondered what exactly his thoughts were when he heard her words. If his subsequent silence delivered any subtle message to the Clerk, he did not acknowledge it. But his response did take her aback.

"Then you are as much in danger as he is," he said calmly. "Regardless of the trueness of his claim to this heritage, he obviously poses a veritable threat to someone of position, and anyone who could hold knowledge of this, is of equal worth in their eyes." He turned to Parrish. "And you sir, must be aware of this, and that is the true nature of the feeble disguise that you have thrust upon the girl."

Parrish sank deeper into his chair. He made no response.

The Clerk rose and crossed to the door, and drew a large bolt across it. "I have a service at seven o'clock in the morning. I must at least make an attempt at sleep before then, though the tidings you have lain upon me will no doubt do their best to prevent that. You can find comfort for yourselves here, I have no doubt?"

"Certainly," Parrish replied. "And thank you for it."

The Clerk held his hands open in an almost ceremonial gesture. "There is much to consider on the morrow. And perhaps you can join me at worship?"

Parrish raised his eyebrows, and looked at Dolly. "Perhaps," he said. The Clerk nodded and withdrew by the further door, leaving them alone with a single candle, and a litany of concerns.

CHAPTER 20

THEN SAID THE AULD MAN

"Dispense with the boyish disguise!" Clerk Michaels proclaimed through a mouthful of breakfast bread. "It will fool no-one in regular company. In military file, it was bound to go unnoticed, but she is too womanly in features to make it resound among others of her sex, if she had occasion to meet them." Parrish glanced up from his barley brose and considered Dolly, but made no response.

"And what would I wear in its stead?" Dolly asked, indignantly. The cleric rose silently and walked to a cupboard by the door. He pulled out an armful of linens and tweeds and flung them across the nearest chair.

"The last Clerk to occupy these quarters had a wife," he said. "I know not the worth or style of these, but make of them what you will. I have seen other women wearing such stuff in the markets and streets of Alnwick, and there is a long coat in the room beyond, that would cover enough of them, regardless." He stared at her as he returned to his seat at the table next to her. "A shame about the cropped hair," he said, "But perhaps a bonnet, or a high collar would hide its severity."

"I like it," said Parrish, almost before he realised it. He looked up and met their matching gazes. He shrugged. "I do. My own wife always wore her hair short, for cleanliness's sake, and I know no other way of it." Dolly felt a hotness at her cheeks and averted her gaze to her own plate. The two men ate on also.

The Clerk hadn't woken them for the service, and had caused some alarm in Parrish's waking mind when he returned with a clatter of eating tools and a potful of boiled oats, with daylight already casting a greyness into the room. He had introduced himself formally as he laid the things upon the wide table, and Parrish had somewhat more reluctantly obliged with an introduction of his own. Dolly kept silent. The Clerk had news of sorts, from earlier in the day. The battalion was to remain at Alnwick for up to two days due to the continuing bad weather, he said, and he had been requested to again attend them at the castle later that morning. The reason for this, hadn't been made clear to him, but he saw nothing extraordinary about it. A cleric, he admitted, offered reassurance to a company of fighting men, especially those who were seemingly so unused to the prospect of military engagement. Talk, he said, was indeed that they were destined for the impending French war, and their stay at their immediate destination would be a short one. What consequences this might have for Moss's predicament, was not addressed by either men, and Dolly was left to juggle her own thoughts on the matter.

By mid-morning, Alec Parrish and Clerk Michaels, an unlikely pair, had left together in a light rain, for duties, disparate but of equal importance in their own minds. Dolly watched them go, and turned a reluctant attention to the pile of clothes that had been left in her charge. There were more garments gathered there, than she herself had ever owned in her whole life. Two long, plain dresses in rough grey cloth were set off by a pair of white

224

shifts and an assortment of long stockings, some worn through at the heel, others at the toe. A colourless apron, much washed but visibly stained, and a dimity cap with long strings lay at the bottom of the pile. Dolly touched her own cheek with the cap, looked down at the ridiculous trousers and baggy jacket she was wearing, and moved out of sight of the long window, a dead woman's clothes gathered in her arms.

Clerk Michaels returned in clear skies in mid-afternoon, looking grim. Dolly was seated by the empty fireplace, her appearance transformed. The cleric looked at her, and nodded. Again, Dolly felt her face flare with embarrassment, and she looked away.

"I have news," he said at last, "But let us wait for Mister Parrish to return before we discuss it."

Dolly's eyes darted towards him. "Is it...?" she stammered the start of a question, but he held up his hand.

"Not bad news," he said gently, "But nevertheless, not what we perhaps wanted to hear."

There was a firm but cautious knock at the door at that moment, and he went to open it. Parrish entered slowly, and at once saw Dolly on the other side of the room. His eyes froze on her momentarily, then turned away. Then they turned towards her again, for a longer time. The cleric watched the other man's features as they softened, his eyes wider, his lips apart. He recognised that look on a man's face, and was troubled by it at that moment. Dolly felt the air heavy between the three of them, and stared hard into the cold ashes. The voice of the holy man broke the spell.

"An exchange of tidings might be beneficial at this point," he said, busying himself with a pile of books on the larger table. "Perhaps you could begin?" He looked up at Parrish.

"I have little to say," Parrish replied. He was a sorry figure, defeated in the cleric's eyes. "I could get no access to the castle, naturally, and the townsfolk are a closed-mouthed lot. The merchants are content with the rumour that the company's stay in their town is to be extended, but there is also mention that desertion is already rife amongst the lower ranks. The continuing talk of a confrontation with the French has sufficiently unnerved many of them, to the point that no-one below officer standing is being allowed beyond the walls of the castle. Moss is undoubtedly incarcerated within also." He sat squarely in a chair and faced the wall. "I am at a loss at how to proceed, frankly."

A long silence ensued. Clerk Michaels pondered for a while then spoke up. "I cannot tell you how to proceed," he said, testily, "But I can shed light upon the current whereabouts of your friend, the man you call Moss." Dolly stood up, the white cap held tightly in her fingers. Parrish looked up at the other man.

"At dawn this morning," he continued, his eyes closed as if in prayer, "a quarter platoon of men escorted the French prisoner, as he is being referred to, in the direction of the fortified rotunda at Haggerston, south of Berwick, where he will be held, questioned, and his eventual fate decided. A Marine Captain called Jopling is on hand to bear witness and provide evidence, and an arresting officer called Carmichael is on hand, seconded from the

Ulster dragoons, to assist with formal identification." The Cleric opened his eyes, and looked at each of them in turn. "With a good road and without the hindrance of a full company, they should be reaching Haggerston as we speak."

"You know this as a fact?" Parrish murmured from deep within himself.

"I do. The Captain of the retiring watch told me as I left after the service. I offered to bring holy solace to any prisoner or casualty, as is my duty. There was none, he told me, and for the reason that I now impart to you."

"Then we are too late," Parrish whispered.

"Too late?" cried Dolly, stepping forward, her eyes ablaze. "Too late? So, we abandon the man to the mercy of his enemies? Your enemies!" she snarled at Parrish. "Where are the noble words you shared with us, in this very room last night, about the remarkable man, the goodness of the man, his selflessness, his worth to those he has helped, all of those things?"

"But we are too late," he said, calmly, firmly. "I stand by last night's words, but he has been snatched from our reach. How could we have known? What could we have done? Who could we turn to?"

"To God, I would suggest," said the Cleric. Parrish glanced at him scornfully, and staunched the reply that his thoughts had prepared in such disdain. Dolly didn't even acknowledge the words, and continued to stare at Parrish, her face a mask of desperate anger.

"Is this suggestion not even worthy of a rebuke, never mind a consideration?" the holy man asked.

"There may be a time for both," Parrish said quietly, "But not at this moment."

Clerk Michaels chuckled at that. He rose and faced them. "Now is indeed the moment," he said. "Time is against us, and I seem to be the only one here with a plan of advancement. I don't ask you to turn to God in devotion, though I'd be gratified enough if that was to be a choice you took. All I suggest is that you lend yourself to God's path, and commit to a pilgrimage, a journey that I feel sure will be of advantage to you. It leaves at midnight, as is the sacred custom, by torchlight, to the Holy Island of Lindisfarne, reaching the flat coastal lands at Dunstanburgh by dawn." The cleric moved to the centre of the room an easily assumed an authoritative air.

"Do you know, perhaps, of the Scotia settlement that holds farming rights, at the bidding of Lady Grey, in this locality? Fellow-countrymen of yours, I believe, with little loyalty to English rule, and a mastery of the coastal waters on that stretch of coastline."

Parrish raised his head slowly. "I have heard tell of it," he said.

"They have little time for my official attendances," Michaels continued, "But in recent years I have had cause to visit them, and have forged a layman's friendship with several of the menfolk." He laughed to himself. "Their attempt at mastering the art of distilling strong drink from their own field crops has proved lamentable, but has at least provided a common interest that we share on a regular, seasonal basis. Moreover, their knowledge of tides and moorings between the ancient slipway of the nearby castle, and those further north, as far as, I would venture to say, the mouth of the Tweed, and points in between, would provide a timely and haste-bidden transport for anyone who wanted to cover such a distance with alacrity."

Parrish was sitting upright by now. He held his hand to his mouth in thought, and stared at the floor for a moment. He looked up at the Cleric. "And say by chance that they could indeed ensure such a speedy passage," he said, "What then? What choice would there be for the journeyman on arrival? I know the castle at Haggerston. I have passed it by countless times. It compares poorly to the fortifications above us at this moment, but is secure none the less. And our friend will be well-guarded. Jopling will keep a close eye, and now this man Carmichael."

"You know of him?" Clerk Michaels asked.

Dolly stepped forward. "He is an ambitious young corporal, just arrived in Newcastle. Moss had cause to have words with him a few nights ago. I did not know that he was present at the arrest, though it should have come as no surprise. But why is he here?"

"His motives would be purely ones of self-advancement, I'm sure," Parrish attested. "Any association with a notable prisoner, especially as arresting officer, would be a true feather in any soldier's cap. The odds continue to stack against us, it seems. And I ask again, what course is open to us, with the man behind stone walls, wherever they may stand?"

The Cleric raised his hand and pointed into the empty air, eyes closed once more. Dolly had begun to see this gesture as a sign of hope, and held her breath.

"I have never myself seen the Haggerston fortification, but I know of one who is very familiar with it. Amongst the clan at the Scotia settlement there is a man called Roland Barnes, a patriarch of sorts, with a brace of sons, many daughters, and a stern wife. She in turn has a sister, who is married to a stonemason, formerly of Berwick, and I feel certain that he has worked in some capacity at this Haggerston, perhaps as an apprentice. They live there still, and the man may have knowledge of its structures and settings. Such knowledge, however slight, may be a boon to us in our endeavours."

Parrish looked at him sharply. "You say "us", like you mean to be part of this tribulation," he said. "Surely you cannot mean it."

Michaels opened his eyes and smiled. "Alas, though I confess to feeling stirred by the thought of this adventure, I am restricted in more ways than one, by infirmity, and also by commitment to other duties. I do, however, feel obligation and justification enough to accompany you on the first part of the journey, should you decide to undertake it, and fashion introductions to possible assistance. I flatter myself that my vouching on your behalf will stand you in good stead with those I have mentioned."

Parrish nodded thoughtfully. "It seems to my mind that these are slender straws for the clutching, but the only straws that present themselves. If nothing else, if the Scotia people are prepared to transport us by water to Berwick, it will gain us the time we have lost in this pursuit. It is a gamble. They owe us nothing, and may react accordingly. We certainly have no means to reward them for whatever help they can provide."

Clerk Michaels looked thoughtfully around the room, at the candlesticks and crosses, the incense cups and jewelled chains, all of which the sternness of common prayer had long-since rejected and abandoned. "Well," he said, with a shake of his head, "There is discussion to be had on that score. But you must ready yourself. You must look like pilgrims." He turned to Dolly. "You can most certainly pass for a parson's wife in that garb, but you sir!" He frowned at Parrish. "You look like a footpad setting out for larceny! I will loan you a suitable outfitting for the ruse. There is rest and food to be taken, before we assemble at ten o' clock by the Bailiffgate. There is a cart and horse available to us. If I may, I shall take the reins myself. I enjoy the thrill of it." He smiled at the thought, and then shook himself back. "Clothes for you, Alec. That's the next thing!" He strode purposefully out of the room, leaving Parrish and Dolly to ponder on the situation.

There was a marked awkwardness between them, that both recognised in their own way.

"I had no intention of abandoning the man," Parrish said quietly without looking at her. "I was genuine in my remarks last night, and equally genuine in my desperation as to how to salvage the situation. At least now there is hope, however slender."

Dolly sat down again, her eyes to the floor. At length, she spoke.

"Are we trying to save the same man?" she said.

Parrish turned sharply. "What do you mean?"

She looked at him. "You and the priest, you talk of this hero, this warrior, this symbol of freedom and righteousness. A saviour!" She almost spat out the word. "I try to think of the man whose meals I made, whose bruises I soothed, whose mouth laughed and yawned and kissed. That man is growin' more distant from me with each new day, not simply because of the miles between us, but because his image in my mind is being etched away, and replaced by the image you seem to have made of him. And if we do save him, rescue him, my heart asks what kind of life we could have together now, in light of all this. Where could we go? What future could there be for us? Not on the Sandgate quay, I know that for certain. What town would have us? What country? And what else but a hindrance would I be to him?"

She threw her head back, and sighed deeply. Once again, Parrish considered the eloquence of her words, and saw at once the very thing Blind Willie had remarked upon, that the girl talked like the songs she sang, in deep, meaningful language, spiced with emotion and a rhythm, that made smart sense of her inner thoughts when she exposed them to daylight. He was entranced by her voice in speech, much as he had been when he had first heard it in song.

"It has been a whirling wind of a time for you, for us all," he said. "There is truth in what you say, but there is also grief, exhaustion and worry. These seeds of doubt are easily sown at times like this. Hold your eyes fast on the goal we have set ourselves, to save an innocent man from the gallows, and once that is achieved, then things may seem clearer."

232

He sensed that his words had fallen short. He stood over her. "If you feel this burden is too much, if you would prefer to remain and avoid the danger that surely awaits us, no-one would think the less of you. And upon my return, whatever the outcome..." He hesitated. She looked up at him.

"I must come with you, of course I must," she said. "However unknown the future may be, that one path is the only certainty. If we ask sacrifice of strangers and those we meet in chance encounters, how can I not be prepared to do as much myself?" She hesitated now. "Last night, I spoke of bein' his wife." She looked away from him. "I knew of no other word to use in a holy man's house. And Moss had used the word himself, in a much less sanctified place! But you must know that I am in no way deceivin' myself by sayin' it. You know the true meanin' of the word, havin' had someone in your life in that role. I'm not even sure it's one I could fill, even assumin' it was asked of me."

Parrish turned away, as if a spell had been broken.

"Rest now," he said, eventually. "There'll be none for us tonight. I shall seek the priest, and get ready for it." He opened the through door and went out. Dolly heard their voices beyond, and sat alone in the musty room, waiting for whatever the hours ahead would have in store.

CHAPTER 21

POOR FOLKS CAN RIDE NOW

A long night's journey towards a shrouded moon being blown across an eastern sky did little to soothe Dolly's profound unease. Alec Parrish had barely spoken to her, after he had roused her with a rough shake in the dim, smoky candlelight of the cleric's house, as a bell close by sounded ten. The holy man himself had appeared soon after, looking grim and grey, and he too had addressed no-one as he busied himself for departure. He'd forgotten to prepare lanterns for the journey, and was blatantly irritated with everyone and everything, but mostly himself. He flung four framed lamps, in varying stages of disrepair on the big table in the centre of the room, and with the eventual help of Parrish, got three of them to show paltry signs of life.

There was a high wind, angering the trees in much the same way as it had on the night of their arrival. As soon as she got outside though, Dolly sensed a new completeness of sorts. Her new clothing, which now included the long, pleated coat and a sturdy pair of boots, stuffed with cotton strips to counter their bigness, brought a comfort and a confidence that she had never experienced before. The men noticed this about her, but still said nothing.

The looming stone castle seemed to watch them from the far end of the street, as they approached the lych-gate of the church, where a man whom the cleric addressed as

Thomas was holding the bridle of a misshapen grey horse, loosely harnessed to a high cart. No sooner had Dolly clambered on to it, facing backwards once more, and bolstered by half-stuffed cornsacks, than the beast began to move, led by Parrish, and with Clerk Michaels still upright on the footboards, gathering the frocks of his churchman's attire. He sat with an undignified lurch and Parrish hoisted himself up at his side.

Their first challenge, beyond a steep downward-sloping roadway, that the horse seemed reluctant to attempt, was a gathering of militiamen with torches at a stone bridge in the deepest dip of the track ahead. As the cart approached, the men clumped together in their very path. The cleric made little attempt to pull back on the reins.

"Take the bridle, someone!" he called, "The beast is liable to fright at flames!"

Two men stepped bravely forward, reaching out towards the head of the animal, and eventually pulled it to a standstill.

"Thank you, brethren," Clerk Michaels gasped, "Though I'd hoped to make a free run up yonder rise, to save the poor nag's wind. It's a climb and a sore job he makes of it. Is there truly need to halt us in this fashion?"

"Where are you off at this hour, Mister?" one of the men asked.

"We are at the start of a pilgrimage to the Holy Island, which we hope to reach by dawn, two days from now. The weather has already delayed us, and the feast of Aidan the saint is almost upon us. By God's decree, we should be making the journey on foot, but my duties here forbade that consideration. Time, as I say, is of the essence"

There was silence from the soldiers, as they each took a turn in peering beneath the flames at the travellers. Dolly stared steadfastly down at her feet, but felt the heat of the flame on her face, as it was thrust up to her.

"I know you, Brother Clerk," the same voice said, "But who are these folk with you? Local people?"

"Locally domiciled, but tragedy has brought them a goodly ways, to offer prayer and contrition, for the absolution of one who is lost," the cleric said, as if in prayer on their behalf. "I cannot speak of it. My meaning must be plain to you, sir. I would commend your understanding to match it."

Another silence ensued, with the torches still raised.

"God's speed then," the soldier finally uttered, "And pray for us also to the saint, upon your safe arrival. Pass with care at the brow of the hill," he added, "There is a carcass of a mare at an unseemly twist, where it fell exhausted three days past. No-one has cared enough to attend to it. You'll catch the stink of it in time enough, I've no doubt, despite the wind."

The cleric thanked him in holy words and slapped the rein on the rump of the grey. Dolly smiled at the cleric's skilful avoidance of the lie, and smiled again that she had wit enough to recognise it. The cart achieved the brow without further hindrance, and the wind mercifully drew away the stench of the dead animal, whereupon Clerk Michaels struck up the same tuneless voicings of the liturgical chants that they had heard him offering to the

236

night on which they'd met. It didn't take much of this to spur Parrish into conversation.

"It worries me that this road is so uncertain," he said, his voice raised against the elements as well as the unkempt voice of the man beside him, "As much in daytime I'd imagine, never mind as it is in darkness. The lanterns do little but bring attention to us, and certainly don't illuminate the way ahead."

Clerk Michaels chuckled. "Ah, this much-maligned steed that leads us, has passed this way many times before. I trust in its sense of direction. And it is a well-worn route, and an ancient one in fact. The mortal remains of the celebrated saint are said to have been carried between these very oaks and larches. The Norsemen also had cause to use it often, though for less godly purposes, as they ventured inland from the coast beyond."

Dolly twisted her head around to catch their attention from behind. "How long will we be travellin'?" she asked, her bones already bruised from the buffeting of the cartwheels. "Surely not until dawn!"

Again the Clerk laughed. The adventure was obviously bringing a measure of enjoyment to him, if not to the others. "No, no, the moon will still be high when we reach our destination, and lucky for us. There is a small shelter, a bothy if you will, formerly used by shepherds and herders, a mile or so to the south of the Scotia settlement. The moonlight is enough to direct us to it. You can rest there for a spell, and I'll walk to the beacon point by the castle beyond. The watchmen will report our arrival. All being well, a boat will come to fetch you at dawn."

At that, it again felt to Dolly that Alec was having doubts about the arrangement. He tapped the wood frame of the cart irritably and raised his voice above the din of its rattle.

"I still ask myself, why would these people feel the need to help us? It seems we are expecting a great deal from them, for nothing in return, and I am reluctant to use the detail of the situation as leverage to convince them that we act justly and in earnest."

"They are used to ferrying souls across the waters to the Farnes," the cleric replied in haste. "It is part of their living that they provide such a service. These are treacherous waters, much affected by seasonal tides, and they have provided rescue and succour for many a mariner and his cargo these many years. They will oblige us, fear not."

"But for what reward?" Parrish retorted. "For the knowledge that justice is being done? Merely that? For that is all we can offer them, surely."

Dolly sensed the cleric stoop carefully, to reach down to his feet. There was a dull ring of metal beneath him. He responded firmly, "Since the bishops forbid ostentatious display of lavish artefacts during services of worship, a redistribution of some of the slighter objects of that nature, can surely not be reproachable. Roland Barnes, our awaiting host, is by nature a grateful man, and has proved so to be in the past. He will appreciate the gesture as much as the prize, and use it discreetly." The Clerk pushed the sacking back into place beneath him. He added wryly, "Just do not accept his liquor, however keenly offered! It is foul-tasting stuff, and would floor an

ox, should one be fool enough to pour it into its stomach!"
He laughed again.

All three slid into silence. The moon was often troubled by clouds, and the ensuing darkness was of some concern to Dolly, but when it cleared, the track was plain to see, stretching back into darkness, along the way they had come. It was too much of an effort for her to turn to see the way they were headed, so she left that concern to those facing it. They crossed a fast-flowing stream, shallow enough to not bother the track, and at which the horse paused and drank briefly at its own volition. The trees had cleared into sweeping fields, unploughed and unplanted, and the road twisted through them at a halting pace. No light of habitation interrupted the darkness, until the tall broken walls of what could have been a mill, loomed up at a sharp turn in their path. It had long been left to nature's will. Dolly convinced herself that she could smell the sea, but still they rattled on without sight of it. Weariness had gripped her before she knew it.

The sweet aroma of Alec's pipe roused her, as he struggled at the side lantern to ignite it. The horse slowed on a rise, and she hoped she would not have to alight and walk to ease its burden, but with a skilful flip of the reins, Clerk Michaels spurred it on, and as they cleared the summit, she heard him say, "There lies the bay, a mile ahead!" She twisted round and indeed saw a solid blackness at odds with the sky, and with the moon's reflection upon it dodging between lines of high bushes, arching towards them.

They sped then through a deep, winding gorge, as dark as anything they had encountered so far, and suddenly veered past a cluster of cottages, standing high to one side. Soon they were skirting the shoreline itself, and the horse began to struggle into thicker grass. Alec jumped down suddenly and took hold of the animal's mane, by way of encouragement. Dolly struggled to do the same, her new pleats proving a challenge and a hindrance. The sods felt soft and deep beneath her ill-fitting boots, when she finally found her footing on the ground.

She could see a building, seemingly little more than a heap of dry stones by a matching wall, and then, directed by the cleric, she edged her way around it to an opening in the gable. There was no door evident. The sea sounded near, somewhere close beneath them. The entrance to the shelter was a jagged pit of blackness, but at once Alec was there with one of the weak lanterns, and she followed him inside. It was dry and eerily quiet, away from the wind and the splash of the tide. A wooden bench, supported by neat rocks, was the only comfort. Clerk Michaels came in behind them, and intoned a brief line of what could have been either a blessing or a curse. He flung down the sacking wrap into a corner, where it landed with a soft clank of heaviness, and went back outside. Alec followed him, and Dolly heard their voices at a distance. He returned alone.

"The priest is away to the beacon," he said. "We can rest easy for a couple of hours perhaps. We'll know the true merit of the journey when he returns."

"Shouldn't one of us have gone with him?" she asked.

240

"The boat will leave from the beach below us when the tide turns," he said, "So he advised us to wait here. Besides, he has prayers to make as he walks, a daily dose of them by obligation, he reckons. They can do us no harm, we can agree on that."

The conversation stumbled to an end. Dolly felt a tiredness overwhelming her. By the yellow light of the lantern, she could see Alec's stooped back, turned away from her, as he busied himself with the remnants of his pipe. After a moment he said, "I'll shutter the lantern now. There's a pitiful drop of oil remaining in it, and we may need it before morning."

Dolly watched the thick blackness pour over them. When Alec spoke again, it was as if the dark had cupped her ear. He sounded closer to her. "Will you sleep now?" he asked softly. "I know you must be troubled, but there's nothing but uncertainty ahead, not least as to where next you'll lay your head." His words and his tone suddenly comforted her, as a lullaby might to a child, or a lover's whisper would to a mate. Was it merely the tiredness that prevented her from knowing which she had heard? The fingers of her hand fluttered, as if reaching out for someone. The darkness was complete around her. The man could have been lying next to her, or perhaps in the farthest corner of the room, she knew not which. Neither did she know now, at that moment, in the fretful need of comfort, which she would have preferred.

Dawn brought a curious twilight into the room, and Dolly was alone in it when she woke. She was cold. Her throat was dry and crisp from the fumes of the dead oil lamp, and she made for the doorway at once. Her eyes

241

were dazzled by the light, as was her mind, by the sight that greeted her. The sky was wider and bluer than she had ever seen it, and the sea gathered itself at her feet like a stain of glass, rolling away across flat yellowed rocks and stone-grey sands, frothing and churning playfully as if rejoicing in a new day. Far over to one side, a small boat was bobbing at the edge of the waves, and a group of men were in conversation, their feet deep in the wet sand. Alec was striding towards her at a pace.

"It's time," he said with some urgency. "They need to scour the far promontory at low tide, they say. Come, it's safer and calmer than I'd hoped, and there's few awake to see us. Come, quickly."

Dolly looked around her towards the land. There was no-one in sight. She pulled up her long skirts and stepped gingerly down to the yellow rocks, mottled with some strange sort of moss-like weed, but dry to her step. She followed Parrish across the sand, and was greeted weakly by Clerk Michaels, who looked more weary than ever. The other two men ignored her and busied themselves with ropes and canvases within the tiny skip.

The cleric gestured candidly towards them and said to Dolly, "That is Roland and his eldest son Allan. They are wary of women, by nature, but respectful. They will deliver you safely to the Holy Island, and from there will arrange transport onward."

"Do they know the reason for all this?" she asked, eying them warily.

"I have told them that a man has been wrongfully accused, and you must reach him in all haste," he said. "But my vagueness has not fooled them, I suspect. They surely recognise that there is more to it, but I have asked no more of them than that which I tell you now. And you can expect no more, I might add. But they will fulfil their given task to the best of their ability, have no doubt."

Dolly looked at him with tender eyes. "Not once have you questioned me as to my faith, my trust in God, as I might have expected from any other man in your position. Not once have you insisted upon my devotion to Him. Why is that?"

"God knows what is in your heart, as much as you do yourself," he replied benignly, "It matters not that I have to leave it to instinct and trust, to know it myself. And I believe I do know it."

"Will we see you again?" she said. "If safety permits it, can we return by way of your door? There is a man who would wish to meet you, to thank you, as I thank you now."

He placed a soothing hand on her arm. "You will be welcome, all of you." She felt he wished to add more words, perhaps of encouragement, even of warning, but Parrish was upon them, urging her into the boat. He led her into the low-swelling water, and she quickly edged herself into the tiny craft. Parrish deftly followed her and she saw him nod towards the older man at the rudder, then turn to the cleric at the tide's edge. He raised his head in stern salute, and Clerk Michaels stared back, raising a fist to his chest, with which he beat twice upon it, as if to encourage a strong heart. It was a curious gesture, to which Parrish merely nodded in return.

The boat climbed a handful of lazy waves and then quickly reached low-swelling water. The younger man vigorously manoeuvred a single oar to get them on their way, and then wordlessly raised a washed-out sail at their rear. Roland, the older man, spoke to him with a thick burr in his voice, and his son pulled up an earthenware jug from below his feet, handing it to Parrish. He uncorked it, and swigged sparingly from it. He clenched his eyes tight as he swallowed, and his body froze momentarily, as if in fright. He looked sternly at Dolly, then passed it to Dolly for her to do the same. She sipped a mere taste, and sensed cold liquid, but with a bitterness to it that suddenly burned like pepper. It fell into her throat like hot ash, and she retched a sharp cough. Parrish looked away. She handed the jug back with a smile, unanswered, to the young man, and then turned to look around her.

The immensity of the ocean, endless, bottomless, filled her chest with breathless fear all at once. She fought to hide it, clasping her eyes shut, and fighting off dizziness from the roll of the swell. There was no sensation of speed, and yet as the sail steered them to one side as they approached the longest spar of land, she was able to see the tiny figure of Clerk Michaels, solitary and still where they'd left him, but now far off and diminishing. Moments later, they rounded the point, and he was gone.

CHAPTER 22

TIL THE TIDE CAME IN

The walls and towers of yet another castle were stretched out, at a tilt, across the new skyline, forming an ominous, sinister backdrop to the journey ahead. Dolly cowered beneath its silent presence, and heard the thick voice of the older man behind her.

"That's Dunstan, the sleeping beast that watches over us," he croaked in a mocking voice. She looked sideways at him, and realised the mocking was directed at the construction of stone, not at herself. "It's empty and crumbling now, with a sorry history of betrayal and deceit. Some greedy hands have reached out for it over the years. And yet there it stands, like a bereft widow, barren and without purpose."

Dolly's eyes widened. "You mean the Norsemen?" she said, "Is that who it's meant to keep away?"

Old Roland laughed bitterly. "No, I do not mean the Norsemen," he said. "They had been and gone long before a stone tasted mortar in the building of that place. The greed was in the English themselves, the lords and ladies who saw our green lands as a remote spot from which to nourish unrest and ambition, and to unseat and overthrow their own kings from a safe distance. They all paid dearly for it, and spread grief and tragedy the countryside around in the doing of it. And now the grand halls and battlements stand empty and rotting, and we are free to live and work in peace. Unlike yourself, I hear."

Dolly glanced at him warily, and at Parrish, his back to her now. "I'm free enough," she said, "But duty binds me to come to the aid of a man, as any woman would, given his innocence."

"Are there children?" he asked.

Dolly started at that. "No, no," she said, too hastily. "But that doesn't matter," she added, "The need he has is still the same. And I am lucky, as he is, to have a friend to assist me." It was an effort to deflect attention from her, and let Parrish take hold of the conversation, but he did not do so. Once more she felt obliged to return to it. "And lucky to have yourself, to hasten our journey to him in this way."

The old man ignored the compliment. "We can take you as far as the Holy Island," he said, flatly. "It will be by way of the Inner Farne, a place where saints and hermits lived, and where the habit is for pilgrims to spend a solitary time, as they feel need to. But we will pass it by and land on the Lindisfarne island, to the farthest end, away from the church-land. There is a causeway marked for passing at low tide, and we should be of an hour where that will be easy passing for you. It is treacherous though, and though a shorter route will present itself to you, plainly, it must not be taken. The sands around it never settle, but for the thin stretches that nestle around the higher dunes, and then it is a short walk across the passage to the safety of the mainland. You go by way of the village of Beal, visible plain enough from the shoreline. From there it is a fair way on to Haggerston. It

246

may be night by the time you see it. That's a distance, I tell you truly."

At that, Parrish slowly turned to face them, stretching his head awkwardly. "The priest said that you could perhaps arrange transport to the mainland," he said. "I am no horseman, but anything that would speed our arrival at Haggerston. Time is against us…"

Roland Barnes stared out beyond him at the water, as if he hadn't heard. Parrish said no more, and turned away. How far could it be, the walk by land, Dolly wondered to herself, and what hour was it now, with the sun high to the south-east, and the sea skimming past them like quicksilver? Already the Dunstan castle was left far behind, and ahead across the waves, she could make out black islands like driftwood, scattered out at a distance across the ocean.

Her thoughts spilled over into wonderings of Moss's welfare, as they had done repeatedly in the days before, but in face of this flat, colourless seascape, she found it harder to push them from her mind, as she had previously managed to do. It was only a week and some days since she had journeyed with him in a boat, smaller than this one, to the mouth of the Tyne. How apprehensive she had been, at what now seemed such a meagre adventure. It had been merely the start of something that had changed her life forever. And here she was again, with Alec Parrish, sat, his back to her, as it had been when she had first clapped eyes on him. She had been wary of him then. She was still wary, and yet he had come to be everything to her, her only companion, unknown to her still, but with a deep bond between them,

247

in the shape of a one-eyed foreigner, whose fate was frighteningly unknown to her.

At the bow, the younger man pulled dried fish and grey bread from a brown leather satchel, and began to break pieces off. He handed pieces to Parrish, and he passed it back to Dolly. Her hunger had been gnawing at her, but she passed it directly to the old man behind her. He declined it and nodded to her to eat it. She thanked him wordlessly, and ate.

The boat sped on, taking a long arc around the first of the islands, and between two smaller ones, close enough for Dolly to see gulls and other birds swarming over it like ants. The sea was full of them too, and with more besides, beasts greased with sea water, like the otters she had seen on the Wear, but so much larger. Closer they came as the boat passed the far point, looking now like bald men left for drowning. Dolly shuddered in revulsion as one, grey and slimy, with round, empty black eyes, passed astern of them. Roland Barnes remarked upon it.

"They are but seals!" he scoffed. "They were mistaken as temptresses and maidens from the deep in the far north. The silkie would come to the dry land, it was said, and tempt young men to their doom on rocks such as those." He nodded to the dribbles of high stone at the long arm of the island. "They were bigger than those pups I suppose."

"And prettier in the face, I'd hope!" Parrish piped up with a casual glance towards them. Roland looked at him sharply, and then cackled a throaty laugh, matched first by his son at the bow, then Dolly too. Alec looked at her and winked his eye with a quick smile. The gesture cut short Dolly's mirth, smothering it with guilt, as she remembered Moss's patch-eyed jest of a similar nature. The laugh of the old man behind her rolled on for a while, and then wilted gradually into silence as the boat journeyed on. The mainland, which they had veered away from earlier, lunged back at them as they approached another long promontory, tipped by a high, slender, uncanny fortress atop a mound overlooking the open sea.

"The Holy Island," said Roland, pointing with a sure finger. "We make the beach beyond in a short time."

They slid on in silence, the light wind filling the sail deeply. The sea beneath them was clear and green, but laden heavy with weed in clumps, like bushes hiding beneath the surface. The expanse of calm water soothed Dolly. The sharp flow of the wooden craft through its smooth wash lulled her. She held out her palm to the breeze, as if to catch its gentleness in her fingers. She sang softly to herself, slowing a jaunty melody from the Sandgate streets of her youth into a lament.

"I was a young maid truly, and I lived in Sandgate Street, I thought to marry a good man, to keep me warm at neet, A goodly body, a bonny body, to be with me 'til noon, But I have married a keelman, and my good days are done."

She smiled at the thought of Bella Roy singing it in the Black Boy, by the stairs one crowded Friday night, long ago, when Dolly had sat with her sister and her new man, cowering inside at the strangeness of the people around her. She la-la'd the melody over again. The men in the boat heard her, and kept their own thoughts on it.

With some manoeuvring of sail and rudder, they veered around the edge of the long island, and were soon slowing into a natural harbour, hemmed on one side by a stone wall. There was no-one in sight. The boat scraped on to shale and jerked to a halt, leaning over suddenly. Dolly scrambled clumsily into the shallow water, with Parrish behind her. The other two men tended to the ropes and sails, and then followed after. From where they stood, this did not seem like an island at all, and Parrish peered across to the trees and long beach to the west of them, at a loss as to which direction to take. Roland Barnes approached them, winding an ancient rope across his arm.

"There is a path from the end of that wall," he said. "It pays off on to the track to the causeway. It will be passable for the next long while, beyond noon, then again before midnight, until the early hours." He pointed off to the north west, where a low rise was the only feature. "That is your goal, by way of Beal Village, and from there the fortress at Haggerston can be seen. Don't expect it to be near to you. But the road is a firm one." He looked firmly at Parrish. "What are your intentions when you get there? To bargain? To plead?" Parrish looked back at him with unconcealed disdain. Roland recognised it, and said, "Surely not to battle your way to justice? Good God man, it is a fortress, a prison to many these past years, and now with added company I hear, soldiers of the king, they say. You are on a fool's quest, and taking a young girl along with you. What promises have you made? What hopes have you installed in a young mind?"

Parrish turned, a flush of anger plain in his face. "We do not have time for this. It will be what it will be. Needs must, and that is plain enough."

"Is this man so important to you?" asked the old man to the other's back. "To the lassie, obviously, but what is he to you, this man, to spark such determination, such foolhardiness?"

Parrish spun round at him. "You are a Scot," he said, "Or have the long years in such a quiet part of England wiped that memory from you? Have you forgotten the struggles our countrymen have had? And moreover, have you forgotten the men that rose up, the heroes, the leaders, the champions, who faced worse odds, harder battles, and yet never shied away from the challenge of them? Well, this man, he is as good as any of them, and by instinct so, like a stag defending his herd. That is the man that we go to deliver from a foe, and one not of his own making. Failure, success, these things matter not at this point. To try, to make an effort on his behalf, that is what is important." He breathed hard at the ground beneath him, and spoke again, in a quieter tone. "And you have done much to enable it by bringing us here, for which you have our gratitude." He turned to Dolly, and said, "Come lass, we have miles to cover." She scurried to him, bowing slightly as she caught the eye of the old man, and the pair of them climbed across towards the knoll above the rocky beach and had reached the clear path in a matter of minutes.

The narrow ridge became a lower track, and stretched off ahead of them. They could soon see the sheen of wet sands that lay between them and the rise of the mainland, but couldn't make out the causeway until they had reached the long line of rough stone markers that guided those who crossed it. The water lapped at them from both sides as they walked. Dolly eyed it suspiciously. The sands beyond looked firm enough, like a strand at low tide, but a leafless branch of dead wood that protruded from it a few steps away, moved mournfully with the ebb of the low waters, like a long wooden spoon in meal slops. There was deep deception around them that was clear.

They walked on wordlessly, wearily, and had finally reached the firmness of rocks in soil and green salt-free grass, when Dolly took time to pause and look back to where they had come from. She recognised the two men in the low cart immediately, despite the distance. When the pale donkey finally drew abreast of them, Roland Barnes barely looked their way. His son threw an arm at the flat cart in invitation, and Dolly and Parrish were upon it and moving at a steady speed before anyone spoke.

"We are not fighting men," Roland said, "Merely farmers and herdsmen, though sired from fighting stock, I dare say. At any rate, we have relatives at Haggerston who might at least be of help to you. And this old mule will at least speed you along at a steady pace, faster than his affronted owner, I hope, when he awakes to find it gone!"

Dolly saw Parrish lean back on his elbows, his eyes closed, perhaps from relief, perhaps from tiredness. The younger Barnes turned and stared back at her briefly, his face expressionless. She wondered about the motives of

252

these men, who had needed holy trinkets as payment for a steady passage across a calm sea, and who now were seemingly prepared to join them in the face of a greater danger. She saw Parrish now had his eyes open, staring at nothing, as if the same thought had entered his own head.

The cart bumped and jostled along painfully. They passed through a gathering of small houses, near which two shabby children sat amongst piles of drying driftwood, but no-one else was roused by the sharp rattle of the wheels.

As they turned out from it, the old man exclaimed, "There!" and pointed vaguely to the north. The two passengers looked across the low fields, and Dolly saw the shape of a high, thin tower, plainly not churchlike, but neither was it a castle by nature. The image of Moss came suddenly to her mind, but along with it, a whirl of voices and faces, of the red-coated Jopling, the sneer of Carmichael, the sightless squint of Willie Purvis, the cold stare of Anty Proud, the shrill taunts of Wool Maggie, and a hundred more shouts, faces, and suspicious eyes. The true nature of their task, now that an end of it was in plain sight, was manifest and unassailable to her. She pulled her coat tighter to her at that thought.

The rough track and the simple cart made the next hour or so a troublesome, painful one. Dolly felt wracked by a mixture of fear and physical exhaustion, and Parrish was grey and frowning to match, when Roland Barnes guided the cart into a narrow track in sight of brown-brick buildings, with the majestic tower of Haggerston watching over them. It was a forbidding sight. There were horses of a military bearing, paddocked far over to one side, with a number of white-shirted men tending to them. Apart from these, and a pair of women with bundles of clothes walking across the opposite field, all was quiet.

It was mid-morning, later perhaps. The four new arrivals upon the scene sat in silence and stared at the strangeness of it. The misshapen tower, the colour of wild oats, the sprawl of trees at its base, the small but sturdy cottages paying homage to it, the pastoral clarity of the place, neither countryside or town, an enclave of opulence hidden away from the truth of the world. Parrish for one had always resented the sight of it, when passing by on the road south, which itself lay within sight of where they now stood. Dolly stared at the highest point of the tower, as if to catch a glimpse of something, or someone. Roland followed her gaze and spoke.

"That is merely a water tower," he said. "The land around is plagued by foul swamps. No fresh water from the Tweed reaches here. That is their only source of water, though I know not how. To the side are the Lord's quarters. Hidden there, behind those trees, is the main building, a curious round structure in the style of European halls, they say. That is where day by day people come and go, eat, pass their dull time." He laughed bitterly, and nodded away further, to beyond all this. "There are stables and barns and the like to the other side. Perhaps that is where you will find your champion." He looked enquiringly at Parrish, who remained uncertain, Dolly saw plainly. At length, he spoke.

"We surely need to see the form of it, the spread of it. Though how to do it without attracting attention..."

At that the younger man, Allan, broke his long silence, in a curious, clipped accent, neither Scots nor English, but somewhere beyond that, which Dolly struggled at first to understand.

"Approach from the main road yonder," he was saying. "As pilgrims, as you are meant to be. To conceal yourselves as anything else would be more of a risk, I reckon."

His father spoke up at that. "Yes, walk plainly around, beyond the tower. You will see the outhouses and byres. There will be no objection to you asking for water in the yard there, or some such excuse for rest." He looked at his son, and continued. "We can harm nothing by paying a visit to your mother's sister and her husband. He has favours that he owes to us, many times over. Though we should say nought on this present circumstance."

Still Parrish hesitated. He spoke eventually. "Those who would testify against him," he said, "The marine captain and the Irish corporal." He nodded towards Dolly. "She is known to them. She could be recognised." Dolly already had this very thing in her mind, but feigned nonchalance.

"They would not recognise me here," she said, "A far-off place from Sandgate, with a different appearance, different clothes and all. And the reason for these clothes and this guise is for exactly such a deceit. What choice else do we have?"

Parrish held up his hand at her. "Yes, yes, all of that, it makes the only sense," he snapped back. "We cannot bide here and debate it. We will skirt around it, as you say, involve ourselves into the service company at the rear, and see the lie of the land." He was irritated, anxious, fearful, and all of them recognised it. He looked squarely at the other two men. "I insist that you come no further with this," he said. "We thank you again for your help. But this is your own homeland, hereabouts. You cannot be seen to be a part of this. You must know that, and know that we realise it too." He held out a firm hand, which was taken by both men in turn. The younger man reached behind him and offered a pale leather drinking-flask to him, with merely a nod. Parrish smiled and accepted it in the same way.

Dolly watched, a turmoil churning within her, of realisation and of hopelessness and much more. She got down from the flat cart and turned towards the farther road, barely glancing back. Parrish then was walking with her, and she instinctively took his arm in hers. He pressed it to his side, without a word, and they strode off together.

CHAPTER 23

SNUG IN THEIR HUDDOCKS

Moss was seated, his back hunched forward and his head low in front of him, when Dolly saw him across the yard. Her gushing heart beat the breath out of her at the sight. The rain had started as she and Parrish had reached the main road north and passed to the west side of the tower. Parrish had lifted her hood across her head, and pulled his roll-brimmed hat firmer down upon his own, in the realisation that the wet spell provided reasonable disguise for them that would afford no remark. They had ambled cautiously into the cobbled entrance, looking in vain for someone to confront.

A single uniformed soldier was dragging bundles and saddles into a wide open double doorway, to keep them from the downpour. As the trooper bustled back for the last of it, Dolly looked in his direction, and saw the defeated figure, half in the darkness of the entrance, but just caught by daylight. Even before he raised his black-haired head at the antics of the trooper, she knew it was Moss. His hands seemed unfettered across his knees. His eye was without the customary patch, and the other squinted through a swelling that matched another on his cheekbone. She heard a sound, and realised it had come from herself, an involuntary sigh of shock, that prompted a sharp nudge from Parrish's arm. He too had seen what she had seen. He easily pushed her in a sideways direction towards a water-butt, as three unjacketed men suddenly barged in from a cross-barred gate beyond. At least one of them noticed the pair of strangers, and Parrish raised a hand in silent greeting. No response was forthcoming. The men made straight for the shelter of the barn, and reclaimed their outerwear. Words were exchanged, and one man eventually approached, still buttoning his tunic.

"What business do you have here?" he asked, not unkindly.

"Sir," Parrish replied quickly with a smile across his mouth, "We stopped off from the road to merely ask for a drink of fresh water, but now a spell of shelter from the damp would also be welcome, if convenient."

"Help yourselves to the water," he replied, showing little curiosity, "And the overhang behind the barrel will draw the rain off you. Have you come far?" The man struggled with straps and buckles, and seemed barely interested. He walked with them to the barrel.

"From the Holy Island," Parrish replied. "We had transport from local folk to the road north, and hoped to reach Berwick by dark. The rainfall is unexpected."

Dolly's eyes tore at her head for another look at Moss, but she resisted it. He had surely heard something of the conversation, and perhaps recognised the voice of his friend, but she doubted that strongly. He had seemed weak and distracted at that first sight, and she wondered what ordeal he had already suffered. Parrish handed her a clay cup from which to drink, and at last she was able to glance back in the other direction as she raised it delicately to her lips. She saw that Moss had resumed the stooped, deflated position, and showed no reaction to their presence. Her heart raced, and she struggled to contain her emotions.

The soldier crossed back away from them at a stride, and they huddled back against the wall to gain the narrow cover from the awning above them. They stood silently for a long while, without purpose. An occasional glance at Moss offered nothing. He was stock-still, bent over, twisted into a shrunken effigy of his former self. Dolly felt a panic, like bile rising into her throat. The rain was heavy, steady now. The soldiers were in unseen conversation within the barn itself. Parrish was upright, erect, yet somehow resigned in his stance. The raindrops tapped away time into a long emptiness. They had come so far, so very far, she thought, and had now wilted away to a pitiful nothing.

Beside her, Dolly felt Parrish stir himself into some sign of movement, perhaps into speech. She herself could think of no words at all. But as she sensed these things, a young soldier appeared at a half door at the far corner of the barn, and called them over, with a shrill, "Come, come in!" as he struggled to latch the two shutters together. Dolly hesitated, but Parrish took her by the wrist and they reached the door as it was about to close. The darkness inside was not complete. Two of the soldiers were hunched over a fire in the furthest corner, which they were still in the process of flowering into full flame. Already the smoke was billowing about, and another half-door was being opened nearer to it. A round-bottomed pan, half full of water with lumps of gristle and root vegetables stood uneasily next to the fire. Dolly peered at it, merely out of curiosity, but another young soldier, still in his shirt sleeves noticed and pulled it to his hidden side with a defensive snarl on his face. It wasn't for sharing.

Virtually the full length of the building lay between them and Moss, still seated and immobile at the opened farther door. The floor was strewn with half-open back packs, ammunition pouches, bed rolls, and loose straw spilling everywhere from the slats above. The stands were empty of horses, but tack and leather-work hung around liberally.

"May we sit a while, sir?" Dolly heard Parrish ask, pointing to an empty dry patch of floor, a stride into the darker corner. The lad at the fire nodded in a carefree fashion, and continued to stoke the flames. Parrish took notice of it, and muttered his thanks. He also took a good look at Moss as he led Dolly to their chosen spot. They sat together and said no more. The men busied themselves, preparing for a meal, with the loud rattle of rain upon the roof drowning out any meaningful conversation between them. No-one asked anything of their two guests, until the oldest of the four soldiers walked over casually after some minutes.

"If our handsome corporal comes in, ye'll have to be out of here, rain or no rain, and make the best of it."

His comrades looked over as one. The man at the fire scoffed in reply. "Ye'll not see him," he said. "He's over there at the dinner table, charming that red haired daughter, and talking himself into a commission. And we're over here with the nags and the hayloft to sleep in."

"Why are you here?" Parrish said. "I've passed this way often on pilgrimage, and never seen soldiers, other than a local watch."

The nearest man threw a hand dismissively in Moss's direction. "We're a company guard for the scoundrel yonder," he said. "He's to be questioned. Some foreign tongue he keeps in his head. Though he's been as silent as the grave these last two days. Ye don't speak Frenchie yourself, do ye?"

Parrish shook his head quickly. "I do not!" he said. "I can't imagine there's many can, not in these parts."

"Likely not," came the reply. The man yawned widely. "There'll be a lieutenant from Stirling in the morning who can handle it. Then maybe we can settle back with the lads and enjoy some block cookin'." He wandered to the half-open door and peered beyond it. "Dark soon enough. And rain for the rest of the night." He looked back at Parrish and Dolly. "You can spend the night here if you will," he said, "But I won't bargain for ye, if the officer turns ye out. Ye'll have to take your chance and head for Berwick." He looked out again. "Though it's hardly a night for it," he added grimly.

A thick darkness soon filled the inside of the stable. The smell of the cooking pot troubled Dolly more than did the smoke that skewed around the place unpredictably from the brightening fire. She had eaten sparingly in the previous few days, and felt painfully empty. The rain drummed steadily on the roof above them. She allowed herself an occasional glance at Moss, but he had not moved a muscle since they had come inside the place. At her side, Parrish seemed agitated,

261

distracted, and his eyes flitted from wall to ceiling, from man to man. At one point, he felt for the liquor flask in his pocket, but then seemed to change his mind.

The soldiers gravitated to the fire, their backs to the couple, and began to eat from the pot, ladling the thin, watery stew onto beaten metal plates. None was offered to Dolly and Parrish, nor provided for the prisoner beyond. Soon it had all been devoured, and with the pot cleared away, the fire brightened and danced into the eaves above them. Dolly could feel the heat from it. One man cracked a slat of grey wood from a section of a bale store, and reduced it to kindling with heel of his boot. Straw, wood and dry sacking were close by but the company paid little heed to it, and there were no beasts in the place to take fright.

A long period of silence followed. Dolly assumed that Parrish would wait until the fire died away, and the men were asleep, before making any attempt at reaching Moss. The thought of it filled her with dread. Her legs were aching and her behind was numb, yet she scarcely dared to move in case it brought notice to herself. Then the youngest of the four men pulled out a short pipe of dark wood, like a drummer's fife, from his pack, and began to clean it with a musket cloth. He blew a note, a long mellow, rich sound, quite unlike the shrill marching sound that Dolly expected. This was a melancholy, lonely sound like the wind through the rigging of sleeping ships at the quayside. The other men ignored the sound, and the lad blew a slow melody from it, true of pitch and trilled as each line began.

"Another one Jamie," said a voice.

"'The Lass o' the Burn' is it?" He started falsely, but then picked up the tune, and then lost it with a curse. "Here's another like it," he said, and picked up a tune familiar enough. "The Waters of Tyne" was well known to Dolly, and Parrish glanced at her with a look that she could not read. She began to hum along to it, but it was in a curious pitch, and she struggled to find her voice.

"Sing up good wife!" said the older trooper suddenly, lighting a long clay pipe with an ember. "Let's hear ye now."

"It's not for a woman's voice," she said, softly, "At once too high or too deep. I cannot reach it."

"Then sing one you know well," said another man, "And Jamie will surely catch it. He's a gift for it."

Dolly's heart suddenly pounded, causing her to reach for a breath. She hesitated.

"Come, sing for the roof over your heads this night," the soldier scoffed at her.

She hummed a line, finding her way into the song, her eyes fixed hard on the clay dirt beneath her. Then she raised her head to the room.

"I was young and lusty," she sang, "I was fair and clear, I was young and lusty, many a 'lang year." The men grew still. She lost any sense that Parrish was next to her. It was to the other man, sitting tethered and bound, that she sang. "Sair fyel'd hinny, sair fyel'd now. Sair fyel'd hinny, Since I kenn'd thou."

There was a soft contented sound from one of the soldiers, and she continued, through the misty meaning of two more verses, and two more gracefully swooping choruses, and into a long silence. Someone by the fire uttered a word of acknowledgement. Dolly pulled her head back against the wall, and lowered it in the direction of the open door, far to the side of her. Only the shadowy form of the broken man was visible in the gloom, but she could see his head was raised, his back straighter, and his face turned towards her in a dark stare of recognition. She turned quickly away from him, but knew that Parrish had seen it too.

"Another song, good wife," said the man with the pipe. "A happier song perhaps, for fighting men far from home! Once more now, before sleep takes us."

"I'll get you water," said Parrish, rising to his feet. Dolly was taken-aback by it. What plan did he have at this moment? She looked up searchingly at him, but he merely turned and walked to the near door, scooping up a small beaker from the floor near the fire. Dolly's mind raced. No stirring tune sprang into it, given her disquiet and concern.

"Sing now lass!" the soldier beseeched her.

"If ye want a besom, for to sweep yer hoose," she sang, mimicking Blind Willie's accent and delivery without having to think about it. Parrish returned before she'd finished and set the cup next to her as he sat down. The listeners were much amused, and the young lad followed it with a jaunty air on his pipe. Another man tapped a wooden slat on the cobbles and the whole scene assumed a jolly, distracted atmosphere.

As the tune came to an end, a voice rang out from the opposite end of the stalls.

"A bonny jig, a bonny, bonny jig!" Corporal Carmichael laughed bitterly. "I know it well from

264

boyhood, before I swore to serve and fulfil my duties to the king. And to obey orders, to remain watchful, and alert, whether in full battle, or as guardians of traitors and scrutineers for a foreign power. You're all strangers to me lads, it is a queer run of fate that has brought us together, but answer to me you must while we are all sent so far from our true paths. So, tell me, is it a hooley, a singing party that we have for ourselves here? For me, fool that I am, took it to be an important mission of security and high importance, with the black gypo in our custody this stormy night!"

The oldest dragoon made to speak. "Corporal Sir, we were bedding down for the night..." Carmichael cut him off sharply.

"Shut up man!" he snapped, and then gentler, with spite in his voice, said, "Just shut up!" He walked slowly over and pushed a fallen ember back into the fire with his boot. "A cosy hearth, is it?" he hissed. "In a wooden stable, with dry straw and sun-bleached logs for a roofing? Well, that ties it all up nicely doesn't it." He turned in anger and spat out a parting order. "Review the bonds on the prisoner, quench that fire, and report to me at the stroke of six for punishment quota." He looked back at them, with arrogant hostility, so common in the middle ranks. "And pleasant dreams lads, I hope the rain doesn't spoil the night for ye." He spun on his heel flamboyantly, and was set for a smart exit, when he became aware of the two figures, huddled low against the dark wall. He looked down at Dolly and Parrish, she with her head hung down, and he looking straight ahead into the middle of the room. "And what do we have here?" he asked in a hiss of a whisper.

The oldest soldier stepped forward after a moment's silence. "Pilgrims sir," he barked, "From the Holy Island yonder. It is the custom of the lower house sir, to offer them shelter. We could do nought but comply with tradition, sir, as guests in the house ourselves."

Dolly's heart rose into her throat. She could feel the dew of sweat across her face, across her chest, her hands clenched into balls of dread at what would happen now.

Carmichael continued to stare for a long moment. "Pilgrims, is it?" he said, softly. "God-fearing folk. Then pray for us, good people, pray for us. And be gone by first light, if you please." He moved on slowly, stopping without a word to stare down at Moss, who had once again assumed the crouched, drop-headed pose that he had formerly struck. Then he walked out into the rain and quickened his pace. Dolly closed her eyes and breathed deeply, but the panic and fear stayed with her.

The soldiers busied themselves in silence, resuming a formal attitude, two fastening their tunics and locating themselves at opposite ends of the stable, as Parrish noticed that it was foot irons that were restraining Moss, as well as cords at his wrist, as these were roughly checked as ordered. The other two men pulled their packs into the darker corners, one of them stamping vaguely on the dying fire as he passed it, and proceeded to arrange bedding wares for themselves. Parrish watched them keenly. Dolly felt herself trembling now, the thought of how chance had played its part in Carmichael not hearing her singing moments earlier. He was not one to recognise her voice, but would surely have questioned the veracity of a pilgrim wife singing for soldiers around a campfire. But Moss had surely heard it, recognised her voice and the song she sang, and would now surely be turning over this knowledge in his bruised mind.

The scene settled into silence, except for the rain squalling mockingly across the roof, and the fire gradually, slowly, fading into a pale, meaningless glow, bereft of light, heat and purpose.

CHAPTER 24

FOR O, IT WAS A FEARFUL SIGHT

A long hour or more passed before Parrish seized the only chance that suggested itself to him. The rain had eased to nothing, the sleeping soldiers nearby snored contentedly, and the two guards were out of sight, beyond the open half-doors. Dolly had fallen into a fitful slumber, despite herself, and suddenly became aware that Parrish was moving slowly but determinedly at her side.

She saw him drain the last of the water from the cup he had brought her, and shake it dry. From his pocket, he eased out the flask of liquor that Allan Barnes had given him when they parted, and cautiously poured the foul liquid from it into the cup. Every move, every raising of his hand, was a delicate manoeuvre. He pocketed the flask, and leaned hard to one side, away from Dolly, where she could see a rough heap of straw skirting a pile of twined bales by the wall, and from it a long, cobbled drain-gulley, running across the floor, directly to the dying ash and embers of the fire. Immediately Dolly saw what he was trying to achieve, but could see no real purpose in it. Nevertheless, she felt her face twist into a look of horror, and her breath clamp itself tightly within her chest.

It took a long time. Parrish had to lean at a deep angle to reach the narrow channel, which itself was anything but clear, blocked along its length by dry dung, straw and who knew what else, and the slope away towards the fire was only slight. The cup was soon drained, but with none of the liquid seemingly reaching its goal. He leaned back and slowly poured out the last of it from the flask. He couldn't risk leaving the flask itself behind, in case it was traced to the Barnes clan. He pushed it back in his pocket and stretched over once more towards the straw. He tilted the cup. The stream of alcohol gained new vitality, and danced playfully on its way, hesitating here, rolling freely there, swelling confidently around unseen obstacle, creeping cautiously at broken corner and dust-filled crevice, but determined on its journey towards the barely glowing embers beyond. But its pace was slow, its strength diminishing, its power waning. A meagre trickle pushed on, straining to reach its goal.

The flare was sudden and shocking. It burst and then skimmed back in a rolling blue flame that Dolly watched with gasping wonder, before Parrish had even finished pouring the last of the liquid. He splashed what was left quickly over the bales, and rolled back just as the flame greedily seized the straw with a sneering crackle. On the other side of the fire, flames had taken hold of a loose pile of straw with a loud snapping sound that roused the sleeping men, who struggled to their feet, just as a thick cloud of grey smoke engulfed them. Dolly herself was frozen in fear, and barely felt Parrish dragging her on to her feet, in time for thick fingers of flame to lunge across the wall where they'd been, and tower above them to the open beams of the hayloft. The guards both appeared at once from outside, in a mess of panic and animated helplessness, as the fire reared in a blazing triumph, high into the roofing. The noise was a roar of power, the smoke spread thickly through the spaces between them, and the long rafters greedily sucked up the rich yellow flames.

"The Black Powder!" someone shouted, and a man lunged forward towards a keg on the floor a stride away, its lid half open, and Dolly felt a painful tug on her shoulder as Parrish pulled her back, blindly in the fumes, towards the farthest door. The smoke cleared for a moment as they tumbled through it, and Dolly saw Moss, standing tall and ready, but still manacled, at the open exit.

The fresh air struck her face as a long, wretched creak from somewhere behind, shot a shower of red sparks into the black sky. Moss rasped a sharp word at them and pulled them both to the side of the building, thrashing through thick bush and crooked branches, just as new voices rang out. A handful of lantern, pale compared to the ever-spreading fire, swung into the cobbled yard. There was a sudden crack of shot, a shell, something, followed by a chorus of wild shouts and more cracking, as powder horns and dry muskets succumbed to the inferno.

All at once the fleeing trio were at the side of an open field, and Dolly saw how Moss was struggling with the chains at his ankles. He cursed loudly as he toppled over, and she ran to his side to help him up, but he pushed her aside with his arm in frustrated anger at his irons. She drew back, feeling hurt and helpless. He clawed himself to his feet, and they moved on once more. Behind them, the long stables were already engulfed in flames. Then, a sudden explosion, the force of which struck Dolly physically, as if a sack of stones had been thrust at her back by mighty arms, splintered the far side of the stable building into a hellish fountain of fiery chaos and scattered debris. A single unearthly shriek spouted out from somewhere in its midst, and howled chillingly above the low thunder of the blast. Dolly was cast to the ground like a scatter of bones, and her head rang like a beaten drum. She lay still for an instant, and felt sure that it was death itself lifting her angrily by her arms, but when she turned her face, it was Alec, scooping her up like a sheaf of barley and dragging her along into safety. Moss too had fallen again and was clambering to his feet as they reached him. He clumsily regained a stride and kept pace at their left. Behind them, Dolly heard repeated slaps like gunshots, and a wild cacophony of voices and shrill panic. Parrish's snarling brogue urged her on, his hands still tight around her shoulders, pushing her blindly into the blackness. Another roar of flame lit up the night behind them, and Dolly's back seared hot from it, then was struck cold by the night, as they skirted a low stone wall. Suddenly, there were horses near them, scattering and galloping in fear, and Dolly realised where they were. The road on which they'd come yesterday was nearby, but Parrish was leading them away from it.

There were voices in front of them now, local people, roused by the noise and the flames, and all three of them crouched instinctively at the sound of them. Parrish suddenly let go of her arms and went forward. He reached a fence, and then called them towards him in a harsh whisper. They climbed through it, Moss with some difficulty, and they halted for a heartbeat. Then Parrish was off again, and Moss threw his legs in front of him like

271

some demented beast, in a vain effort to make speed. Dolly ran at his side helplessly. She turned her head towards him, but his face was tilted away from her in his effort to keep up. His breath rasped and snarled from his mouth like that of a fleeing, savage animal, and Dolly fought back her fear of it. She instinctively veered towards Alec, as if to find safety in his wake.

The fire was burning easily and brightly far behind them, but they were well away from its light by now. There had been one more rattle of burning shot, and now that had all but ceased. Surely by now, Dolly reasoned in her mind, Moss at least, if not the two pilgrims also, would have been missed, and most likely blamed, and a search would be soon underway. The escapees were free but adrift in a strange darkness.

It was the old grey mule that saved them, tethered contentedly by the gatepost of a cottage, set away from the others, at the edge of the settlement. It was the same animal that had brought them here. Parrish saw it and hissed at the others, "Stay there!" before loping another fence and disappearing. They both dropped to their knees, and almost immediately, Moss wrapped his massive arms around Dolly from behind, and pushed his tousled head into her neck.

"Dolly, Dolly," he whispered into her ear. "*Non ci posso credere. Dolly, Mia Cara!*" She tensed, and felt her whole body stiffen. She twisted round to face him, her heart thumping, but his face was shrouded, hidden. His voice cracked, his words were noises of emotion, but of pain, of joy, of fear? She couldn't tell. She gripped his hand with

272

hers, and tried to wring out the confusion within her, but it stubbornly remained.

Beyond the fence, Parrish was across the lane, and then stopped suddenly, as several tall figures emerged from the side of the darkened building a stride or two in front of him. He froze and then recognised a throaty voice from the mere single word that it spoke.

"Inferno!" said Roland Barnes, as he watched the flaming building lean into a slow, fiery collapse.

"Roland Barnes!" Parrish hissed from nearby. "Here!"

All the men wheeled round as one, and Roland stepped forward.

"Pilgrim? Is that you?"

"It is," came the reply. "And any help you can give us would be welcome, if only a firm direction away from this place!"

The fire away behind them danced and shouted in the night. Anxious moments passed and then Dolly heard them; strange ruffling, pounding noises, approaching from the lane beyond. Then the hiss once again of Parrish's whisper. Moss rose and threw himself bodily over the twisted fence, turning back to help Dolly over the same. Two horses, their hooves wrapped in sacking, plodded and edged around the narrow track. Roland Barnes was still securing the feet of one. They were saddleless, but bridled, and Parrish urged them to mount.

"My legs are bound close!" Moss said. "I cannot stride a horse." Dolly herself held back, never having ridden before.

Roland spoke up. "Hoist yourself side on behind me," he said. "Use yonder fencing to raise to it. And lass, behind your man there, the same way. Hurry!"

They did as bidden, though not without a struggle and some pain on Moss's part. Alec pulled Dolly up and she stretched herself over the beast like a man. She reached her arms around Parrish and held him tightly, and found a comfort in it. But then she was taken aback by the unsteadiness of the arrangement, and felt like she was sure to fall, such was the wide back, and jolting stride of the animal. They moved off down the dark track, slowly at first, then picking up a worrying speed as Roland veered off into open land after a short while. The chaos and madness of the burning buildings were immediately out of sight.

The horses pounded on, seemingly in a random direction, ebbing and flowing, climbing and tumbling, across thickly grassed lands still steeped in inky blackness, and sodden underfoot. More than once, Parrish and Dolly teetered on the edge of tumbling, for Alec himself was a poor horseman, but Moss seemed at awkward ease on the other. On they went, wordlessly, for a long, endless, bruising time, until suddenly they were in sight and smell of the dark, broiling sea. Not now the smooth pond on which they had sailed the day before, the waves roared a mocking challenge to any man who dared to venture forth amongst them. Roland slowed them down to a languid pace, and drew alongside them.

"The tide is not yet up, but wild as this, the way across to the island will be a hazardous one. If the marking stones are covered, there is not light enough to keep to

274

them, even in a passable depth. But what other choices we have, I fail to see."

Moss spoke up from behind him. "The sea covers the pathway?" he asked in astonishment.

"It does indeed," answered Roland, "And to stray from it is to perish in shifting sand and deep waters."

"We must risk it!" said Parrish at once. "Those behind us will have scoured the north road in both directions by now, and the land around, and know that this is the only alternative. And see!" He pointed to the east. "The dawn is upon us. They will have us in clear sight from a long way off."

The greyness of sunrise behind thick cloud had come upon them quickly. Without another word, Roland pushed his horse on, and Parrish did the same. The track was firm, and they made good progress to the start of the causeway. Then there was little sign of it beneath the rippling water, and Roland's horse reared back from it. His heels pressed it forward, and the second animal took courage from that. The stone markers were visible enough, barely covered by water, once the riders were almost on top of them, but to anticipate their position while moving forward was more of a challenge. Progress became slower and slower, until Roland dismounted and led his beast, with Moss clinging at a clumsy angle, balancing across its back. The pace became steadier with this, but the depth of water increased as they crossed, and Roland was knee-deep before too long. He stopped briefly and stared ahead to gauge the distance remaining, and then pulled on the bridle again. Dolly clung tightly to Alec, and closed her eyes, until she felt the water at her own feet, high up the horse's flank. The beast's footfall seemed sure enough however, and when Dolly looked up and peered ahead, it seemed Roland was through the deepest stretch. He looked back reassuringly. But as he did so, he abruptly cast his gaze beyond them, with a sudden stretch of his neck.

They all looked to the rear, knowing what they would see. Five or six horsemen, including a red coated figure on a stocky grey, taking up the rear, were on the bankside, overlooking the start of the causeway, and beginning to trot down towards it. The leader rode confidently, with purpose. Dolly knew instinctively, even at such a distance, it was Carmichael. They were perhaps half a mile, probably less, behind them. Roland realised that it was impossible for him to remount in haste, and set off at a brisk pace on foot, splashing through the ankle-deep water, pulling the horse after him. He was soon breathless, and threw up his arms in frustration. Moss slid down and signalled for him to remount, and then he himself jumped back up behind, belly-down across the animal, his chained feet dangling, his head bobbing comically. They had reached the fork in the track where a slender path would lead to the moorings and Roland's tiny boat, and the horses easily climbed the rocky dune to where it veered away.

From that vantage, Roland took time to look back. Parrish and Dolly drew abreast of him and did the same. The light from the east was clearer now, and though it was hard to make out detail, it was plain to see that the pursuers hadn't found it easy going, and were in some difficulty. The sound of high, desperate voices reached them on the wind. Parrish turned and shielded his eyes against it.

"There's a loose horse on the ridge!" he said.

"And another, maybe the grey!" said Roland. "If just one man reaches us. We are unarmed!"

Parrish steadied his mount and eased Dolly from behind him to the ground. He dropped down behind her, and held her shoulder reassuringly. Moss too struggled from the other horse, and staggered to find balance several paces away. They all stood statue-like, straining eyes and ears in the direction of their pursuers.

There were men moving, wading far from the true path of the causeway, visibly struggling with the depth of water. Not one had broken free from the pack to gain ground enough to follow them. Another bare horse could be seen galloping south along the beach, away from the rest, and the voices were becoming fainter and fewer in number. Dolly stared, not knowing, and not wanting to know, exactly what she was watching. The distant figures were scattered, spread across the scene in chaotic abandon, as if vying with each other in some crazy game of ball. To-and-fro they darted, then slowing, then wilting, then vanishing, as the treacherous shoreline swallowed them up. The lead man, Carmichael for certain, had dropped into a thrashing, splashing confusion of desperate panic and then was still. Others followed suit. In minutes, for surely that was all it took, the causeway seemed empty, rippling with the incoming tide, the surviving horses grazing innocently among the higher grass, and no sign of a man living. The men and

Dolly stood in shocked silence. The treacherous tide had taken their part and done its worst on their behalf.

One single horse, the grey, stood aimlessly in firmer shallows. Then from behind it, uncertainly, a single, red-coated, hatless form emerged from the water. He hesitated at his mount, then advanced, cautiously, passing beyond the steed, carrying in one hand a shapeless bundle, and in the other, a long Brown Bess musket.

As they watched, the cautious figure of Jopling grew surer, steadier, occasionally stooping to search out the submerged marking stones, until Dolly heard Roland Barnes murmur beside her, "He'll soon have reached the firm path. He's clear of the shallows." At that point, Jopling raised the loaded musket smartly to his shoulder, took a rapid aim and fired. The onlookers saw the smoke blossom upwards, and then the report of the shot and the splat of the ball in the sand beside them sounded almost simultaneously. Parrish swore and they all cowered, except Moss, who stood tall and erect, his hand over his missing eye, somehow focusing on the red-coated man. Dolly looked up and saw Jopling emerge like a phantom from the curtain of smoke. He was already reloading. He raised the match to his lips and breathed it into life, set the hammer, and hoisted the gun to his shoulder. She stooped low once more as he fired again, the smoke springing forth as before, then another absurd moment of nothingness, followed by a deeper report across the water, just as another ball splashed to its fruitless end, but nearer this time, the ripples from its landing enough to reach the onlookers in a short moment. The shooter was again filling his weapon, and was soon splashing through shallows, near enough for the sound of feet through saltwater to be heard above the roaring tide at their backs. Dolly heard Parrish shout out a warning for them to remount, to leave, but Moss was unmoved by it. Jopling grew closer and closer still, close enough for the splash of his step to match the footfall, and then he stopped, checking the hammer of his gun for dryness, and was about to raise it again.

Moss crouched down quickly, but then stood again. Dolly stared up at him, and then noticed that he held in his hand a rounded stone, about the size of a small apple, that he squeezed once and balanced for weight. He leaned back and his arm arched around. He flung the stone towards the other man with a fierce movement that leapt from his entire body. He staggered over his iron bindings, but regained his balance at once. Dolly saw Parrish stand up suddenly, his gaze following the projectile as if it was a soaring bird. As she herself turned to Jopling, she saw his head drop back, as the stone hit him squarely on the forehead with a hard, dull sound like a butcher's hammer on fresh bone. The musket fell away from his hands and he dropped solidly, face-down in the shallow salt water beneath him.

Dolly caught her breath sharply, her hand at her face, as Parrish loped past her, running towards the fallen man. Moss stood motionless, watching the scene intently. Parrish slowed as he reached the motionless man, and Dolly saw him gently prod him with his foot, and stare down at him for a moment. He knelt cautiously, and raised the motionless body by the shoulder, and then let him roll back into the water. He walked steadily back to the others, wiping his hands in an almost symbolic gesture. As he reached Moss, he looked at him briefly, and said, "Balilla," and then walked on. Moss looked down to the ground beneath him, and made no reply.

CHAPTER 25

SHE'LL SOON BE FIT TO SAIL AWAY

With a click of his tongue, Roland Barnes pulled both mounts away sharply by their loose reins, and led them off towards the lip of the tiny harbour that lay at the foot of the rise. The others all stood where they were, spread apart from each other, in a stunned silence. Roland took out a short-bladed fisherman's knife, and began to cut away the soaked sacking from the hooves of the animals. Moss slowly turned his head to watch him, and then said, "If only my feet would taste freedom so easily!" Roland looked up.

"Come with me now," he said. "I must take these horses yonder for safe keeping, until my son and brother return for them. There are tools there, in the holdings. Surely enough to cut those irons from you."

Without another word, they moved off together, along the short curve of the small bay, where a motley set of boatsheds was perched. Dolly realised that she was watching them go. The horses seemed carefree and obedient, and she felt an instant of relief that the enormity of what she had just witnessed could drip away like water from her eyes. But immediately it all swept over her again, burned in the vision of her memory. The horror of it swam before her, unsteadily, mercilessly. She closed her eyes, as if to banish it. She felt a hand on her high arm, steady but looser than before, and looked up into Alec Parrish's face. His eyes were old, tired, creased with ruthlessness, yet now soothing and reassuring. His voice was too.

"Come lass," he said.

He almost led her off the brow of the rise and into stony sand towards the lapping water. Dolly sat down on a broken creel, as if exhausted, with Parrish standing still and silent beside her. She looked up at him at last, but he didn't match her gaze.

"Are there more soldiers coming?" she asked in a resigned, weary voice.

Parrish turned to her, and seemed uncertain in his reply. "They will come eventually, but they're billeted a distance away from the castle. And there's business enough there to occupy them for the short while. But when they see the others haven't returned…"

Dolly reached down and took a fistful of sand, clenched it tightly, and then hurled it away from her, as if it was the bitterness of her thoughts.

"Did they deserve to perish like that?" she asked, the passion cracking in her voice. "Does any man? The water claimed my own father, and now it claims my enemies. And yet, I feel almost as much regret for them as I did for him."

Parrish turned away, almost scornfully now. "Their arrogance, their thirst for power is what brought them to their end," he said. "And brought freedom for your man, the man you love, a man to whom power and arrogance mean nothing. You shouldn't rejoice in what happened, but neither should you mourn. And you are free of them now, to have a life with him, the man you have chosen."

At those odd, wistful last few words, she glanced up at

him. She saw him look down at the sparse pebbles beneath his feet, and kick his boots into the wet sand.

"But what good will I be to him now?" she said. "Look what they've done to him. I don't mean the cruel bruises and the shame of it, I mean that they've turned him back to what he once was. A man who kills other men. A hero. A leader. Even you, you called him by that name!" Parrish looked at her sharply. "I heard you," she said, "'Balilla!' that's what you called him. And that's who he is. He's not Moss any more. Maybe he never was. When he was a river worker on the Tyne, and I was there to feed and clothe him, that was plain enough, but now, he can never return to that. And nor can I. What future is there for either of us." She hesitated. "I could better serve you," she murmured, almost to herself. She sensed how his body reacted to her words. She looked up at him again. "I don't care for you the way I did for him, and neither you for me I'm sure, but I could be with you, and happy at that, in a world that is familiar to us both. I've listened to you, heard how you speak to others. You're a learned man, in your strange Scotch voice. I know that Moss has stood up for all that is right, and fought in its name, but that was in his own country. You stand up for the people of *this* land, *my* land. I would stand at your side in that. After all that has happened, I would want to do that. I would *have* to do that. And he could find a new life in his own land, and a woman of his own kind, who would be worthy of him."

Parrish stood, looking down at her. She raised her eyes again, and saw a look of confusion, surprise, perhaps hope, upon his grey face. Then he shook it clear with a snort of anger.

"You talk such damned foolish stuff lassie!" he said sharply. "You know nothing of me. These few days were but a duty that we shared, and one which I have fulfilled, but one which you have yet to see through to its end. You and I, we are barely a pile of pebbles in the scheme of these things, compared to what that man yonder has yet to achieve. Do you think you would be content with me in my hovel on the Byker ballasts, or wherever I care to settle, knowing that you let slip a man who could be an inspiration to so many, and to whom you too are an inspiration? Forget what you once were, the Dillen Doll, or whatever the blind fiddler called you, and grasp what you have become. These threads you carry on your back, they are a new skin for you, with many more to come, to match a hundred different climates, and different places. Wherever you go, people will come to know the name of Balilla, and one day, that name may well rise into the stuff of legend." He reached out slowly, touching her cheek with his finger-tips, and paused for a heartbeat. "But every man of myth and legend, even those ancient gods from Roman times, each one had a goddess by his side, often wiser and stronger than the god himself." He smiled at the look of wonder on her face. "You'll soon forget these days we have shared," he said, "And be hungry for better ones. And I the same. I will move on, as I always have done. Believe me!"

She cowered from his words, and was then aware that Moss and Roland Barnes were striding towards them from across the sands. Parrish became aware of them too, and turned sharply away from her, towards the open sea beyond.

Roland approached and spoke quickly. "I shall take you to the Staple Island, on the outer Farnes, and from there you can take a barque, east across to Holland or Denmark, once the traders have chosen their course. This is a tidal mooring for them, when leaving the rivers to the south. I can arrange passage for you, but we must hurry." He peered out to sea, and pointed to a group of three low-masted schooners lying still beyond the furthest islands. "You see, they will leave on the next high tide tonight. With this sea, it may take us some hours to clear the breaker rocks at Longstone and elsewhere, and without my son to help me, it will be heavy work."

Moss spoke up. In the new daylight, he looked worn and bruised, his lost eye now covered by a rough cloth, tied behind his head. There was blood, dried into his chin, and below his ear. The rest of his bruised body was mercifully hidden. But his voice was strong, his words full of purpose, though none were directed to Dolly. "I can handle sail and ropes," he said. "Shout hard your instruction, my head is like bells inside it!"

Roland nodded and turned to Parrish. "You and the lassie take centre place and hang on well. We could maybe even tie you, against unexpected rolling and suchlike."

Parrish raised a hand in front of him. "I will not be coming with you," he said firmly. "There may be more to do here, and I am unknown in the affair. I shall stay, and pass the care of my friends to you Master Barnes, with my gratitude once again."

Moss looked at him, and spoke warmly. "My friend, there is still much danger here. I do not see the need for you to stay behind."

Parrish smiled, "There are things I must do, even back in Newcastle. These are dangerous times everywhere, and I cannot walk away from them." He held out his hand. "Go now," he said, "I may well follow you later, but for now, travel safely."

Moss shook his hand and placed the other on his shoulder. Then he turned towards Barnes and gestured for him to lead. They moved off, and were soon in conversation. Parrish averted his eyes from Dolly, but sensed that she had risen, and was standing motionless, a step away from him. He slowly turned towards her, and met her gaze. Her head was bare, her cropped hair hardly ruffled by the wind. There was a smudge of dirt on her pale cheek, and her stature was strong, straight and womanly, with no sign of the weakness that she'd carried with her when they had first met. Her eyes were clear, bright, but tinged with a pain perhaps. There was a long moment between them, and then he tipped his head in the direction of the waiting vessel. She dropped her gaze, and turned away towards it. Parrish watched her walk away, and sensed no limp, no slowness in her step.

Within a short while, the little boat that was carrying them had turned and made for the open sea to the east, and the wind had taken its sails. Parrish walked along the high path until he caught sight of it, making good speed in the open water. He watched it for a long time and then eventually he lost sight of its mast as it cleared the point of the long, low black shape that was the next island.

Then he turned away slowly westwards, to wait for the next low tide and a safer causeway.

CHAPTER 26

AND THERE SHALL BE TIES

Winter came early to the Tyne. There was talk of the river freezing over, as it had done three years previously, rendering the keels and brigs helpless and motionless, and vessels of all sizes and origins drifting aimlessly at anchor off shore at Tynemouth, for a week, before they abandoned the river altogether and tried for harbours further south. The businessmen of Sunderland and Kingston were rubbing their hands together and hoping for a repeat of that season, while the Hostmen of Newcastle looked at gloomy skies and wrapped themselves in thick wool and mouldy furs and prepared for the worst.

Already their plans for new coal staithes and deeper, longer keelboats had been thwarted, and once the true nature of the recent theft of the papers and parchments from the Guildhall were known to the public, the threat against the local workforce had become common knowledge too, and agitators like the man Turnbull, who had once been privy to the inner sanctums of Tyneside business dealings, were now stirring up unrest and dissatisfaction amongst the working men of Sandgate. The Hostmen knew they would prevail eventually, and the threat of a cold winter, while proving costly in the short term, might well be an advantage to them in the long run. They, like the rest of the city, prepared to dig in for a long, difficult season.

On the Town Moor, the new barracks at Fenham were taking shape, but the Green cuffs had the sure impression that their cosy tenure in this city was not to be a long one. War with France was still a topic of conversation amongst all ranks, some of it more informed than the rest, and the patriotic rise of local private militia was rendering their position somewhat obsolete. Local men, especially those in service to wealthy lords and landowners in countryside regions, found themselves being offered wage, uniform, training and prestige by signing up to these companies, most of them in the belief that they would never have to raise a musket in anger. Some would discover, in the years ahead, that they had been sorely mistaken on that account.

After the unfortunate loss of Corporal Carmichael, drowned at the incident at The Farnes, and widely considered by the men under his command to have had the makings of an officer, a group of new and stricter mid-ranking regulars had been seconded from other companies, and the local people became less used to seeing young dragoons and troopers carousing through the city streets at night. The local pubs and alehouses were none-the-worse for it. Much the same set of characters frequented the same haunts, and talk of pressgangs and suspicious strangers had gradually ebbed away as topics of regular conversation.

It was around this time that a quiet, cautious man of small stature and amiable manner, first appeared on the Sandgate quayside, by the name of Henry Parker. His speech had a strange twist to it, and it was said that he had lived the first part of his life in the far western counties of England, where he was known as an artist and painter of some renown. He had arrived in Newcastle, intrigued by the many published editions of poetry and verse that were emerging from the educated pens of professional men, caught on the tide of literary enthusiasm that the new printing presses had instigated. But when he had confronted and interacted with these men upon his arrival in the city, he had found them arrogant and aloof, and besmirched by their own self-importance. More to his tastes, and more to the teasing of his artistic inclinations, were the shabby characters who roamed the quayside and the taverns, both men and women, a cast of eccentrics in strange, outlandish attire with habits to match.

These were the people who he eventually approached, and coaxed to sit in his draughty upper room in the Groatmarket, to pose for portraits in all their everyday glory. Initially singly, he gradually won over much of their confidences, enough to suggest a majestic group portrait, to commemorate the camaraderie and unique flavour of this outlandish brotherhood, in an effort to depict the real, deep side of Tyneside and its inhabitants.

He had sat in the Flying Horse night after night as winter encroached, suffering the frowns and scowls of the landlord Harrison Marley, and his dismissive opinion that few, if any, of these eccentrics would agree to be part of this haughty venture. Henry Parker sat and watched them all closely in spite of this, and soon recognised that, due to his outgoing nature as well as his obvious infirmity, central to the company at all times was the blind fiddler known as Willie Purvis. Indeed, Harrison

Marley agreed, that if Blind Willie could be persuaded to join up for the adventure, then most if not all of the other characters would fall into place behind him. So it was that Parker wooed and coaxed his way into Blind Willie's society, and began the protracted process whereby a painting of all of them would eventually be achieved. It was as much Willie's venture as Parker's, despite the lack of sight of the former, and the unique vision of the latter.

"Now, ye'd need to have Captain Starky," Blind Willie had decreed over another cup of Spanish Juice, giving no attention or respect to the seaman in the corner who was bellowing a tuneless shanty from the Indies to a swaying crowd of drinkers. The room was noisy, packed against the cold outside, and squirming like a rat's nest with excitement. "Starky's a man of military stature," Willie acclaimed loudly over the surrounding din, "And would make a fine picture for any ordinary man to admire. And Bold Archy, who would be maudlin' if he was left behind, close as he is to Starky himself. Ralphy the Hawk, undoubtedly, and Tommy Ferns, a blind man like mesel' but without the abundance of talent as Ah enjoy with it. And women! Bella Roy, Auld Judy, beauty that she is! Peggy Grundy, a popular lass, with a face that any passin' body would recognise hereabout, and ye'd need that, to prove a certain popularity amongst the folks."

Across the room, at that moment, a new song erupted, almost tunefully, from a young lad with his father's hat and pipe to smooth him into the company.

"Fresh Ah come from Sandgate Street!" he sang.

"Dolly! Dolly!" the room responded as one.

"My best friend there to meet, Dol Li A!"

Drinks and smoke were left untouched, as everyone bellowed back the chorus of the song.

"Dolly the Dillen Doll, Dolly, Dolly! Dolly the Dillen Doll, Dol Li A!"

Parker leaned in towards Willie, whom he saw was almost alone in not joining in with the rest.

"And this woman, Dolly," he said over the din. "Surely she should be in the painting. I hear her name and her song in every alehouse in town. Where is she? Can we include her along with the rest?"

Willie was silent for a moment. "Ah, Dolly. No, no," he said quietly. He raised his voice a little. "She's long gone. Long gone, that lass. There's few that know where, and fewer still that even remember her. She'd be in here, at one time, most nights, but she was a reticent body. People would hardly notice her. Until she sang a bit song, and then they'd notice the voice of it, and wonder where it was coming from, given the weakness of the look of her. She was nowt but a dung bird, like the rest of us, but she grew into a linnet, and flew away to the company of kings and princes. She'd have been a smudge of beauty on that picture of yours, make no mistake!" He laughed, and nodded to himself and clenched his unseeing eyes, as if to squeeze something into his imagination. "But she's long gone, long gone," he added wistfully. The people around him bellowed her name again. "This is my sang, ye know!" he suddenly exclaimed. "Ah made it for her mesel'. But people forget these things. We'll all be forgotten eventually, paintin' or no paintin'."

He smiled into his drink and the song went on. Another verse, and then another, with the chorus bouncing back louder than even before.

"Dolly Coxon pawned her sark! Dolly! Dolly! For to join the baggage cart! Dol Li A!"

In the corner, by the far door, a solitary figure stood, a pace back from the raucous crowd. His dark eyes stared unseeing, down into a deeper place than the sand-strewn floor beneath him could even hint at. If anyone had dared look searchingly into his clouded face, they would have barely seen a movement, though the sliver of a smile flickered once perhaps, then was straight-ways swallowed into bitterness with a grimace that further creased the grimy lines between his eyebrows.

When the eyes closed slowly, no-one could be fooled that it was the lull of the voices or the sweetness of the tune that were the cause of it. The boisterous chanting of a name though, therein lay the undoing. To most of the rest of the company, it surely meant little, but to a few, and especially to him, it sowed seeds of wondering and speculation, that no resolution seemed ever likely to quench. News from foreign parts was a rare commodity, even in a seaport as busy as this one. Perhaps a Spring thaw would bring with it the makings of a fresh page in a wayward tale, but real stories of war and conflict across a grey sea, only hindered the chance of hope and its fanciful musings. Vivid images were easily lost in times like these. And this song? It would be sung again, and then again perhaps, but the name, and eventually the words and the melody, would surely be forgotten. And such a slight thing it was, no match for the true spirit it represented.

His eyes opened once more. He swilled the last mouthful of ale around the bottom of his cup with a thoughtful hand, and felt the wash of noise roll over him. He was content to leave the booming chorus to those unkempt voices around him. The fingers of his other hand, inside his long pocket, softly clenched and unclenched around the silky garment that he had saved from the pawnshop's possession. In a society of brash and bold, displaced and misshapen individuals, those around and about saw him to be a quiet, unsociable man. They allowed his errant comings and goings, and tended to leave him to his own thoughts and concerns. He never acknowledged it, but nevertheless, this was how Alec Parrish knew his life would always have to be.